A Hint of Scandal

BOOK 9: THE SINS & SCANDALS SERIES

KELLY BOYCE

The Sins & Scandals Series

While there are those who spend their time in modest pursuits, upholding propriety befitting the lords and ladies of the ton, it would seem that for others scandal is just a sin away...

AN INVITATION TO SCANDAL
A SCANDALOUS PASSION
A SINFUL TEMPTATION
THE LADY'S SINFUL SECRET
SURRENDER TO SCANDAL
A SINNER NO MORE
THE SWEETEST SIN
A MOST SCANDALOUS CHRISTMAS
A HINT OF SCANDAL

For my sister, Alyson.
No one, in the history of the world, has ever laughed as hard
at hanging pictures as we.

Chapter One

"Cut off?"

Temperance Lindwell stared at her father, waiting for him to complete his sentence, because surely he could not mean what he had just said. Even he, blustery as he could be at times, had enough sense not to toss his own daughter out onto the street. Didn't he?

"Without a penny to your name."

Then again, perhaps she had misjudged. As he returned her stare, blatant and unapologetic, the realization that he did indeed mean what he said, settled in with startling clarity. He'd had enough. Would brook no further refusals. Had reached his limits.

Unfortunately, however, so had she.

"Very well then." Temperance straightened her shoulders and gave her father a stiff nod. Now was not the time to discuss the matter or what she planned to do about it. Mother and Constance were waiting on them to leave for Lord and Lady Frontenac's fete. Constance had been looking forward to the event all week and Temperance refused to ruin her twin sister's excitement.

"Then you will do as I say?" Father raised one eyebrow, not appearing convinced at her easy acquiescence. He knew her too well.

"I will consider your ultimatum and give you my final decision on the matter by the end of the week." She kept her voice steady, speaking to him in the same manner she had seen him use when dealing with his business associates. But in the end, all she accomplished was perhaps buying herself a little more time and no more than that. When Leopold Lindwell put a plan into action, he did not back down. He considered retreat a weakness.

As did she. She was her father's daughter, after all.

And her plan was to avoid marriage this Season. And for each Season that followed. Perhaps if her parents had bothered to listen to her during the numerous times she attempted to speak to them about her reticence toward marriage, they might not have come to this crossroads of ultimatums. But they hadn't.

And so now, here they were.

"You have been a constant disappointment, Temperance." Her father sighed and shook his head.

Constant disappointment.

How often had she heard that in the past two years? Too many. Once upon a time, she'd been their shining star, the belle of all the balls. But that time ended the moment she'd broken her engagement with Beauregard Montgomery.

Father had never forgiven her the embarrassment her refusal had caused him and, determined to save face, he'd whisked them all across the ocean to London. He was determined to regain standing in New York's Society by achieving the grand coup of marrying his daughters off to titled gentlemen.

Whether his daughters wanted to marry a titled lord and

live in London, away from everything and everyone they knew, had never been discussed.

Temperance echoed her father's sigh and stared at the books lining the shelves along the wall. Books that belonged to someone else—the owner of the home who had let it to her family. Everything in this house, save the clothes they wore and a few other sundry items, belonged to someone else. They were interlopers into a Society that did not want them. That tolerated them only because of a loose connection to the Duke of Franklyn. Though their fortune was revered in New York, London scoffed at it. As if its newness somehow changed its value.

Regardless, her parents expected Temperance and Constance to suffer through another Season of being looked down upon by the very ton into which they were expected to marry.

Her father did not bother to address the deadline she'd set forth as he walked past her to the great hall where Mother and Constance waited. He expected obedience, assumed a victory not truly in evidence. In his mind, his threat of leaving her penniless on the side of a road like a pauper was sufficient to bring her to heel. He could think of no worse fate to befall her.

But she could. And the loss of wealth and prestige she would suffer as a result were a small price to pay.

Constance gave her a sympathetic glance when she joined them a moment later. Temperance had not discussed her plans with her sister, a fact that niggled at her. She discussed everything with her twin and vice versa. They shared a closeness Temperance had yet to experience with another individual. A trust and belief that went unrivaled. Perhaps if she could find that with a man, she might find the idea of marriage more palatable. But she knew better than to believe in a man's lofty promises of love and trust and fidelity.

No, marriage was not for her. She had other plans. Unfortunately, those plans included leaving Constance behind. How did she find the words to say such a thing to the one person she'd shared her entire life with—her secrets and dreams and heartbreak and humiliation? But, notwithstanding being twins and despite their close connection, they were different people. Constance had dreams of her own and, unlike Temperance, those dreams centered on marriage and family. She didn't see either of these things as a sentence to be endured, but a pleasure and a purpose. Temperance feared her sister's thinking might have been somewhat warped by the romantic novels she tried to hide under her pillow, but there was little to be done about that.

Regardless, they were meant for different destinies, though the reality of this, the very thought of leaving her sister behind to avoid her father's dictates, pained her to no end.

The trip from their leased townhouse in Mayfair to the Frontenac's imposing home in Grosvenor Square remained mired in a tense silence save for the conversation she and Constance shared through nothing more than their facial expressions. They had perfected the skill over the years and it proved quite beneficial when they did not wish to have their parents privy to their talks. Such as now.

Constance raised one eyebrow. *Is Father upset with you?*

Temperance twisted her mouth to one side. *Like an angry bear poked with a stick.*

You being the one that held the stick, of course. Constance tilted her blonde head to one side; the fat curls brushing against her bare shoulders. Temperance had always considered her sister the pretty one, with her sweet expressions and delicate features, unlike her own, which were bolder, darker, and fiercer in their construction.

Temperance shrugged one shoulder in response and offered an apologetic half smile.

A sigh escaped Constance and a sad facsimile of Temperance's half smile rested upon her lips.

Guilt stabbed at Temperance. She did not want to hurt her sister or bring strife upon the family. But she could not go on like this, caught in a strange limbo where the life offered was not the one she wanted, and the one she wanted meant giving up the one person she held most dear.

But what other choice did she have?

"I have come to loathe these things," James said, glancing around the ballroom at Lord and Lady Frontenac's stately home, just a handful of doors down from his own. If he was a smart man—and he liked to think he was—he would slip out to the terrace and disappear into the dark night. If he hurried, it would take but a few moments to arrive back at his own doorstep in time for a brief nightcap, a quick stop into the nursery to check on his brand new nephew, and maybe a little reading before he turned in for the night.

Unfortunately, that scenario meant leaving his great-aunt behind and that would create its own problems. The great Lady Dalridge would not take kindly to being left high and dry.

"They are a necessary evil," Alex said. "Is that not what you told me near this time last year?"

James glanced at his oldest and dearest friend—now his brother-in-law—who had the audacity to smirk at him, and weighed the pros and cons of planting a facer on him in the middle of the festivities. Likely not the best idea. His sister would be most displeased about it and he did hate disappointing her, especially so soon after she'd delivered his dear nephew, William, named after their father. "Do you not have somewhere else you can be?"

Alex clasped his hands behind his back and shifted his feet, looking every bit the duke he would someday be. "As a matter of fact, I would much rather be at home with Hen. Unfortunately, she has banished me from the nursery this night upon claims my hovering was wearing on her last nerve."

"Hardly surprising. She indicated to me you were becoming rather annoying." Then again, she'd said the same thing to him when he'd attempted to protest attending the event in favor of staying home.

Alex shot him a sideways glare. "And she told me I had to ensure you did not try to sneak out early, so perhaps if we wish to make my wife happy with both of us, we'd best set to the task of getting through this evening and finding you a wife."

"I do not need a wife."

"Every titled gentleman needs a wife if they hope to acquire an heir. Those two things go hand in hand, last time I checked. Now, unless you wish to see the great title of Marquess of Ridgemont go to that shoddy cousin of yours, you'd best consider the bounty of desirables before us. It isn't as if you have to love her madly, although I do recommend it quite highly."

The muscles in James neck tightened involuntarily. He had loved madly once, as his companion well knew. But the woman had not loved him back. Instead, she'd married another man—Alex. The marriage had ended in disaster and James still bore the scars of not being able to stop the pain experienced on all sides. He had no interest in a repeat performance. A good, docile wife would suit well enough.

Alex nodded toward a group of ladies huddled nearby. "How about Lady Charlotte Overton?"

James shook his head. "Pleasant nature and certainly

pretty enough, but her uncle is an absolute bastard that I have no wish to associate with, nor call family."

"Then perhaps one of Lord Caldwell's daughters. Given he has three and no sons, you'd be doing him a great service. All are pretty to one degree or another and most are pleasant, from what I am told. Perhaps the eldest, Eugenie?"

"Too prudish."

"Then the middle, Rosalind?"

"Too controversial in her thoughts and deeds."

Alex sighed. "What of the youngest, Marianne."

"Too young."

"Then what about Lady Mary Blanchard?"

"Too pompous."

"Lady Felicity Markham?"

"Too nasally."

"Miss Temperance Lindwell?"

A laugh erupted from James and he turned to look at Alex. "One of your American cousins? Are you mad?"

"*Distant* cousins," Alex stressed. "And regardless, they are obscenely wealthy—"

"As am I."

"They are beautiful—"

"As are many others."

"And once Lindwell marries his daughters off to titled gentlemen, he and his wife will pack up and leave England to return to New York, an event that would please my father greatly. Do you not wish to please the great Duke of Franklyn?"

"Worthy attempt, my friend, but as much as I greatly esteem your father, the answer is a resounding no. I have no desire to marry a crass American girl."

"I think you are being near-sighted on this. Given there are two, you can choose the one most to your liking—the very pretty brunette with a sharp mind or the lovely blonde with a pleasing and gentle demeanor. Both are educated, though I understand Temperance took more to that than Constance, and if that is not enough, even your own sister insists they are not that bad."

Not that bad. Coming from Hen that was rather damning praise.

"Hen finds a kind word to say about everyone, whether deserved or not. Regardless, I am not marrying an American. When the time comes, I will marry a proper English lass, thank you very much."

"It is unfortunate that you feel that way," Alex said, scanning the crowd before him. "As I may have indicated to the eldest Miss Lindwell that you were looking forward to dancing the upcoming waltz with her."

James shot Alex a deadly glare. "There is a very good chance I will murder you in your sleep tonight."

Alex shrugged, clearly unconcerned by the threat of his imminent demise. "You're rather ornery, you know. Perhaps it is not so much a wife you need most at the moment, but a mistress. A woman who can tend to your more, uh, baser needs so that you are not such a bear to be around. Honestly, man, when was the last time you actually—"

"This is hardly the time and place to discuss that matter." James glanced quickly around them, but no one appeared interested in their conversation, save for old Lady Blanchard, who waved her fan in front of her face and batted her eyelashes at him. Most unsettling.

Alex lowered his voice and leaned a bit closer. "I am only suggesting there are several relatively young, handsome widows here this very night, that would be more than happy to assist you in alleviating the frustration you must be feeling given you haven't lain with a woman in—"

"Enough!"

Several heads turned their way including his great-aunt

seated several chairs away. Lady Dalridge raised one eyebrow at him, a look easily translated into displeasure over his sudden outburst. Bloody hell. James clenched his jaw and forced an apologetic smile.

It did not improve his mood in the least that Alex appeared most amused by his reaction. He quickly changed the subject. "Which Lindwell girl is the eldest? I thought they were twins."

"Indeed they are, but Temperance—the brunette—came first and that is the one you are to dance with."

James groaned. The more outspoken of the two. Wonderful. "She is a bloody bluestocking."

"I grant you, she has some rather...progressive...ideas, but is that not better than listening to someone prattle on about who served what at some tea and what fripperies they wore to attend it?"

James continued to glare. "Progressive? Is that what we're calling it?"

He had heard through the grapevine Miss Lindwell had been seen having many animated conversations with Miss Rosalind Caldwell. A situation bound to end badly.

"When is this waltz to begin?" he asked through gritted teeth.

Alex smiled, showing a distinct lack of sympathy or regret for James's current plight. "In about twenty minutes or so, I believe."

"Then I still have time for a stiff drink in the billiards room first."

"Indeed you do."

"Good." He would need all the fortification he could find to get through the rest of this evening.

James spun on his heel and stalked from the ballroom, ignoring Alex's amused laughter following behind him.

Chapter Two

Miss Lindwell had barely spoken to James since the waltz began, a fact he found rather off putting, given he was a marquess and she a young lady hungry to marry a titled gentleman. One would think she'd put a bit more effort into cultivating his attention. Bat an eye, offer a coquettish smile. Something.

Instead, she'd done nothing more than respond to his questions with one-worded answers, never once meeting his gaze as she did so. It was the height of rudeness and did nothing to cultivate his favor, if that was her hope.

Then again, according to his sister, it was Mr. and Mrs. Lindwell who were most hungry for their daughters to hitch their saddle onto some poor unsuspecting lord and ride him all the way to the altar.

Deuce it! That was not the image he needed in his head when he held one of said daughters in his arms. And, as Alex had indicated, Temperance Lindwell was indeed attractive, despite her American-ness.

Was that a thing?

He shook his head. It hardly mattered. The point was he

found her quite fetching with thick hair the shade of dark chocolate and skin that held a healthy glow about it. And—though he would deny this, should anyone make the suggestion—the fact that she ignored him was oddly intriguing. He wasn't used to being ignored. He was but one and thirty, hardly long in the tooth, handsome, wealthy, and in possession of a title that stretched back seven generations. He was—even he must admit—a damn good catch.

What unmarried woman in her right mind wouldn't set her cap for him?

He studied Miss Lindwell as he spun her about the dance floor, adding a bit of a flourish as he did so, though that failed to garner any reaction at all. Bloody hell. What was her problem? Perhaps he should try trampling her toes. Maybe that might grab her notice.

Devil take it. Is that what he'd been reduced to? Stomping a lady's feet to gain an ounce of attention?

Maybe Alex was right. Maybe he did need to get himself a mistress.

Perhaps he should pay Hawksmoor a visit on the morrow and see whom he might suggest. Despite being newly married and somewhat reformed, The Hawk held more knowledge about the inner workings and secret desires of the ton than anyone. If a young, comely widow was interested in throwing her lot in with a handsome lord in need of certain carnal pleasures, perhaps Hawk might—

"Forgive my bluntness, Lord Ridgemont, but I feel the need to be upfront on a certain matter."

Miss Lindwell's verbal interruption of his thoughts startled him and he had to react quickly to adjust his step, which faltered slightly in surprise.

"Do tell? And what matter is it you feel the need to make me aware of?" He could not begin to imagine, given the one-worded answers he'd thus far received from her.

"I feel I should make it clear that my agreeing to dance with you this evening should not, in any way, be misconstrued."

"Misconstrued?"

"Yes. I hope you are aware that my consent to your request—"

"My request?"

"That I save this dance for you."

James shook his head. Alex had arranged the dance without his knowledge. What exactly had his friend said to her? He bit his tongue to keep from informing her of such, however. It would be rude to do so and while he did not care for Miss Lindwell, he was still a gentleman.

"I see. And what message did you fear your acceptance of this *request* might indicate?"

James pictured several different ways in which he would make Alex pay for cornering him into suffering this moment.

"That my agreement to your request indicated an interest in you that went beyond a quick turn about the dance floor."

He blinked. He had heard of the eldest Lindwell daughter's penchant for plain speaking, but this was the first time he'd been on the receiving end of her particular brand of bold claims.

How did one respond to such a statement?

He spun her around the ballroom, expertly avoiding the bumbling Lord Plimpton who had sadly been born with two left feet, neither of which could dance.

"I can assure you, Miss Lindwell, that I have in no way made any such assumption toward your interest in me."

"Or lack thereof," she added, making her feelings on the matter clear. As if he'd had any doubt from her earlier claim of disinterest.

"Or lack thereof," he muttered, issuing a tight smile to

convey that was the end of this particular topic of conversation.

Miss Lindwell's shoulders sagged in what James could only assume was relief. His pride stung a bit on that one. Given his standing in Society, there were any number of young ladies that would jump at the chance to marry into a family whose lineage was long and whose title held much cache. Was that not what her family wanted, after all?

"Good." She gave a swift nod, but apparently was not quite finished hammering at his pride, as now that she had begun to speak, she seemed disinclined to stop. "Because despite my parents' most fervent hopes, I have no intention of marrying you or one of your ilk."

One of his *ilk*? What the bloody hell did that mean?

"I beg your pardon, but what exactly—"

She cut him off. "Do not take offense, my lord—"

Far too late on that account.

"—but I simply find your type rather...uninteresting. Uninspiring, really."

Uninteresting? Uninspiring?

Her forthrightness took him off guard and, once again, he stumbled, forcing him to pull her closer to regain his footing.

"Is that so?" He sputtered. Because how else did one respond to such a derogatory characterization? "And what have I done to acquire such lofty praise, Miss Lindwell?"

"I've noticed that you English lords and ladies take very little in the way of chances," she said, her voice plain and clear as she spoke and James had no choice but to hear what she said given they were locked in this godforsaken waltz for at least the next several minutes.

"Chances?" What the devil did that mean?

"Yes. You prefer your status quo, going about as you always have in your antiquated ways where Society is built upon the backs of those less fortunate ,yet it is those who have everything who reap the rewards."

Was it possible for an American to have a thought fly through their head without blurting said thought out? "I suspect every society has its own tier system of some sort. Are you to tell me America is any different?"

Miss Lindwell shrugged and the waves of dark hair that cascaded down from where they were gathered at the crown of her head bobbed against her bare shoulders. It was rather distracting. She had very lovely shoulders.

"Of course not. Those of us that inhabit the new world brought with it the archaic ideas of the places we left, and there are those who insist on keeping them in place. But the difference between the new world and the old is that if one should choose to break free of those strictures, one can rise high and elevate their station in life. Take my father, for example."

"Must we," James muttered. He found Leopold Lindwell loud and full of himself. But if Miss Lindwell heard James, she gave no indication and instead barreled forward with her dissertation on everything wrong with England and everything that was right with America.

"My father came from nothing. His father had died shortly after arriving in America. My father was but a child at the time and his mother worked herself to the bone to put a meager amount of food on the table for her children. If my father had been in England, that same fate would have been his future. Struggle, poverty, illness created by both of these things. But instead, my father took every opportunity to better himself. His education came through experience. He worked hard and he took chances. And it was the ability to do this, to have that opportunity to take chances that allowed him to build an empire. He has earned the respect of his peers and is now held in high esteem."

James glanced over Miss Lindwell's shoulder at the band playing upon the raised dais. They did not appear to be ending their rendition of the slow French waltz any time soon.

"Are all you Americans so boastful?"

She shot him a cutting glare. "It isn't boasting. It is stating facts. And the fact is, had my father lived here, such behavior would have been looked down upon, as if he were trying to jump himself up, live beyond his *station* simply because he wished a better life for his children than the one he'd had. He would have been reviled for his love of hard work and the joy he found in being successful. A way of thinking I consider nothing short of destructive and demeaning, having no benefit toward those who, by fluke of birth, were not born into the aristocracy."

"My, but how little you think of us. These last two— three? —Seasons spent attempting to marry one of us must have thoroughly taxed your sensibilities in this regard."

"As I've stated earlier, Lord Ridgemont, I have no intentions of marrying one of you. Or marrying at all, for that matter."

What kind of preposterous thinking was that?

She was far too pretty to hole herself away in a convent and likely too outspoken for the sisters of whatever holy order would deign to put up with her. How *he* had put up with her for the past four minutes baffled him.

He took a deep breath and reined in his irritation. "I am certain there is a gentleman out there that shall be quite aggrieved to learn about your disinclination toward marriage, Miss Lindwell, but I can assure you, with all due certainty, that I am not that man."

He should have left it at that, but his curiosity got the better of him.

"What exactly do you plan on doing with yourself if you do not marry?"

She tossed her head back, giving James a perfect view of the line of her jaw. Strong and defined, it should not have been attractive on a woman. And yet it was, somehow suiting its owner with ease.

"I am educated and resourceful, my lord. I believe I would make a wonderful teacher for the next generation."

"Indeed." God help the young minds she would infect with her dangerous rhetoric. A generation of bluestockings is what they'd end up with, if it were left to her.

"Someone must teach them that the old ways are not set in stone and that they can rise up from humble beginnings and be whatever they choose. It's quite clear you and your ilk have no intention of doing so."

There was that word again. James gnashed his teeth as he struggled to find some calm in the stormy barrage of her unwarranted attack upon him and his *ilk*. But there was no calm to be found.

He attempted a placid expression; more for appearances, should anyone look their way, than because he felt it. Because he did not. Anger roiled inside of him, fed by her pomposity that she had the right to judge what she did not know or understand.

But James refused to be goaded. The last thing he needed was to have the suggestion made in the society rags that he had engaged in a rather heated discussion with the American heiress. It would not do and likely his great-aunt would have strong words with him should such a thing happen. As much as Lady Dalridge loved gossip, she preferred it to be about other people.

James plastered a false smile upon his face. "I suppose, Miss Lindwell, that such unrelenting rudeness is not your fault. I can only assume that you cannot help yourself. You are, after all, an American and therefore given to far less civilized social behaviors than my particular *ilk*."

She stiffened in his arms. "Less civilized?"

Well now, that got a bit of a rise, didn't it? Victory tugged at the corner of James's mouth, but he held his smile in check. "Indeed. It is this inability to conduct yourselves in a proper and polite manner that makes it difficult for you to fit into our world, no matter how desperately you try."

"I assure you, *my lord*, I am not trying."

"But your parents certainly are, aren't they? Given the egregious number of parties they have thrown since your arrival to London. Clearly, a vain attempt to buy you a position within our Society and our way of life. The very life you claim to loathe."

"I do loathe—"

He didn't let her finish. He was on a roll now and while the part of him that had been trained relentlessly in the fine art of gentlemanly behavior advised caution, the ire he had stoked within her and the way it made her eyes flash overrode his better sense.

"Honestly, Miss Lindwell, there is nothing so gauche as watching you Americans throw around your newfound riches like a child in a candy store, in the pathetic hope of linking your *ilk* to a lofty English title." He raised an eyebrow and pulled out his most arrogant tone. "As if such a thing could be purchased."

Then he tsked and shook his head.

In hindsight, it was likely not the best way for a gentleman to behave. Definitely not while in the middle of the ballroom at Lord and Lady Frontenac's well-attended fete. And most certainly not as the music ended, allowing all those nearest them to hear the solid smack of Miss Lindwell's palm as it landed against his cheek with enough force to cause his eyes to water.

Deuce it! Where had she learned to hit like that?

He might have asked her, but by the time his vision

cleared, all that was left of Miss Lindwell was the haughty stiffness of her lovely shoulders as she stalked from the ballroom, cutting a path through a very shocked crowd.

James rubbed at the spot on his cheek.

"Americans," he said, addressing the other partygoers, with a small laugh—though merry was the last thing he felt. He had behaved abominably, allowing himself to be goaded by a woman who clearly did not know the first thing about his heritage and the people who had forged it.

Regardless, the proper thing—the *gentlemanly* thing—to do would be to apologize. Even if she didn't deserve it. Even if it was the last thing he wanted to do.

Because that is what a civilized English gentleman did.

With an inward groan, James made his way from the ballroom to find Miss Lindwell.

Temperance let the night air cool the burn of anger and embarrassment raging across her face in equal measure. How dare that awful man say such...such... awful things about her family! That they bordered on the truth only made his claims all the more hurtful. Clearly, avoiding marriage to men such as Lord Ridgemont was the best decision she had made in a long time.

Slapping his lordship, however—no matter how much he had deserved it—was likely the worst. Her father would be incensed once word reached him. Her mother mortified. If she hadn't sealed her fate before, she had done so now. She only hoped her actions—and the ones she was about to take—did not have a detrimental effect on Constance.

Temperance pulled her wrap closer. The thin silk did little to protect her from the damp spring air. At this rate, the long waves of her hair that Melinda had worked so diligently to tame would turn to frizz before she returned to the ballroom. More reason for Mother to find disfavor with her.

With a sigh, she glanced around the gardens then down the lane that led to the street beyond. Miss Rosalind Caldwell was nowhere to be found. Had she witnessed Temperance's physical outburst toward Lord Ridgemont and changed her mind about discussing the possibility of Temperance taking the position of headmistress at the newly built school for young girls?

The devil! She should have contained herself. Lord Ridgemont had intentionally goaded her with his ridiculous notions and she had allowed him. If she could not show restraint where that pompous gentleman was concerned, how would she ever maintain her composure with children likely to test the limits of her patience and their own boundaries?

But, surely Rosalind—as she insisted on being referred to —would understand and overlook this temporary gaffe. Despite being the second daughter to a baron, the lady was a very enlightened thinker. Rosalind's opinions with respect to educating the minds of young girls, especially those who would otherwise find themselves toiling in service for the rest of their lives, or worse, echoed Temperance's own beliefs.

"Where are you?" she muttered into the dark night. Rosalind had agreed to meet with her away from the party, to ensure their conversation was not overheard. The last thing Temperance needed was word of her plans getting back to Mother and Father before she could implement them. If that were to happen, she would likely find herself locked in one of the upstairs bedrooms, never to see the light of day until she was dragged kicking and screaming to the altar, forced to marry a man she did not want. She shivered, both from the damp air and the horrid thought of her potential fate.

Temperance reached for the small pin watch she'd hidden within the bodice of her dress and unclipped it, holding it up to the thin strands of moonlight that fought its way through breaks in the cloud. In her attempt to escape the ballroom and the brouhaha her slap was likely to cause, she'd arrived at their appointed spot earlier than planned.

The sound of carriage wheels in the distance grabbed her attention and a moment later, a hackney stopped at the end of the long drive near the front of the house. Had Rosalind decided to hold their conversation in a carriage to protect them from the weather and any prying eyes?

Temperance took a few steps forward then stopped. An unexpected discomfort roiled in the pit of her stomach. Just nerves. This was a drastic undertaking, after all. It was natural to be nervous. She took a deep breath and pressed her hand against her heart.

"Courage," she whispered and took a few more steps toward the awaiting carriage.

The driver set the brake on the hackney and stepped down from the driver's box. Temperance watched as he opened the door to the carriage and noted the man's ill-fitted livery. She had heard the Caldwells were in a bit of a financial pinch, but could they not at least tailor their servants' livery properly? No wonder Lord Caldwell was desperate to marry off his three daughters. Clearly, it was the only way to ensure they were not left destitute, given he had no sons to take up the baronage upon his demise.

Another reason women needed to be educated. If they were educated, they could hold positions that would allow them to support themselves. And perhaps—though this was a thought she did not speak aloud for fear of being accused of sedition—they might eventually be regarded as persons by law and not the property of some man.

The driver stepped away from the open door of the hackney. The hint of a red dress rustled in the breeze within. Temperance had not seen Rosalind this evening and therefore had no idea if she had been wearing red, though the color seemed a rather flagrant choice for one as serious-minded as the middle Caldwell daughter.

The driver faced her and executed a short bow. "Miss Lindwell?"

"Y-yes." She took a few steps forward, but the roiling in her stomach refused to abate. Was she making the right choice? She wasn't one given to rash decisions and she'd thought long and hard about this course of action. If she wished to avoid marriage to what amounted to an English version of Beauregard, boldness was required. So why the second thoughts now that the moment was upon her?

The driver swept an arm toward the open carriage door. A rather grand gesture, as was the wide grin upon his face. Then again, likely the Caldwells were not in a position to hire the highest quality of servants. When economies had to be considered, certain niceties fell by the wayside.

She took another deep breath and set her shoulders back, slipping her pin watch into the pocket sewn into her gown. This was it. Her chance to take control of her life and make it her own, instead of spending her days controlled by her father or husband.

Temperance nodded at the driver and marched with purpose toward the hackney.

Toward her future.

Chapter Three

What the devil did she think she was she doing?

James took a step closer from the shadows as he watched with growing curiosity Miss Lindwell's retreating back. She strode with obvious purpose toward a rather rough looking hackney where a shabbily dressed liveryman held the door opened for her.

Was she running off? Meeting some gentleman—and he used that term loosely, as what gentleman would send such a shoddy transport for a lady? Had he stumbled upon a tryst?

James stopped. If so, he wanted no part of this. A smart gentleman would do an about face, return to the ballroom and put the matter out of his mind. It wasn't his business what Miss Lindwell did or whom she did it with. If she wished to ruin her reputation by partaking in some salacious assignation with whoever awaited within the carriage, what business was it of his?

None.

Then why were his feet not moving?

He glanced down at his Hessians that shone to perfection despite the weak thread of moonlight from above. He really must compliment Gregory on his attention to detail. His new valet was worth his weight in gold. It had been well worth incurring the ire of Lord Bloomsby to steal him away.

James looked up once more. Miss Lindwell drew closer to the carriage. She had not seen him. Was not aware her shenanigans were no longer being carried out in secrecy. Should he call her out? If so, he must do so now before she stepped inside the carriage and potentially ruined herself.

Would that be such a disaster? She had already claimed no interest whatsoever in marriage. What woman did that? He shook his head. Miss Temperance Lindwell was a complete puzzle to him. Physically, she embodied every aspect he would normally find appealing. A little taller than the norm, which given his own height was a bit of a blessing. Luscious dark hair —he'd always had a preference for brunettes. And a face that was an entrancing mixture of both beauty and intelligence. A far improvement over many of the young ladies he'd conversed with this evening, who'd proved empty and vacuous.

Then again, none of them had slapped him across the cheek.

Nor did any of them hold such unsettling ideas as never marrying. Or choosing to forgo having children of her own in favor of educating the masses and elevating the working class above their station. Her determination toward the betterment of others stunned him.

And perhaps even fascinated him a little, if he were being honest.

Then again, honesty could be highly overrated and blast it —she was going to do herself a complete disservice if she stepped foot inside that carriage! James groaned. Was there no one else that might relieve him of the duty of saving Miss Lindwell from herself? The shadows revealed no one. It was up to him and he could not, in good conscience, simply stand by and allow her to stumble into ruin.

He was a gentleman, after all. Born and bred to protect the fairer gender, even from themselves and their own folly.

"Miss Lindwell!" James hissed her name, careful not to shout and draw the notice of anyone who might have slipped outside into the gardens for a tryst of their own. If he was to do this, the last thing he needed was to be overheard and have the events misconstrued, thinking *he* was the gentleman she was secretly meeting in the shadowy lane.

Only ten feet from the hackney, Miss Lindwell spun on her heel at the sound of her name. Beyond her, James caught sight of red skirts billowing inside the carriage as the breeze kicked up around them. He stopped.

Skirts? Well, that was unexpected. Was Miss Lindwell—? I mean, he had heard of women who preferred...that is, who showed a certain preference for the fairer sex. A preference he could readily understand, but he had never suspected that Miss Lindwell leaned in that particular direction.

"What are you—" Miss Lindwell stopped then shook her head, flicking a hand at him as if to shoo him off. "Go away. This is none of your business."

He could not argue with her on that point. However, he was here now and his gentlemanly instincts refused to let him leave. Something about the situation rubbed him the wrong way.

Perhaps it was the nervous quiver in Miss Lindwell's tone. Or the way the lady sitting inside the hackney had yet to show herself.

"Who is in the carriage? Show yourself there!"

"Hush!" Miss Lindwell hissed and took a step toward him. "This is none of your concern. Go away. Miss Caldwell and I wish to have a conversation outside the noise and commotion of the ballroom and we do not require your *permission* to do so."

He disliked the way she stressed the word permission, as if

he was attempting to exert his influence upon her. Clearly, he wasn't. He was merely trying to stop her from doing something foolish. Because he had a sense there was more going on than her claim of having a conversation with Miss Caldwell—

James stopped then looked at the hint of red skirts still visible within the carriage. Lady Caldwell had stopped him on his way to search for Miss Lindwell and she'd had each of her three daughters with her. None of whom had been adorned in a scandalous red gown. Cream for the eldest, a soft rose for the youngest and rather plain navy for the middle. Not a red among them.

What the bloody hell was going on here?

James jabbed a finger at the awaiting hackney. "That is not Miss Caldwell."

"I beg your pardon, it most certainly is." But her voice wavered as she cast a quick look over her shoulder. That was enough for the hair on the back of James's neck to prickle. Something was amiss. But before he could act upon instinct, mayhem broke out.

"Blast it! Grab the chit!"

Despite the skirts, the voice that came out of the hackney was several octaves too low to belong to any woman.

James didn't hesitate. He broke into a run at the same time the unexpected voice caused Miss Lindwell to spin about on her heel to face the occupant of the hackney. The liveryman acted upon the command and grabbed her by the arm, hauling her awkwardly against him before shoving her toward the open door of the hackney.

"Unhand me, you smelly oaf!" Miss Lindwell swung her free hand and boxed the liveryman about the ears. He cringed just as James reached him and pulled him away from her.

"Get back to the ballroom," James ordered as he struggled with the wiry and surprisingly strong liveryman. Bloody hell, this thing was getting well out of control.

But a quick glance showed the occupant of the hackney had a hold of her and was attempting to drag her inside.

What the deuce was going on? He shoved at the liveryman to disengage the man and pull Miss Lindwell to safety.

A pistol appeared over Miss Lindwell's shoulder and the heavily bearded face of a man in a red dress appeared. "Stop where yer at, m'lord or I'll shoot ye where ye stand."

For a fleeting second, James considered the man's dictate. Then decided against it. If he did not dispense of these criminals, there was no telling what they would do to an innocent such as Miss Lindwell. And devil take it, if they thought he would simply walk away and allow that to happen, they were both as stupid as they looked. He rushed at the man.

The pistol snapped but nothing happened. A misfire. Both James and the man froze, stunned. Then James took advantage and lunged toward him. His opponent threw the pistol at him. He ducked, but not far enough and the hard metal bounced off the side of his head. He winced and stumbled slightly to his left, vaguely aware of Miss Lindwell twisting around and leveling the right hook he'd been privy to earlier against her captor.

Clearly, the man had been as unprepared for the blow as he had been, and he staggered back, falling into the hackney.

James opened his mouth to command Miss Lindwell to run to safety but the words never had a chance to leave his mouth as something hard and heavy crashed into the back of his skull. Suddenly, the cloudy night sky erupted with a thousand brilliant stars. Then just as suddenly, his knees went out from under him.

And then there was nothing.

Temperance pulled back the curtain covering the window and let in what little light was available. They had already left Grosvenor Square and were heading away from the city proper from the looks of things.

Where were they taking them? And why?

She glared down at Lord Ridgemont's prone form that had been dumped rudely at her feet inside the carriage. They were alone, their captors having both taken to the driver's box above, likely to further discuss the daft plan that had brought them here.

Despite their obvious success thus far, whatever foolish notion precipitating their actions remained as dimwitted now as when they began. Neither her family, nor the ton, would stand by and allow such mistreatment of their members. And heaven help the two fools when Lady Dalridge got her hands on them for kidnapping her beloved great-nephew. Although, had his lordship not swooped in to play the white knight, as if any of what was transpiring was his business, she would have handily escaped and returned to the ballroom unharmed.

She glared down at him again. The liveryman had picked up the thrown pistol and hit Lord Ridgemont soundly on the back of the head. He'd dropped like a stone and not moved of his own accord since.

What had he been thinking? She had not needed rescue. Growing up with one of her older brothers being well versed in the pugilistic arts did have its benefits, after all. Though Collin had instructed her never to use what he had taught her unless she found herself under dire circumstances where it was her only alternative.

Thankfully, this was only the second time she'd had to employ those skills—discounting the slap she'd landed upon Lord Ridgemont earlier this evening. And granted there was still some argument among those close to her as to whether or not the first time had been warranted as well. Regardless, she was indebted to her darling brother for imparting the knowledge and she would be sure to thank him profusely, should she ever see him again.

An event that would not be in question had Lord Ridgemont not seen fit to interfere. Her strike had set her free from her captor's grip and she'd already hiked up her skirts to sprint back up the lane to safety when Lord Ridgemont managed to ruin everything. Had he not gotten himself knocked unconscious, she could have made her escape. But she could hardly just leave him behind, defenseless.

Now look at them!

Temperance leaned over her lap to get a closer look. His long body was unceremoniously folded into the interior of the carriage. They had originally tossed him onto the seat across from her, but he'd quickly slid off to land at her feet when the hackney jolted into action. She'd tried to stop his fall, but he'd been too heavy, his limbs long and unwieldy.

She nudged him with the toe of her slipper. No response. Temperance twisted her lips to one side. Their captors had planned to leave him behind, though in no position to tell the tale of what had happened or identify either of them.

"Stick 'im with a blade and leave 'im in the bushes."

The command came from her captor wearing the horrific red dress—clearly the leader of the two.

"Kill 'im? That'll get us bloody hanged!"

"And you think kidnapping this chit won't if his lordship can identify us? Now take care of it. Maybe the grand Mr. Lindwell will be more willin' to pay a pretty quid if'n he thinks his precious daughter might meet the same fate."

Kidnapping? They were kidnapping her?

"You will do no such thing," Temperance had commanded, stopping her struggle to get away from the leader. "Leave his lordship be. Likely, you have rattled the poor man's brains to such a state he won't even recall the events of this evening. If you leave him be, I shall come quietly."

Surely Father would pay the ransom with all due haste and she'd be back home within a day. Two at the most.

The imposter of a liveryman shrugged and rubbed his jaw. "She makes a solid point, Ferris."

"Foolish wanker, you used my name! Bloody hell. Fine. But I ain't leavin' him behind. May be we can get two ransoms out of this night to make up for the extra hardship. Get 'is lordship in the carriage and hurry up about it before anyone realizes either of 'em are missing from their fancy party."

Any hope they would leave Lord Ridgemont behind so he might offer some assistance in tracking down the fools who had abducted her faded, as they were both shoved into the carriage.

Now look at him. Unconscious and of no use whatsoever. There was no telling how badly he was hurt as he had yet to awaken. This night had gone from bad, to worse, to epically horrible.

Temperance reached down and shook his lordship's shoulder. "Lord Ridgemont?" She kept her voice low and steady. Nothing.

She peeled off her silk glove and held her hand in front of his nose and mouth. Relief washed over her as his warm breath brushed against her skin. He was alive. That was something, at least. He'd be far more useful to her that way.

She tapped his cheek, smooth, warm, and recently shaven. "Lord Ridgemont?"

Again nothing.

Temperance let out a huff of frustration. She needed him awake and mobile. She was not so innocent she did not understand the dangers of being alone and unprotected with men of low morals. Besides, if the opportunity for escape presented itself, she hoped to take it. Not something she could attempt while Lord Ridgemont was inert and unresponsive. Despite her earlier irritation with him, she was not about to abandon him with their captors and attempt a bid for freedom on her own. If they made good on their earlier threat to end him, she'd never forgive herself.

The carriage rocked back and forth and she glanced out the window. They had left the cobbled streets and the terrain had turned rougher. Buildings and derelict houses replaced the grander homes of Grosvenor Square and the scent of the Thames permeated the walls of the hackney. Here and there, figures drifted out of the shadows then back in, but none stayed long enough for her to call out for help. Not that they would even hear if she did. The carriage traveled swiftly with little heed to safety or comfort. If they were to escape, it was up to her.

Temperance leaned closer to Lord Ridgemont's ear, bracing her other hand on the seat to steady her from the rocky ride.

"My lord?" What was his first name? Benedict? No, that was Lord Glenmor. Nicholas? Drat, no. That belonged to Lord Blackbourne. Thomas, perhaps? Yes, that was it. "Thomas, are you hurt?" The name slid off her tongue, an intimate whisper in the dark that left her unsettled in a way that had nothing to do with their current predicament. She brushed the emotion away.

Lord Ridgemont let out a groan and his hand that rested near her foot fumbled, his long fingers slipping around her ankle.

Good heavens! She froze as shock and something else—something warm and liquid and oddly comforting—shot up her leg at the inappropriate contact. She swallowed and attempted to remove her leg from his grasp but Lord Ridgemont held fast, as if the contact was the only thing tethering him to this world.

"Lord Ridgemont?"

"If you are going to breach etiquette and refer to me by my given name, you may wish to use the correct one, which is James, not Thomas," he said, his voice strained. Yet not so much that he couldn't manage a proper set down at her incorrect name usage and social gaffe. Under different circumstances, and directed at someone else, she may have been impressed.

She took a fortifying breath. "There are any number of things I might call you after you interfered, and I am certain I shall get to all of them in the near future, but for now, I would like to ascertain the extent of your injuries."

"Interfered? I was attempting to save you." He released her ankle and cold air rushed in to replace the warm band where his fingers had teased her skin through her silk stocking. He attempted to push himself up, but collapsed under his own weight and groaned.

"Yes, well, bravo. Well done," she muttered. "Stop trying to get up."

Temperance leaned forward and reached down to feel the back of his head where he'd been struck. His hair was damp and when she pulled her hand away and held it up to the window, a dark stain covered it.

"You're bleeding." She did her best to keep the fear from her voice. She knew little of such injuries, but surely, this could not be good for a body.

"Bloody hell," he muttered.

"Something like that." Temperance leaned forward again and reached for the hem of her gown, lifting it up to expose her linen shift. Finding the seam, she pulled with all her might until the tear of fabric echoed inside the carriage.

"You have very lovely calves, Miss Lindwell. Although I hope, you would not be taking advantage of my current state to expose yourself and create a situation whereupon I would be forced to offer marriage to save your reputation."

His suggestion took her by surprise, though it was difficult to know whether he issued it with any kind of seriousness. She pulled on the linen once again until the strip hung loosely from her shift. One last pull and it was free.

"Don't flatter yourself, my lord. I have no interest in marriage, least of all to you."

"You wound me."

"I highly doubt it."

A quiet chuckle, followed by a groan filled the space around them. How he could find anything humorous in their current situation baffled her. And yet it buoyed her at the same time. If they could both keep a level head, perhaps they would find a way out of this mess sooner rather than later.

"Do you think you are able to sit up with assistance? I need to bandage your wound to stop the bleeding."

Lord Ridgemont attempted to lift himself from the floor of the hackney to no avail. "I believe you will have to come down to my level."

She looked at the space between the two seats. It was fully occupied by his lordship. "There is no room for me."

Lord Ridgemont shifted slightly, moving onto his back with a long moan. "You shall have to straddle me."

His bold words took her aback. "I beg your pardon?"

"Please do not take my suggestion as an invitation, Miss Lindwell. It is simply the only option. If you are able to straddle me, perhaps we can work together to pull me into a seated position whereby you can wrap the bandage around my head. Unless, of course, you possess the ability of levitation, then by all means..." He rolled his hand in the air.

She pressed her lips together. It was shame irritation could not float a body in the air because, if so, their problems would be solved. As it were, he was too heavy for her to pull into a seated position without his assistance. But straddle him? The suggestion sounded horribly salacious. And, despite the circumstances, oddly exciting. Honestly, one would think she'd been the one knocked on the head!

She swallowed and draped the linen over her shoulders as she balanced her hands on the seats on either side of her as the carriage bumped along at breakneck speed. But with both hands holding her steady over him, she had no way to lift her skirts enough to ensure her feet did not get tangled in them. She hovered over him trying to find the best solution.

"Is there a problem, Miss Lindwell?"

She looked down. He had opened his eyes and heaven help her, but she must look like a complete fool, hovering over him like a looming apparition unsure of what to do next.

Temperance cleared her throat and attempted a neutral tone. "My skirts are in the way. If I become tangled in them I will not be able to move properly to get you into a seated position."

Not that there was anything proper about this situation. If one were to review, she had been kidnapped, was being transported somewhere unfamiliar by two brigands that had already suggested killing Lord Ridgemont, said lord had fondled her ankle, and now she was about to straddle him like a common doxy!

The fear and hysteria she'd held at bay thus far crept closer.

Lord Ridgemont moved and before she understood what he was about, his fingers fumbled about her ankles and her skirts began to slide up her legs, along with his hands. Temperance jolted at the sensation, the intimacy of such a touch beyond anything she'd ever experienced. She could not move. Did not want to.

The carriage lurched, rising up and falling down as if the wheel had hit a deep rut. Temperance's hands bounced off the seats to either side of her and she pitched forward, landing hard against his lordship and forcing his hands farther up her legs until they rested on her bare thighs.

She froze. Lord Ridgemont's breath brushed harshly against her neck. Temperance closed her eyes and tried to regain her composure but heaven above, how did she do that when his hands hovered only inches from her—

He moved beneath her. Dear sweet lord—she was sitting on his private parts!

"Are you hurt, Miss Lindwell?"

She shook her head, her voice stuck somewhere in her throat.

"This is a bit of a pickle, I suppose."

She nodded.

Lord Ridgemont cleared his throat and removed his hands from her thighs, their slow retreat leaving a trail of heat behind, branding her skin in a way she expected would take a long time to fade.

He shifted and placed his hands on her hips. Temperance closed her eyes. He held her firm and lifted her off his private parts to sit farther down on her lap. For all that was holy, she should have insisted her captors leave him behind. Surely, the strange and confusing torture of his hands making themselves familiar with every inch of her body was far worse a torment than whatever her kidnappers had in mind.

"Perhaps if you could put your arms around me and pull up, I can push from the floor and we can wrestle me into a seated position. Do you think you might be able to do this?"

"Yes." The word croaked out of her. She would do just about anything to end the miasma of confusing emotions churning like a tempest inside of her.

Temperance slipped her arms around him and on his count, pulled him upward with all her might. It took several tries before they managed to maneuver him into a somewhat seated position.

Temperance took a deep breath to steady her nerves. Despite still sitting upon his lap with nothing protecting her skin from the rough wool of his trousers, she breathed a little easier. Unfortunately, each inhale brought with it the masculine scent of him.

Beneath them, the uneven rumble of the carriage wheels brought home the severity of their situation. She gave herself a mental shake. *Get control of yourself, for goodness sake! You're not some foolish girl. There is work to be done.*

"My lord, if you have no objection, I am going to untie your cravat and use it to press against your wound. Then I shall wind the strip of linen from my—" Temperance stumbled then regained her composure. "—from my shift and wind that about your head to hold it in place."

"Do what you must, although I should inform you Gregory will not be pleased to see his hard work tossed off in such a manner."

"Gregory?"

"My valet."

"I see. Well, perhaps you could extend my humblest apologies to Gregory and explain to him I thought this a better use of the cravat, given your current situation. Now try to hold steady."

Lord Ridgemont's skin, beneath the expertly tied cravat, was hot to the touch and she hoped it was not indicative of a fever from the severity of his wound. Could such a wound cause a fever? Oh, bother! Why was it in all the books she had read and studied at the Litchfield Female Academy, not one of them gave her a better indication of what to do in situations such as this?

She pursed her lips. Likely, because no one expected the proper ladies of Litchfield would find themselves straddling a lord of the realm in such a scandalous manner whilst being spirited out of London by two bungling kidnappers to places unknown. No, those ladies sent to the Academy were expected to pair up with the proper gentlemen from the Litchfield Law Academy and marry. Upon marriage the lady was to birth a passel of proper children to continue the family lineage and make her husband proud, all while said husband mucked about with his lover and left his wife all but forgotten once she had done her duty.

How close she had come to meeting such a horrid fate.

She jerked at the knot—mentally cursing Gregory for his expertise—and Lord Ridgemont grunted.

"Forgive me."

"If I did not know better I would think you were trying to strangle me."

"If I courted your untimely demise, I would have let our new friends driving this carriage leave you dead in the bushes as they had wanted."

For a moment, Lord Ridgemont said nothing and Temperance managed to undo the knot.

"They wanted to kill me?"

Chapter Four

"**O**f course, they did. You're a liability, I would think."

Miss Lindwell shifted her weight and James winced. He wasn't sure how much longer he could allow her to rest upon him in such a manner without the evidence of what it did to him becoming embarrassingly obvious.

"A liability?" Likely, this was the first time anyone had suggested he was anything but an asset.

"They did not want you to be able to identify them and suggested it best if they eliminate you as a witness."

She delivered this reasoning with an indifference to their situation that left James baffled. He knew few women of his acquaintance that would be taking these current circumstances with such a level head. Most would be all but catatonic or in the throes of hysterics.

"Then how is it that I am here and not bleeding out in the bushes?"

She reached behind him, forcing James to lean forward, his mouth only inches from the delectable décolleté that he had found quite tempting earlier in the evening. Miss

Lindwell may be an outspoken bluestocking, but she was a stunningly beautiful one without doubt.

And she smelled positively wonderful. Like something deep and woodsy. Untamed.

Oh, bloody hell!

"You are here because I agreed to come along willingly if they did not kill you. They agreed, but determined they could not risk leaving a witness behind, so they tossed you in here with me."

She had saved him. The truth of this fact settled around him with a discomfort that rivaled the throbbing in his skull—not to mention farther south—for supremacy.

He was not used to being saved. Had never been saved, come to think of it. If anything, he was the one who was always saving others. Or trying to, at least. He hadn't always been successful in that regard and those failures haunted him to this day.

She pulled him closer until his mouth rested against her soft skin, shoving the dark thoughts from his head. One of them, at least. God help him.

He flinched as she placed the folded cravat against the incessant pounding at the base of his skull then tapped his shoulder. "Straighten up."

He did as she bade and she wound the torn piece of linen from her shift around his head, tying a tight knot at the side next to his ear.

"There, that should hold. Do you think you can push yourself up onto the seat?"

He didn't. Despite the strange rush of heat and awareness heightening his senses, his limbs were weak as a babe's and any sudden movement sent his head tumbling as if it had been tossed into the murk.

"Perhaps it best I stay put."

"Hm. Yes, I suppose." She shifted off him to kneel in the

small space between his body and the seat she'd occupied only moments ago. "Better they believe you to be no threat to them until we need you to be."

"Yes. Exactly." Whether or not he would be ready when she needed him to be was not worth considering. He would do whatever he must to keep her safe.

"Well, get some sleep then. I have a feeling they are taking us well outside of London, so we may in for a long trip. Do you mind if I—" She nestled into his side, surprising him.

"What are you—"

"I lost my shawl in the scuffle and it is cold in here. I'm afraid my gown was not made for such weather. It was meant for traipsing about ballrooms in the hopes of enticing some poor, unsuspecting gentleman."

Her admission surprised him. "I thought you did not care to entice any gentleman—unsuspecting or otherwise."

"I do not, but I am not the one who designed the dress."

"And you are truly opposed to marriage?" The idea continued to baffle him. What woman would not want to marry? "I see no advantage to such thinking."

Her shoulder shrugged against him as she settled in. "I see no advantage to marriage. Tell me, would you willingly enter into a situation that left you as nothing more than a piece of chattel to be dealt with and used as seen fit by the whims of another?"

"No, but—" He stopped. Is that what women thought? Surely, not all. His sister was happily married. In fact, he'd never seen her so happy. Then again, Alex did not treat Hen as chattel and James would bet his life that his best friend did not consider her as such. She was an integral part of his life, decisions, and consideration on all matters. And what of Lord and Lady Hawksmoor? Or the Sheridans? The Laythams? The Bowens and Kingsleys? "Not all men think this way."

"But all men are *allowed* to think that way, a fact I take

great exception to. I prefer that the only voice I answer to be my own. I am perfectly capable of making my own decisions and do not need someone else to do so for me."

The heat of her body seeped into his and the tension in his muscles eased somewhat. He gingerly rested his head against hers.

"If our current situation is any indication of your decision making ability, Miss Lindwell, you may want to rethink your strategy."

She lifted her head and James winced at the movement. Bloody hell, but everything hurt. How was it a simple conk on the cranium could make every single muscle ache in response? Or was that from being callously tossed into the back of the carriage and bounced about as they rode roughshod for parts unknown?

"Might I remind you, it was my current quick thinking and decision making that kept you from landing in the bushes with a knife piercing your heart."

The reminder pinched his ego and he shifted uncomfortably against it, but the sensation refused to abate. He did not care to be indebted to others, especially an opinionated harpy such as Miss Temperance Lindwell, whose backward ideas were nothing short of ludicrous. Regardless, the fact remained, if she hadn't made the deal of trading her freedom for his life, he'd likely be dead right now.

Cold invaded his blood stream as the reality of that thought perforated the pain in his head, sinking in.

Dead.

Because he had tried to save a woman.

Had he known that possibility existed when he'd stood on the pathway outside Lord Frontenac's home, would he have let well enough alone? Would he have turned away and left Miss Lindwell to her fate, saving himself and the future generations who would bear the title Marquess of Ridgemont?

No. He would not have. He did not know how to.

Saving damsels in distress was something of a hobby for him, was it not? Or at least trying to.

Ruth's image floated up from the sacred place where he kept his memories of her stored, but his remembrance had grown a bit fuzzy around the edges. He could see the dark hair, the lithe figure, but when his heart called out to her, it was not her face he saw when she turned about.

James jolted and blinked into the dark as Miss Lindwell's countenance faded in his mind's eye. Several long moments passed before the shock wore off and his heartbeat returned to normal.

Clearly, the hit to his head had caused temporary brain damage.

***

Despite her best attempts to stay awake and maintain some sense of where they were going, the darkness and warmth of Lord Ridgemont's body had lulled her to sleep. A fact Temperance had not been aware of until a sudden bump startled her awake and brought to the forefront sore joints and aching muscles, compliments of the bumpy ride, damp air, and struggle of earlier in the evening. Next to her, she could hear the steady in and out of Lord Ridgemont's breathing. At least something was working in their favor. His wound concerned her, almost as much as the fear they may not be able to escape their captors. And if they did, would they even know which way to run?

She craned her neck to see out the window, but nothing about the landscape looked familiar in the dim morning light and fear crept in. What would become of them? What if their captors decided to go ahead and do away with Lord Ridgemont? He was in no condition to fight off two attackers. And without his protection, what would happen to her? If they were concerned with his lordship identifying them enough to kill him, would they not have the same concern with her? Once they had the ransom money, what reason would they have to keep her alive?

Doubt took root. She may not get out of this situation alive.

Above them, the voices of their captors drifted down. They were squabbling once more, like unruly children arguing over a toy they both wanted. A vision of her two brothers flashed through her mind and her heart pulled. How she missed them both. Especially now. Would she ever see them again? It had already been half a decade since Daniel left to seek his own future, instead of the one Father had insisted he accept. She had not heard a word from him since. The abandonment stung, but worse was the fear that something horrible had happened to him.

What if she died here without ever discovering the truth?

"Are you awake?" Lord Ridgemont interrupted her anxious thoughts with his low whisper, his familiar voice arresting the fear before its claws sank too deep into her heart.

"Yes."

"I think we should attempt to make our escape. It's important we get you to safety. I do not mean to be crass, Miss Lindwell, but there is no telling what these men have planned—"

"They plan to hold me for ransom," Temperance said.

"Yes, but what I am referring to—"

"I know what you are referring to." She was not a complete fool and she'd be a bold-faced liar if she claimed not to have the same concern. "But I am worth more to them unharmed, my lord. As damaged goods, I will not fetch as high a price from my father."

"And what makes you think they know this?"

"I will make it clear, should it come to that." She straightened, reluctantly pushing away from the warmth of Lord Ridgemont's side. It was difficult to think straight and strategize when all she wanted was to sink against him and let the illusion of security ensconce her. But that's all it was. An illusion. If Lord Ridgemont acted rashly, things could go from bad to worse in a fast minute. There was only one solution.

"I need you to pretend to still be unconscious."

"I will do no such thing," he hissed, the affront at such a suggestion evident from the flash of anger in his deep blue eyes and the firm set of his jaw.

She shot him a glare and held a finger against her lips to remind him to keep quiet. "You must." Temperance shook her head and stood, lifting herself back into the seat she had occupied earlier. Good heavens, but her bones hurt from all the rattling.

"I can see no advantage to—"

She cut him off. "There are two of them, maybe more. You are injured and in no condition to fight them off. We must assess our situation before we act imprudently. If they believe you are no threat, it will allow us an element of surprise once you have regained your wits and strength."

Lord Ridgemont's body stiffened and his mouth pulled into a firm line. "I can assure you, my wits are—"

"Lord Ridgemont," Temperance said, keeping her voice low. "They are more likely to keep us together if they think you require care. I will make it clear to them that they will fetch a hefty price for your safe return as well. This will give us time to determine our whereabouts and formulate a proper plan for escape."

He pulled his mouth tight once more until a white line appeared along the perimeter of his lips, standing out against his already pale skin. His lack of healthy color told her he still suffered the effects of his injuries.

The carriage came to an abrupt halt and Temperance had to grab the edge of the seat to keep from being tossed forward onto Lord Ridgemont. Outside, the squabbling had ceased and the carriage jostled as one or both of their captors jumped to the ground.

Temperance leaned forward, her mouth close to his lordship, her voice urgent. "Lord Ridgemont, this is our best chance. Please!"

He issued one last glare then gave a curt nod, slipping back down into his previously prone position. His dark lashes closed, casting a shadow against his stark cheekbones. Temperance had little time to appreciate the beauty of this as the door to the carriage jerked open and their two captors stood in the opening.

Beyond them was nothing but an endless landscape of tall brown grass and sparse bushes matted with pockets of snow that had yet to yield to the spring thaw. They had clearly traveled north. And landed in the middle of nowhere.

Desperation clawed at Temperance's insides. What would they do now?

Chapter Five

~~~

It took all of James's will to not react when the buffoons pulled him unceremoniously out of the carriage, first by his feet until his backside landed on the box placed beneath him—how kind of them to not let him land on cold, hard ground—then by his underarms as they dragged him over the rough terrain.

He opened one of his eyes by a narrow slit, careful not to give himself away as one of their captors kept pace near his hip, the miscreant's hand gripped tightly on Miss Lindwell's arm. The landscape gave little away. The snow packed around the dead grass indicated they had traveled north, but other than that, he could not place their location. The land rose up to meet the horizon and, based on the positioning of the sun he guessed it to be late-morning, perhaps early afternoon. Which would explain the growling in his stomach.

Had their captors made provisions to feed them? They didn't strike him as the most forward thinking of men, but surely, even they would realize they could not starve their prisoners and hope to claim a hefty ransom. Besides, he required proper sustenance to regain his strength and get them out of this mess. As it was, his body ached and pained, his head throbbed and he was parched. Not that he hadn't experienced such maladies after a party before, but usually such came after too much brandy and a proper tumbling about with a rather ribald lady of untold acrobatic abilities.

"In here," the leader barked before pulling ahead and dragging Miss Lindwell along with him. A few seconds later, James's feet bumped over the threshold of what appeared to be a small crofter's cottage, the reverberation sending shards of pain shooting through his skull.

He closed his eyes and did his best to memorize the twists and turns that took them from the front door to where they ended up. It wasn't difficult. The room they were taken to was a short distance from the front door. Suddenly, James was released and left to fall to the floor. He winced and groaned in pain, instinct propelling him to push up from the floor to retaliate, but Miss Lindwell's hands on his shoulders stayed his actions before he could fully react.

Bloody hell! He could not wait to be free to deal with these reprobates and make they pay for what they had done. What they were doing. What they might still do. But much as he loathed to admit it, Miss Lindwell's plan was sound. He must lead them to believe he was not a threat so that he might soon show them how erroneous an assumption they had made in that regard.

"Be careful," she admonished. "This is a lord of the realm. You cannot treat him like a sack of grain."

"We's can treat 'im 'owever we want. And it ain't like he can tell the difference like he is. We corked 'im good."

"Tie his lordship up."

A hot breath shot out of Miss Lindwell and brushed against his face, bringing the swift reminder of earlier, when she'd nestled against him and fallen fast asleep, her breath tickling his skin that had once been covered by his cravat.

"You will do no such thing! He is injured and in need of care. If you are not going to provide that, then at least leave him untied and help me get him onto the bed so that he might rest comfortably. If any harm comes to him, you will find yourself in a fine pickle that you well might not escape. It is to your advantage that he is kept well."

There was a grunt of frustration, followed by a curt, "Do what the chit says."

James was lifted once again and tossed face down on the musty smelling straw mattress; limbs splayed out like a drunken sot who'd passed out before hitting the covers. A few seconds later the door to the room closed with the unmistakable sound of the lock clicking into place.

"Lord Ridgemont? Are you quite well?" Miss Lindwell had placed a hand over his where it rested near the edge of the bed. She kept her voice so low he could barely hear it, except for the fact that somewhere between getting bonked on the head and arriving here to this cold, foul smelling hellhole, he had trained himself to hear her.

"I have had better days, Miss Lindwell. I am not going to lie."

"And have you had worse?"

He meant to tell her no, but that was a lie. Because he'd had worse days. Much worse. But she did not need to know that and he did not care to discuss it. Still, when he opened his mouth, the truth, to some extent, slipped out. "Indeed, I have."

"Ah, well—" The bed depressed where she sat upon it, "—then it appears we finally have something in common."

James opened one eye and glanced up at her then rolled over onto his side, the motion causing him to grimace as the room spun. He waited a moment for the world around him to settle and then studied his companion for a moment. Her hair had come undone in the initial struggle, and now cascaded down her back in dark, chocolate waves. Behind her, a small window let in the natural light, casting a halo around her. James remained still and studied her for a long moment.

What could she have experienced in her gilded life that would be worse than this? From what Alex had told him, Miss Temperance Lindwell had led a charmed life. Raised up in wealth and position in New York City, the belle of every ball she'd attended, well educated and considered by all to be in firm position of an intelligent mind, staggering beauty, and embarrassingly large dowry.

"You're staring, my lord."

"I am trying to sort you out."

She offered him a half smile and a little bit of the fire he'd seen earlier returned to her dark eyes. "Well, best of luck with that. My family has been attempting to do the same for many years with very little success."

"How curious." God help him, but he wanted to reach up and curl a finger in the dark hank of hair that fell over her shoulder, just to see if it was truly as soft as it appeared.

"Curious?"

"Yes, I think so." Though no more so than this strange physical reaction he had to her. What would she do if he reached up and touched that silken curl? Likely slap him soundly again. He moved his jaw from side to side, though the skin had stopped stinging hours ago, the memory lingered. "Most women of my acquaintance are quite plain in their wants and needs. They wish for marriage and family. To be well provided for and taken care of. But not you. I find that curious."

Miss Lindwell lifted one shapely eyebrow in a way that reminded him of the way his friend, Lord Hawksmoor, had of looking at a person, as if he could see through the words spoken into the actual intent lurking behind all that remained unsaid. A rather unsettling thought.

"Then perhaps you aren't looking deep enough, my lord. As most women I know have many kinds of hidden depths. Just because something isn't visible on the surface does not mean it doesn't exist. Take your sister, for instance. I bet you coddled her most of her life simply because she had burns upon her neck and body. You thought that made her weak and in need of protection—"

"She did need my protection!" And he had protected her with everything he was worth. Had he been more diligent in doing this earlier in her life, perhaps the fire would have never left its mark upon her skin.

"Hush!" She pressed her fingers against his lips then quickly pulled them away as if she'd touched a hot stove. "I have met your sister, my lord, and I can attest to the fact that I know few women with the reserve of strength she possesses."

James made to argue but found he could not. Miss Lindwell was right, as he had discovered over the past year. The young girl he had cared for after the fire that had destroyed their home and killed their parents had grown into one of the most resilient women he had ever known. The frail thing that had clung to life after fire had ravaged her one side of her body now possessed the fortitude of a warrior, while giving the appearance of being nothing more than a tiny slip of a woman with a sweet nature. It had taken James a long time to discover this, yet Miss Lindwell claimed to have seen it upon first meet.

Was James truly so blind?

He shook his head at the ridiculous suggestion, then wished he hadn't as his brain rattled around inside his skull. Deuce it! How long before the pounding in his head ceased so he could think clearly and get them out of here.

"Regardless," he said, pushing aside their current conversation for one of more import. "I do not want you to fear. I will see us out of this situation and return you safely to your family."

"Is that so?"

Was she smirking?

"Yes. And why are you smiling? Do you find this situation amusing?" Perhaps she was addled. Or in denial. They had been kidnapped for heaven's sake and she did not appear to be exhibiting any sign of fear over this fact. Did she not understand the danger they were in? Did she think she could just slap their captors across the face for their rude behavior and walk away?

"What I find amusing is your suggestion that you are in any position to rectify our current situation. Why, you can't even sit up."

"I beg your pardon? I most certainly can."

"Then, by all means, my lord..." Her voice trailed off but the challenge in it was undeniable.

Shit.

James pursed his lips together and braced his elbows against the straw mattress—good Lord, did something just move beneath him? Were there mice in this god-awful thing? He forced the thought away and pushed himself into a sitting position.

The room swirled and dipped and spun, forcing him to close his eyes or face the very real possibility of tossing up whatever he had last eaten.

"Are you quite well, my lord? You look a little peaked."

James bit down to keep from telling her his current thoughts on her observations. Despite Miss Lindwell's irritating nature, he would not give over to behaving as anything but the utmost gentleman. They were in a precarious situation and he could not risk degrading it further by hurting her tender feelings and causing her to dig in her heels.

"I am quite fine, Miss Lindwell, but I thank you for your

concern." He opened his eyes and waited a solid moment before the world righted itself. For a fleeting second, he thought he witnessed concern etched into her pretty features. Then again, he also thought he saw stars when his head swirled, so clearly he was imagining things.

"Very well," she said, in her usual brisk, matter-of-fact tone. "Then I think it best I try to get the lay of the land, as it were."

He did not care for the sound of that. "Meaning?"

Miss Lindwell stood and crossed the room to the door. "Meaning I think it best if I get a sense of where everything is. It will likely help us later. Also—" she cleared her throat and looked away from him but not before a hint of pink burst onto her cheeks. "—I need to take care of some *personal* business."

"What possible personal business could you—"

She shot him a desperate look.

"Oh!" It was his turn to clear his throat and look away, embarrassed to be discussing such matters with a lady. "Right. Of course. But I do not like the idea of you going out there alone."

"I am hardly about to invite you along to the powder room."

He looked back toward her. "I am quite certain this cottage does not have a powder room."

"Well, there must be a watering closet somewhere!" By now, she had started to shift from one foot to the other and back again, as if speaking of it was making matters worse.

"I'm certain there is something, but as I said, I do not think it safe for you to go with these men on your own. There is no telling what they might do."

She ignored his warning and banged on the door. "Hello! Hello, out there!"

James winced. "Miss Lindwell, please wait until I can at least get to my feet and—"

She spun on her heel and faced him. "Lord Ridgemont, I have been waiting for the length of our trip and I can assure you that I cannot wait another minute." She turned once more and called out, banging her fist against the door until the sound of footsteps echoed in the hallway and the door was unlocked and thrown open, forcing her to stumble back.

James turned to swing his legs over the edge of the bed, but the movement caused the room to tilt and spin at precarious angles until his vision dimmed. Though he sensed he was falling, the knowledge seemed like a faraway memory that disappeared like a wisp of smoke hitting cold air.

Temperance could not recall ever knowing such sweet relief. Despite the rough nature of the small watering closet and the knowledge that one of her captors was standing directly outside like a sentry, she wallowed in the release. Though once her business was done, reality crept in once more.

She was being held hostage.

With Lord Ridgemont. An injured Lord Ridgemont, at that.

Given her thoughts and opinions on the lofty lord and his pompous ways, she had to concede having him here made the situation a little more palatable. At least as much as being a hostage could be palatable. And much as she despised admitting it, his presence bolstered her inner fortitude.

She was not alone. He would protect her. Or rather, he would if he could manage to go more than two minutes without passing out.

His head wound concerned her greatly. She had little experience with such things, but surely, the fact that Lord Ridgemont kept losing consciousness could not be a good sign. Or was that normal after someone had received a swift hit to the head the way he had? And not just one hit, but two. When her captor threw the pistol when it misfired, she'd witnessed it bounce sharply off Lord Ridgemont's temple. Apparently, two blows were how many it took to get through his stubborn skull.

Temperance jumped as the door to the small closet banged and shuddered. "Hurry it up in there."

She took a deep breath and stood, straightening her gown that was now sullied and ruined from her ordeal. She would be brave. She would not give into fear. She would find a way out of this for both of them.

Failure was not an option.

One more deep breath and then she pulled the door open and stepped outside to meet the glare of her captor. Now that she'd had a better look at him, he seemed familiar to her, but she couldn't place him.

Temperance narrowed her gaze. "Have we met before?"

"Oh la," he said, with a wave of his hand and a put a feminine lilt to his voice. "I suppose ya don't notice your servants, do ya? Too busy falutin' around with yer pretty nose stuck in the air."

Her servant? She narrowed her gaze and studied him. Father had gone overboard when it came to hiring staff, filling the home with more than was truly needed, in her opinion. But Mother had insisted their wealth be on display in every way possible so as to attract a titled lord in need of a cash influx. The whole notion of it had filled Temperance with disgust. As if she was to be sold off to the highest bidder.

She searched the man's face and worked her memory until his image connected with a location. "Niles. You work in the stables."

He would have readied the carriage for them, which is how he knew she'd be at the Frontenac's party. But how had he known she would be meeting Rosalind in that particular spot? Was his cohort from Lord Caldwell's employ? Had the two seen an opportunity and concocted this ridiculous plan?

Then again, how ridiculous was it in the end? It had worked, after all. At least so far.

"Never you mind my name. Now git back to the room." He gave her a shove and Temperance's fancy satin slippers caught on the edge of a raised floorboard, nearly tripping her up. She caught herself in time and shot a hard glare back at Niles.At some point, she and Lord Ridgemont would have to make their escape and the realization that her manner of dress —a fancy ball gown and satin slippers left her at a horrible disadvantage given the terrain and chilly, damp climate. Would she even survive? Or would she succumb to the elements? What if it rained? Or, heaven forbid, snowed?

Breathe. Don't think about that. Take one hour at a time. The rest will fall into place.

And if it didn't, well, surely whatever fate awaited her out in the wild was a far cry better than what might await her in this house.

Chapter Six

J ames stirred, pulling himself out of the deep darkness. Where was he? He blinked, but the dark was unrelenting, the only hint of light through the window opposite him where the first trace of sunrise had begun to show on the horizon. An unrelenting ache pressed against his skull.

Had he gone on some kind of bender? He closed his eyes and dropped his head back. He was on a bed—a very uncomfortable bed, at that—and the air around him reeked of mustiness, neglect, and something else he preferred not to think too hard upon. A thick quilt had been tossed over him and a warm body curled up next to him.

A warm *female* body, given the curvature nestled against his side, providing the only warmth available in the cold room beyond the quilt. Perhaps it was the cold that explained why both he and the lady in question were fully clothed.

Tension filled him.

Think man!

James fought through the murk and throbbing in his brain until the events that had brought him here found their way to the surface and settled around him. Filled him with alarm.

They'd been kidnapped. The other part of the *they*—the warm body next to him—being Miss Temperance Lindwell. And bloody hell, he'd fallen asleep!

Guilt stabbed through him. How was he to protect Miss Lindwell from the two miscreants who had abducted them if he couldn't even keep his damn eyes open? The last thing he remembered, she had left the room to take care of personal business. He had tried to stop her from going off alone with one of the men and then—

And then nothing.

His guts twisted. He hadn't fallen asleep. He'd passed out.

He had failed her.

What had happened while he lay incapacitated? Had they taken her away? Harmed her? She was back now—clearly—but what had occurred in the interim? The way she'd nestled herself against his side suggested she was fine, but James had learned long ago that appearances could be most deceiving and that women had a way of masking their pain in a myriad of ways.

Temperance's earlier words floated back. Her claim that women possessed multiple layers to their characters, many of which remained undetected by men who only skimmed the surface. Was he one of those men? He had seen Ruth's pain, but only when it was too late to truly understand its depth. Too late to pull her back from the edge. Too late to stop her from her ultimate destruction.

He forced the memory away before it overtook him. He could not afford to be dragged down into the dark. He needed to keep his wits about him. To protect the lady whose life and well-being now rested in his hands. Or, more accurately, against his side.

What if one of the men had—

James stopped the thought and gave it a hard shove from his brain. He could not countenance the thought that she had been harmed in such a way while he lay dead to the world. The idea that he had failed to protect her was inconceivable.

Not that such a failure would be his first.

He bit down on the memory and squeezed his eyes shut. Not now. Not here.

"Miss Lindwell?"

She stirred, pressing soft and warm against him. Parts of him stirred as well but he ignored the sensation. It was to be expected. Alex had been right in his assumption that it had been too long since James had taken care of things in that regard. He'd been too busy of late dealing with his sister's less than warm reception into Society, his attempts to get Alex to rejoin the land of the living and stop hiding away at Breckenridge, and the events that brought the two people most dear to him together.

He'd had no time to consider more carnal pleasures and now was hardly the time or place to indulge in such fantasies. And Miss Lindwell was definitely not the woman to be indulging in them with.

What the deuce? Where had that thought come from? The sooner he got them out of here, the better. For both their sakes.

James nudged his bedmate, brushing against something soft and pliable. He swallowed. Not helpful.

"Miss Lindwell," he repeated, a little louder this time.

She squirmed slightly then her body stiffened and pulled away from him.

He captured her with his arm and pulled her back, bringing her warmth, and the quilt, to rest against him once more.

"Unhand me," she said, the sharpness in her tone indicating she had regained a wakeful state.

"Then quit stealing the one and only blanket. It is cold as ice in here." Or it felt that way after the heat of her body left his. She must have experienced it too, as despite her dictate, she made no motion to move away again.

Her shoulders sagged against his chest and she let out a sigh. "It is at that."

"Have I been asleep long?"

"Yes. I'm not sure how long. I drifted off as well."

"And when you left the room...did anything—" James hesitated. How did one approach such a delicate subject? "That is to say, did they...were they...respectful?"

"You may relax, my lord. My honor remains intact. Nothing untoward occurred. I did, however, discover that the gentleman in the livery was an employee of our household. He worked in the stables."

This certainly answered the question of how they knew to find her at the Frontenac's that night. "And the other man? Did he look familiar to you?"

She shook her heard and her dark hair brushed against his chin. Despite their ordeal, it smelled divine, as if she had soaked it in delicate rose petals. It helped cover up the fusty odor wafting up from the mattress they lay upon, though just barely. "I've scoured my brain to place him but I cannot. I wondered if perhaps he was a member of Baron Caldwell's household and that is how he knew I would be meeting Rosalind."

James had wondered the same thing. He'd also wondered something else. "Pray tell, what reason did you have for meeting Miss Caldwell under such cloak and dagger methods?"

"We wished to discuss a matter without it being overheard

and spread about. Gossip is rife within the ton, my lord, in case you weren't aware."

He was only too aware. But what misdeeds were she and Miss Caldwell getting up to that required such secrecy? If anyone's habits and personalities were well matched to Miss Lindwell's it would be that of Baron Caldwell's middle daughter. Known for her outspoken and often controversial views, it was all Lord and Lady Caldwell could do to keep the one daughter's reputation from affecting the eldest and youngest daughters from finding proper husbands. Rumor had it they had all but given up hope of Rosalind marrying. No gentleman dared look her way. Her strong opinions scared off even the most stalwart of lords.

"What exactly did you and Miss Caldwell need to discuss? You weren't planning an overthrow of the crown, were you? I'd hate to have to turn you both in for treason."

"I'm sure you'd be happy to be well rid of me."

"I was thinking more of Miss Caldwell. Hen is rather fond of her."

Something akin to a short laugh came from Miss Lindwell followed by a brief silence before she spoke again. "I was meeting with Rosalind because I wished to accept her offer of becoming headmistress of the new school for young women that she—"

"You were seeking employment?" The very idea baffled him. Her family had more money than Croesus! What need did she have of employment?

"Not seeking—accepting. And you need not say it with such derision as if I were courting the plague."

"Not the plague, but definitely ruination."

"Ruination against what? Marriage? Oh dear, whatever shall I do? Oh, I know, I shall find employment so that I do not need rely on some lofty lord's whims of whether he does or does not find me suitable, or will or won't let me do what I wish, or go where I want, or say what I think."

Her sarcasm was duly noted and not the least bit appreciated. "I cannot for the life of me see what you find so repulsive about marriage."

He, for one, had always looked fondly upon the institution. Not that he'd hurried into it, though once upon a time he had planned to. That didn't work out to his favor, however, as Ruth had chosen Alex instead, but had she not...

Had she not, perhaps she'd be alive still.

Or perhaps not. Ruth had always been a melancholy sort, never quite satisfied with whatever state she found herself in. Perhaps she would have found him lacking, or his attentions not enough. Or too much.

He pushed the thought away. There was little point in meandering down that particular path. Ruth was gone. Alex had remarried and found the happiness that had eluded him in his first marriage. And James was—

Well, he was currently in a rather bad situation with a woman who barely tolerated him and a head wound that pounded inside his skull and left him off balance, making a hasty escape difficult at best. And yet, still a necessity. They had both seen their abductors. Miss Lindwell knew the identity of one of them. It put the criminals in a risky spot. Even if the ransom was paid, there was no guarantee they would simply be allowed to waltz out of this dilapidated crofter's cottage and be on their way.

Which meant they must find a way to leave before it came to that.

"I fear we must make our escape sooner rather than later, Miss Lindwell. I cannot guarantee our captors will be agreeable to simply letting us go. Our ability to identify them has put us in a rather precarious position. They may make the decision to eliminate the risk."

He did not care to speak so blatantly about what might befall them, but sugarcoating the matter did them no service. Besides, likely Miss Lindwell was not the type who would appreciate it if he did. She was given to plain speaking.

"I agree. Do you have a sense of where we are?"

He shook his head. Bad idea. The darkness that surrounded him swirled and he reached out to steady himself, though given his prone position, he was unlikely to fall anywhere. Miss Lindwell's hand covered his and too late he realized what he'd reached for was her.

"What is it?"

"Forgive me. My brain has yet to resettle itself, it appears." He should remove his hand, but her fingers had entwined in his and provided an anchor that rooted him. "To answer your question, I am unsure about our whereabouts beyond to say farther north, based on the length and speed of our travel and the colder climate. However, I am certain there must be a village close by."

In truth, he was certain of nothing at this point, but he didn't want her to worry that he did not have a proper handle on the situation. He would protect her. Keep her safe. There was no other option.

"And which direction do you believe this village to be in?"

That much he could not say. "Did you see any hint of a village along the way?" She'd had a better vantage point from her position on the seat.

"No, none. However, the road we traveled, before we turned down the lane that led here, continued on into the distance. How far, or to where, I cannot say."

"Then I suspect if we continue on in that direction, we shall come upon civilization of some sort eventually. Once we reach it, I will demand we are provided with shelter and we can then make arrangements to return to London with all due haste."

He made it sound easy, but the reality lay far beyond that. There was no telling how far they would have to travel before they found a village or settlement of some sort. Nor could he ignore the fact that neither of them was dressed for a long journey in inclement or cold weather, two things that were rife this time of year in northern England. He may be able to manage, but Miss Lindwell had nothing more to wear but a silk gown and satin slippers. Regardless, they could not stay here and wait for a ransom to be paid, hoping they would be released and sent on their way at the end of it.

Their best bet was to make a run for it. To get as far away as possible before their captors realized they were gone. And they would have to make their way on foot. Attempting to relieve their captors of their horses would cause too much commotion and raise the alarm. They must sneak away with all due stealth and speed while their abductors slept.

"What makes you think anyone will be willing to stick their neck out for two oddly dressed strangers that show up unannounced to demand lodging and sustenance?"

James turned to look at her. The sun had risen farther during their conversation and dawn's light now caressed her features infusing them with a surreal beauty. "I will simply introduce myself."

She scoffed at him. "And this will magically send everyone to do your bidding, will it?"

"Of course. I am a lord of the realm. The Seventh Marquess of Ridgemont. Why would they not?" Good God. He truly did sound like a pompous ass, didn't he? Was this what she had been referring to earlier?

"How lovely it must be to have everyone fall at your feet, eagerly awaiting your lofty orders. And what proof do they have that you are whom you say? You look a little worse for wear and I no better. For all they know, we could have set upon an unsuspecting couple and been the ones to do them harm, not vice versa."

He pulled his hand from hers and turned onto his side slowly so as not to set his brain to spinning. "I beg your pardon, I am a very reliable and trustworthy individual."

"According to whom?"

"According to all those who know me."

She flicked a hand in the air as if to dismiss his claim. "But these strangers do not know you. Likely, they have never even heard of the Marquess of Ridgemont. For all they know, you've pulled that name out of a hat and are no more a member of the peerage than they."

"Are you always this contrary?"

"Are you always this arrogant?"

"I am not arrogant. I am...confident."

"Is that what you call it here in jolly ole England? Well, fiddle dee dee."

"Fiddle dee what?"

She huffed and shifted to face him. "Do not take offense, my lord, but likely the only thing about you that will convince them you are who you claim to be is the haughty way you have of addressing others."

"Haughty?"

"Yes."

"For your information—" He stopped and fumbled with the pocket of his jacket until his fingers brushed against the cool gold exterior of his watch and pulled it out to hold up to her. The weak rays of sun illuminated its shiny exterior and the swirling markings etched into its top. "I have this."

"A watch?"

"Not just any watch. This watch was passed down from my father and his before that. It bears the Ridgemont coat of arms. A clear indication I am who I say I am."

"Unless, along with the clothing, you also stole the watch from the real Lord Ridgemont."

"I *am* the real Lord Ridgemont!"

She shrugged. "What proof do they have of that?"

James gritted his teeth and wrapped his fingers around the watch, shoving it back into his pocket. "You are the most disagreeable of women. Has anyone ever told you that? Is it any wonder no man in his right mind has offered for you?"

A hint of pain rippled across her pretty features and remorse washed over James, but before he could offer a proper apology, Miss Lindwell turned away from him and tossed the quilt aside, swinging her feet over the edge of the bed giving him a brief flash of her stocking covered ankle.

"We should see if our captors would at least feed us. I am famished."

"Yes, of course." He should apologize for his rude remark. Under different circumstances, she likely could have her pick of many of the lesser-ranked lords. There was any number of them in dire need of a cash infusion to keep their lifestyle and properties afloat. Badly managed estates abounded. But her parents were insistent only a higher-ranking lord would do for their daughters. A fact that irked the lower ranking lords and disgusted the higher, resulting in neither group making an offer to either of the Misses Lindwells.

As Miss Lindwell put on her satin slippers and made her way to the bedroom door, she glanced over her shoulder at him. "Regardless of what we do after we leave here, I agree with your assessment that we should make our escape. I do not trust these men to keep their word any more than you do. However, if we wish to get farther than the front door without you collapsing, I believe a day or two of convalescing is in order."

That it was he who kept them from leaving hit him with unexpected severity. He had promised himself he would keep her safe, yet so far, he had done a dismal job of it. Her reminder of such, whether intended or not, was like a nettle burrowed deep beneath the skin.

He must get better and he must see her to safety. No other outcome would be tolerated.

Chapter Seven

The dish their captors served could best be described as the worst kind of gruel. Temperance wasn't even sure what it was supposed to be, save for a grayish mush with a few pieces of mutton, perhaps, and what appeared to be a generous helping of barley. Beyond that, she recognized nothing.

She choked the offering down, hoping the meat was not rancid and that the sustenance would bolster her flagging energy. It had been three full days since their arrival at the cottage and a routine had been established. Morning ablations as she was marched to the water closet and provided with a bowl of ice-cold water to wash up with in the bedroom she shared with Lord Ridgemont. As if she would take care of such things in front of him.

Temperance pushed the disgusting offering around in her bowl. Her appetite had left her since this morning's trip to the watering closet. The precariousness of her position was brought home to roost when Niles leaned in, his fetid breath brushing against her skin until she thought she might be ill.

"Tell me, 'as the lofty lord made a full recovery? Ferris ain't too keen on keepin' the man free and able to walk about."

"I can assure you, Lord Ridgemont remains quite unsteady on his feet. You've seen him. He can barely sit up without losing consciousness." Granted, she'd practically had to beg his lordship to appear in a weakened state any time one of their captors came to take her to the watering closet, leaving him behind with a chamber pot. If they determined him to be a threat, likely, they would tie both of them up, and then any hope of escape would be lost. "The blow to his head has left him quite addled. Sometimes he isn't even sure where he is. Or who he is."

"Well, you best make sure you keep 'im docile, so's we don't have to tie the bugger up," Niles said. "Maybe give 'im an eyeful of what ye got under them fancy skirts. Maybe I get a bit 'o that myself before we 'and you back to your family, hm?"

The suggestion had sickened her, crawling over her skin like a slime she couldn't wash away. She had forced herself not to respond, and she did not reveal Niles's suggestion to Lord Ridgemont for fear of what he may do. But one thing was clear—they needed to leave sooner, rather than later. The hungry look in Niles's eyes increased with each interaction. She could not risk letting it go any further than a look. If either of their captors tried to take advantage of her, Lord Ridgemont would feel the need to protect her virtue, and likely get them both killed in the process.

She sighed and scowled down at her meal. After returning from her morning ablutions, breakfast had consisted of a piece of stale bread and a bowl of tepid porridge. The suppertime gruel set before her now was a small improvement, though barely.

The time in between the two meals, Temperance spent pacing the room, devising a plan of escape that had developed no further than their original plan. Escape to the road, find someone to give them shelter and ultimately help them get back to London.

While the daylight hours dragged, it was the nighttime that was the worst. The temperature dropped significantly and their captors refused to provide wood for the small stove, convinced they would try to burn the place down. A ridiculous assessment, given the door to their room was constantly locked, the suggestion seemed a bit counter-productive, leaving them to burn, but their captors apparently lacked the intelligence to understand this. She did, however, manage to convince them to bring an extra quilt, though it was in worse condition than the one they already had and offered little in the way of extra warmth.

The situation left Temperance with no other choice but to sleep next to his lordship for warmth. Inevitably, at some point through the night she would awaken and find their limbs had become intertwined and he'd curled his body against her back, one arm wrapped around her middle holding her close. It was the absolute height of impropriety and as shocking as such an unexpected intimacy was; it was in those moments when she relaxed. When she felt safe. Protected.

Pride and modesty dictated she push him away, but the need for warmth and for those few moments of peace before the sunrise brought forth the truth of their predicament, were too intoxicating to give up.

With each sunrise, the lack of a detailed escape plan raised its ugly head, leaving her unsettled throughout the long day. There were too many unknowns. What if the nearest homestead or village was a full day's walk away? Or more? Would she make it wearing nothing more than a pair of satin slippers?

Would Lord Ridgemont be well enough for such rigorous travel? What if he passed out again? Then what? Did she stay with him? Go for help and leave him to the mercy of anyone who might come upon him, their captors included?

"You're making that face again."

Lord Ridgemont's irritatingly calm voice interrupted her thoughts and she set her spoon on the edge of the bowl, her lukewarm meal losing what little appetizing appeal her hunger had lent it.

Temperance pushed away from the small table near the cold stove and began to pace once again. "I am thinking about our escape."

"Given your expression, I take it you are not pleased with our options."

They had discussed them from every angle but continued to come back around to the same parameters. Escape at night, head for the road, find shelter. It was as simple and as difficult as that. The problem was, what would happen in between each of these events, no one could predict.

She sighed and turned to stare out the window to the field beyond. Their window faced the front of the cottage and was on the ground floor. Not especially smart on the part of their captors, but she was not one to complain. Perhaps their inexperience in such matters would work in their favor. Then again, perhaps it would cause their captors to panic and react foolishly. There were far too many variables to take into account and it had her stomach tied into knots.

She pressed her palm against the cold glass. It was warped and unclear in spots creating an eerie picture of the landscape beyond once the sun began its descent.

"Perhaps we will hear from Father tomorrow and need not worry about such matters of our escape."

Temperance did not hold her breath in this regard. She

had angered Father the night of the Frontenac's party to a degree she had not seen since she had broken off her engagement with Beauregard. What if he thought this a good opportunity to teach her a lesson? Or that she was not worth the amount of ransom requested? Perhaps, much as he had done with her brother Daniel, he would turn his back on her without blinking an eye.

Lord Ridgemont joined her at the window, standing close enough that once again she could feel the warmth from his body push against her. He had offered her his wool jacket the first day and continued the offer each day after that, but she had refused. She did not want to do anything that might hinder his recovery. As it was, he could now rise from the bed without fear of losing consciousness, and his balance had returned, though he claimed a bit of a headache remained.

"Receiving word from your father or my family could take some time. Are you willing to wait that long and hope it will all turn out in the end?"

It was a reasonable question. There was no telling how long it would take before word came—if it came at all. What if their captors did not take that into account and their supplies ran out? What if Niles' lascivious comments became actions? Or their captors decided to cut their losses, eliminate the witnesses, and make a run for it?

"No," she whispered, staring at Lord Ridgemont's distorted reflection in the glass. "I am not."

He nodded and lifted a hand to rest upon her shoulder. The three-day growth of whiskers had made him even more handsome and his calming presence was the one thing that had kept her from losing her mind and giving in to the fear that constantly chaffed at her. Much as she loathed admitting it, his lordship had proven to be more of a help than a hindrance and she could not imagine what it might have been like—what might have befallen her—should their captors have killed him.

Not that she would ever admit such to him.

His hand slipped away from the bare skin on her shoulders, leaving behind a rush of cold that raised the gooseflesh on her skin. Oh, how she longed to be warm again. To curl up in front of a roaring fire with a book in her lap and not a care in the world. How long had it been since she'd experienced such a sensation? Certainly, well before her family had reached London.

The ropes holding the misshapen straw mattress on the bed creaked as Lord Ridgemont sat down upon it. "We should discuss what might happen upon our return to London."

His statement startled her and she spun on her heel. "Whatever do you mean?"

He raised one eyebrow that partially disappeared beneath the dark lock of hair that had drooped forward now that they had removed the makeshift bandage from his head.

"We have been left alone in this room, sharing a bed, for several nights now. If such information should be discovered, or even alluded to, it will leave you ruined. The only recourse will be for the two of us to marry."

He sounded as unenthused by the idea as she felt.

"I have no intention of marrying you. And we have not engaged in any activity that would leave me compromised, so there is nothing to worry over. Besides, no one is aware that we shared a room. It will all be supposition on their part with no facts to support their claims." Her cheeks burned and she turned back to the window to prevent Lord Ridgemont from seeing the effect of discussing matters had on her.

She was not an innocent. Or rather she was, in the literal sense. She had never engaged in the carnal behaviors shared between a man and woman, but she was well read enough to understand what they were. And confident enough in her knowledge to equivocally state that her relationship with Lord Ridgemont had never once breached the parameters of said behaviors.

"Whether we have *engaged* in them or not does not matter. It will be the perception that we did that will ruin you. Gossip doesn't require proof to be ruinous." He rose and his hand touched upon the footboard of the bed as if he still needed to balance himself before moving ahead. Perhaps he was not as healed as he claimed; yet when he approached her, his gait was steady and strong.

"And I have told you that I am not interested in marriage and therefore do not need to have my reputation saved. You may rest easy that you will not have to offer for me upon our return to London."

He reached her in a few steps and crossed his arms. He had taken his jacket off after offering it to her and though she had refused, he had not put it back on. He must be cold. He had to be. Why, her own hands felt like blocks of ice at the end of her arms and she had to remove her ridiculous shoes on a regular basis to rub the feeling back into her toes. Why he insisted on leaving his jacket off baffled her. Was this some kind of silent protest on his behalf because she had refused his offer? If so, it was a foolish one.

Likely as foolish as her own refusal to take him up on his offer.

Sometimes it was difficult to tell which of them was more stubborn. If she had been of a more reasonable temperament, she might have suggested they share it back and forth, but, despite her name, temperance had never been something she excelled at, a fact that did not appear to be changing any time soon.

Pride goeth before the fall, Constance had repeatedly told her. Her heart lurched. Would she ever see her sister again?

No. She would not think like that. Of course, she would

see Constance again. There was no question. She would find a way out of this predicament; take her place as headmistress of Miss Caldwell's school for young girls and everything would be fine.

"Everything will *not* be fine," Lord Ridgemont said, staring down at her with a dark look.

Had she spoken that aloud? Bother. This captivity was causing her to lose her senses.

"It isn't just marriage that you will require your reputation for," he continued.

Temperance held his gaze. Goodness, but he had the loveliest blue eyes. They were a deep blue flecked with shards of black. When you stared into them for too long, it was as if you were falling into a spinning kaleidoscope. Quite disconcerting.

"Whatever do you mean?"

"You will also need your reputation if you have any hope of taking on the role of headmistress of Miss Caldwell's school. Unless you think families will willingly send their daughters to be governed by a woman of ill repute."

"Ill repute?" The word stung. It harkened a little too close to threats once made by another man. A man she had trusted with her heart only to discover he took that trust rather lightly. So lightly, that he thought nothing of tossing it about as if it was a small, unimportant thing. A man who cared so little, he had boldly threatened to ruin her reputation when she had the audacity to break off their engagement.

"You need to be reasonable, Miss Lindwell. Word will get out, and even if I claim to the highest heavens that nothing untoward occurred, it will not matter. I may be considered a gentleman, but I am also a man. There will always be doubt that all propriety was upheld, especially when Society is all too aware of how desperate your parents are to marry their daughters to a title."

Temperance sucked in a breath and took a step back to put distance between her and Lord Ridgemont's vile accusation. "Are you saying you think my parents arranged this abduction for the sake of forcing your hand in marriage?"

He held up a hand against her outrage. "Don't be ridiculous. How would they have known I would even be out there. But your parents' goals are well known, and I should not be surprised to see the suggestion whispered and bandied about. Don't you understand?" He removed the space between them and his hands, cold as ice, took hold of her arms. "It is the whispers that destroy you. They spread through Society like a sickness, infecting everything they touch."

If she didn't know better, Temperance would think Lord Ridgemont actually cared about what happened to her in this regard. She shrugged off the thought along with his touch. Both made it difficult to think straight.

"Then if it comes to that, I will simply return to New York." Not that anything waited for her there but the remnants of another scandal. When she had ended her engagement, Beauregard had made good on his threats. He'd claimed her moral character was lacking and not up to the standards of the Montgomery name. The suggestion, vague as it was, had been enough. She did not need Lord Ridgemont's reminder of how misinformation and lies could ruin a person's hopes and dreams. She had already lived it.

Yet here she was, confronting it once again. Facing the destruction of a future she had thought to claim as her own. A future that was meant to protect her from such cares as innuendo and gossip.

She turned away and walked to the bed then thought better of it and changed direction toward the small table pressed against the opposite wall. "How can you so willingly suggest we marry when you have no desire to spend more than five minutes in my company?"

"In case you've not noticed, I have spent far more than five minutes in your company of late."

"Because you have had no other choice."

"True. Though I will admit you are not as heinously annoying as I once presumed."

"That's rather damning praise."

He smiled at her and the expression shot straight into her heart with such unexpected velocity that for a brief moment she could not breathe. Could not blink. Could do nothing but stare at that beautiful smile as if it was a polished diamond discovered under a pile of rubbish. Not that the rest of Lord Ridgemont was rubbish. In fact, there was little about him physically that she could find fault with. He was tall and lean and well muscled, a fact she'd discovered when he'd wound his body around hers at night seeking warmth. His face was as handsome as one could get, with his midnight hair and blue eyes that sparkled with both intelligence and, she would allow, a certain amount of humor.

But that smile. Heaven above, if that didn't simply cause the rest to pale in comparison.

Lord Ridgemont placed a hand over his heart as he approached her. "I do know how to flatter the ladies. And while, I admit, you would not be my first choice as bride and, likely, my great-aunt will raise a holy raucous upon the mere suggestion, it is the right thing to do to protect your reputation."

As far as proposals went, she'd heard better. Then again, flowery language hadn't made the sentiment true the last time around, had it? At least Lord Ridgemont's was an honest assessment of facts even if it did lack the romantic soppiness a lady might wish to hear. Not her, in particular. She was not given to such silly mawkishness. But some ladies might prefer it.

"Regardless of your suggestion, my lord, I remain steadfast

in my original claim toward marriage and my not partaking in it."

His smile softened, but the effect of it remained. "Tell me, what is it exactly that has turned you off marriage to such a degree? Your cousin told me you were once affianced, so you haven't always felt this way. Was your engagement such a horrid affair it left you with a sour taste in your mouth?"

Embarrassment rushed at her from all sides and heat spread across her chest then raced up her neck until it pooled in her cheeks. What did Lord Rothbury know of her previous situation? Had her parents spoken of it? And even if they had, she had never revealed all the salacious details of what she had discovered.

"Given the rather intense blush you are currently exhibiting, I will assume the answer to that question is *yes.*" He looked down at her with that piercing gaze he had, as if he possessed the power to see inside of her to where she hid her deepest secrets. It made her want to run and hide.

"I do not know what you're talking about." Because what other choice did she have but to deny?

"Hm." He took her hand, surprising her with the sudden intimacy so that she did not resist when he pulled her toward the bed and sat down, guiding her to sit next to him. "Tell me about this former engagement."

"I—I will do no such thing." She was not about to trot out the whole sordid affair for him to dissect it piece by piece. Or for her to relive the pain and humiliation of it. She had put the matter behind her. Moved on. Determined it was not a road worth traveling down again. A heart could only withstand so much pain before it stopped working and she did not care to meet that threshold. Nor did she care to have her fate tied to someone so closely that they held such power to hurt. No, it was better to be alone. To keep your heart safe from those who cared little whether they broke it or not.

Lord Ridgemont squeezed her hand. "I think you must tell me. If we are to be married, it is only fair I know all there is to know about you. How else am I to protect you from the insidious whispers and gossip and what not?"

The man was truly infuriating. Did he honestly think she would bare her soul to him simply because he dictated she do so? But, of course, he did. He was the Seventh Marquess of Ridgemont and all that rot.

"Lord Ridgemont, please allow me to be perfectly clear—"

"By all means." He let go of her hand and flopped back on the bed, letting his legs dangle over the end. It forced her to turn to face him and when she did, he smiled up at her and she stumbled over her words, hating the effect that one simple gesture had on her.

"I am not going to marry you. Not now, not later, not ever."

"That's a rather finite answer. And please, call me James. If we are to be betrothed, I think it allowable we may refer to each other by our given names. Now, about this former fiancé, was he a brute? A gambler? A philanderer?"

The blush she'd experienced earlier rushed back.

"A-ha!" He wagged a finger at her. "A philanderer then. Such a pity. Well, you need not worry about that on my account. I am as faithful as a hound."

Temperance pulled her lips in, an attempt to hold back her irritation. The man had not listened to a single word she'd said. Instead, he ran on with his foolish notions and presumptions and assumed she would just follow along, as if her own feelings about the matter were of no importance. Typical.

"When we put this hellish—"

His brows dipped creating a crease between them. "Good heavens, Temperance. Language."

"—experience behind us, I hope never to see you again, *my lord*. I do not think I can make it any more clear than that."

"My dear girl, you can say such things six ways to Sunday. It does not alter the reality. If you have any hope of living any kind of life, you must marry and given that I have been thrown into this mess with you, it is my responsibility to protect you and keep your reputation intact as best I can. Trust me, I am no less aggrieved by the situation than you, but it is what it is and in the end, marriage serves both our purposes. As much as you will now require a husband to maintain any hope of a good reputation, I require a wife to provide me with an heir. We may as well focus on the positive and make the best of things."

"Provide you with an heir? What am I, a brood mare?"

"If so, you are a very fetching one. Though you do snore which is a bit annoying, however, where we will have separate bedchambers, I'm certain I can overlook that—"

"I do not snore!"

Lord Ridgemont pushed himself up on his elbows and the recalcitrant lock of dark hair fell over his brow.

Temperance folded her fingers into her palm to resist brushing it out of the way.

"How would you know if you snore? You are asleep when it occurs."

"Because I—I just know. Besides, Constance would have said something to me if such nonsense were true and she hasn't, so obviously you are mistaken." Then again, her sister slept like the dead.

He smiled again and something inside her shifted, as if whatever it was that had been out of place only now found the spot where it belonged and decided to settle in.

Temperance pushed off the bed and stalked to the window. "You are the most annoying individual I have ever had the displeasure to meet."

"Even more so than your former betrothed, the philanderer?"

Temperance winced, his words hitting their mark though his sudden contrition indicated that had not been his intent.

"Forgive me, Temperance, that was uncalled for. I did not mean to—"

She spun on her heel, unaware he had approached her from behind. She took a step back, but her retreat was inhibited by the windowsill. "I am not interested in your apologies, my lord—"

"James."

She gritted her teeth. She wondered if her captors would consider a request to move her to a room of her own.

"Given that we will be forced to spend at least a few more days in each other's company, perhaps it would be best if we stopped conversing. I am not interested in anything you have to say and you do not listen to anything I say."

"Not true. I have heard every word you've said. I simply find much of it a bit foolish and shortsighted. Besides, if we are to formulate a plan to escape, we shall have to speak to one another."

He was too close. His masculine scent filled the air around her and his stature blocked everything else in the room from her sight. It was as if he had taken over her world, becoming the end all and be all. An idea that frightened her far more than she should allow.

She needed to get away from him. Away from here. And given his lordship was now in fine enough form to irritate her to such a degree, surely he could also withstand the rigors of their escape.

"Very well then. Let us formulate our plan and execute it with all due haste. The sooner we do, the sooner I can depart from your company and that will make me a very happy woman indeed."

Lord Ridgemont's lips quirked to one side and his eyes sparkled and that thing, whatever it was, that had shifted inside of her now warmed and bloomed in her chest until she had no other choice but to shove the feeling back down.

"Please stop looking at me in that manner."

His smile grew and he took a step closer. "What manner is that?"

She pursed her lips and took a deep breath. The ground beneath her grew uncertain. "You know very well what you are doing. You're trying to charm me so that I might come around to your way of thinking."

"I assure you, I am doing no such thing." He took another step. "Is it working?"

Good heavens! The man was a cad. This was not fair play. "Stay where you are, sir. I am not some simpering miss who will be seduced into doing your bidding simply because you—"

"You talk too much, my dear."

James slid an arm about her waist and hauled her into him, his body as hard and uncompromising as rock. Temperance was unprepared for the swift movement. Or for the way air whooshed out of her lungs at the unexpected thrill of feeling his body against hers. This was much different from when they shared the bed. He'd always been at her back then. But this—this was face to face. Like the waltz they had shared, only much closer. So much so, that she could feel the outline of his hard thigh press into her, and the rise and fall of his chest. His hands slid close to the curve of her buttocks and a deep ache pulled within her.

"Ah, finally. Silence!"

She opened her mouth to respond, with what, she did not know. Nor did he allow her time to come up with anything as his mouth descended upon hers and every word she had ever known whirled about in her mind like a tempest. She flattened her hands against his chest to push him away, but as his lips teased hers, strength abandoned her and her knees buckled slightly.

Heaven help her!

She had been kissed before. Beauregard had given her a handful of kisses during their courtship, though none had left her legs a wobbly mess and her stomach filled with the battering wings of a thousand little birds. His kisses had been...what? She could not recall Normal, likely. Perfunctory.

But this...

Oh, this was so much more than normal or perfunctory. This was clouds being pushed aside and the warmth of sunlight beating down upon you. This was the difference between safely trotting and giving your stead free rein to run like the wind. This was—

Oh, this was nothing short of glorious! And—

And over.

Temperance stumbled backward, forcing James to reach for her once more only this time to steady her, not sweep her back into his arms to experience again the rapture that mouth of his could inflict.

"Have I finally rendered you speechless?"

The rush of the kiss fell away with hasty purpose, leaving her as irritated as she had been before he'd kissed her senseless. And senseless was only too apt a description of what she'd experienced. Because had she any sense at all, she'd have pushed him away the instant his hands landed upon her. Instead, she'd allowed him to touch her, to kiss her, to show her a weakness she had not been aware she possessed.

One she did not know how to overcome.

Save with anger.

She balled up her hand but his fingers slid around her wrist, his thumb pressing into her palm until she released her clenched fist.

"Uh, uh. Save your energy, my dear. You'll need it for our escape."

"Release me this instant."

"I think not. At least not until you promise not to level another right hook upon me. You pack quite a wallop and I would prefer not to be on the receiving end of yet another. Who taught you to hit like that, anyway?"

"My brother."

He raised one dark eyebrow and surprise brightened his eyes. "Brother? I was not aware you had a brother."

"I have two."

"I see. Well, then I commend whichever one taught you how to swing like a man, but I would much prefer if you saved your energy for when we will need it most."

"Then stop kissing me."

He smiled and her knees did that thing again that made standing difficult. "Now that will be a difficult promise to keep. You have very soft lips and I find I enjoyed our kiss far more than I had anticipated. It bodes well for when we are married, don't you think?"

Temperance ground her teeth together. "For the last time, I am not—"

"—marrying me. Yes, yes. So you say. But I think you will change your mind. I'm quite a catch, you know. However, for the sake of harmony, I promise I will not kiss you again on two conditions."

She didn't like the sound of this, but curiosity loosened her tongue. "What two conditions?"

"That, one, you agree to wear my jacket when we escape."

"Fine." She had no desire to freeze to death before reaching safety. "What is the second condition?"

"That you ask me."

"Ask you what?"

"To give you another kiss."

She laughed at his audacity. "I can assure you, my lord, that will never happen."

He smiled. "Then you should have no difficulty agreeing to my terms."

"Very well. I agree."

A mischievous glint shone in his eyes and Temperance was left with the sensation she'd just made a pact with the devil.

Chapter Eight

"Hush." James waved at Temperance who, after a good night's sleep, was busy suggesting any manner of schemes to allow them to escape. The door lock, they could pick open with one of the few hairpins that had survived the initial scuffle with her captors. It was an old trick he'd learned long ago, but as for the rest of their plan, it was all over the place as they attempted to factor in different variables. For now, however, James needed his partner in crime to stop her chatter so he might hear the conversation occurring on the other side of the door and farther on down the hall.

For once, she did not argue, but rather joined him at the door, nudging him slightly to gain access to where the key fitted into the door. She pressed her ear against the metal, bringing her face perilously close to his groin. He gritted his teeth. Ever since the kiss they'd shared the day before, he'd been on edge and having her mouth hovering near the area most affected did not help matters.

James stepped away from her while still keeping his own ear pressed against the crack between the door and its frame.

He could only catch snippets of the two men arguing, but what he heard sent a cold chill down his spine.

"Why ain't they answered yet? Coswald said 'e'd be back to us by today and the day's almost done with." Niles's agitated voice had turned raspy, fear edging around it.

Below him, Temperance gasped. He glanced down and met her gaze.

"Coswald is our stable master," she whispered.

Great.

Ferris's sharp rebuke echoed down the hall. "The man's a halfwit. I shoulda never let you convince me to let 'im act as the intermediary. Likely 'e'll end up gettin' thrown in gaol and we'll have the Runners landin' on our doorstep at any minute! This is wha' I get for lettin' a bunch of idiots convince me this would work."

"If you listened to a bunch of idiots, wha's that make you? The bloody leader of the bunch, I'd say!"

The sound of flesh upon flesh echoed in the hallway and the wall reverberated with the impact of a body being thrown against it. The scuffle lasted only a few seconds before Niles stuttered out an apology. It had little impact on Ferris.

"Your fool friend shoulda been 'ere today with the money and I'm tellin' you this right now, if Coswald don't bloody well show up come two sunrises hence then we're gonna be slittin' some throats and I'm gonna be on my merry way. I ain't leavin' no bloody witnesses to point a finger at me and I sure as 'ell ain't hangin' from no bloody noose for no one, 'specially the likes of some lofty lord and lady."

"She ain't no lady, she's an American."

"And you better hope that makes her da willin' to pay up faster than most because in two days I'm leavin' but I ain't leavin' no witnesses behind."

The conversation tapered off as the two traveled beyond earshot, but it had been enough. The fear in Temperance's gaze was absolute, as was her silence. There was nothing left to say, only do.

James had less than two days to fashion an escape plan and get them both to safety.

I t was relatively basic as far as plans went.

James had noted that their captors preferred to spend their evenings drinking whatever strong brew they had procured. Their raucous laughter and drunken feuding filtered down the hallway well into the night. Some time, shortly before sunrise, it would grow deathly quiet, signifying the two men had given in to the drink and fallen into a dead sleep.

The timing of this would allow them to escape shortly before daylight ascended. They would use the light of the moon to guide their way down the lane to the main road. Once on it, they would continue on in the hopes of finding a homestead or village, or some type of shelter before their captors awoke from their alcoholic induced slumber and came in search of them. The ground outside appeared frozen, which should work in their favor as far as disguising any tracks that would give them away.

James biggest concern was Temperance's clothing. Or lack thereof. The temperatures were still quite cool and would be even more so at such an early hour before the sun rose to warm the air and chase the frosty dew from the ground. Her dress, perfectly suited for grabbing the attention of a titled lord, was completely ill suited for running through the country-side in the dark of night. Her shawl had been lost in the melee. She had at least agreed to wear his jacket for warmth, but that did not address the matter of her ridiculous shoes. They were hardly made for such rough terrain. Given they needed to put as much distance between them and their captors as quickly as possible, they could not afford to be slowed down.

Taking one of the horses was not a viable option. The noise made in saddling the horses would alert their captors to their plans before they even mounted up. If it were just he, James was certain he could outrun the sots. But with satin slippers, it was unlikely Temperance could go faster than the men. They'd capture her and James would have no choice but to stay by her side. There was no telling what the men would do to her if he were not there to protect her.

James stared at down at the quilt as Temperance stared silently out the window.

"Perhaps we can tear the quilt into smaller portions and wrap them around your feet?" It would provide some warmth and a bit of protection against the rocks and uneven ground they would encounter.

He'd half expected her to reject the idea—she could be contrary at the best of times—but she appeared to mull the suggestion over, sticking her feet out from beneath the stained hem of her gown and staring over at the quilt. Over the past day, as the time for their escape grew closer, her agitation had started to show. Agitation edged with fear.

"That might work." She bit her lower lip and slowly dragged her teeth over it, a simple, unconscious gesture that somehow managed to create a burst of need within him. Which made no sense. He did not want this woman.

Liar. The word whispered in his mind, echoing through him. He shook it off. Temperance Lindwell was the antithesis of everything he sought in a wife. Yes, he would marry her. Honor dictated he must, given their living situation over the past several days. But nothing about the prospective union sparked any hint of joy in him.

Except for that kiss.

God help him, that kiss.

But a kiss was not enough to forge a strong and proper marriage like the one his parents had modeled. Though, such a kiss as they had shared could certainly make up for—

"I suppose it will do."

Temperance's assessment threw James. Had he spoken aloud? Heat crept up his throat then stopped abruptly as she rose from her chair and walked to the bed, picking up the edge of the quilt. "It is old enough that we should find a loose seam where we might be able to tear the material. We can use strips from the bed sheets, or my chemise if we must, to tie them securely around my feet."

"Yes. Of course. Good thinking." At least one of them had their thoughts going in the right direction.

He never should have kissed her. It had been a sudden, rash decision, directed from somewhere far beneath his brain. Had it been his brain that had taken part in the decision making process, it would have set him right. It would have told him that opening that particular Pandora's box was a dangerous thing indeed.

It would have reminded him that saving damsels in distress was not an area where he particularly excelled.

But it was too late now. Because he *had* kissed her. And now he must save her. And then, inevitably, he must marry her.

The door creaked, the sound echoing through the hallway. They both froze, Temperance's fingers fisting into the back of his shirt. She was close enough he could feel the warmth of her pushing against his spine. He waited. There was no indication from the other end of the hall that they had been heard.

With slow movements, James walked, keeping his steps soft as they made their way toward the front door. The wrapped strips of quilt around Temperance's feet made her silent as a wraith. Hopefully, they would hold up to the rigors of the road. If not, he was more than prepared to carry her on his back if it meant getting her to safety. Now that they were on their way, the urge to protect her, to ensure her safe return to her family, became tantamount.

But first, they needed to get out of this cottage without detection.

James reached around and found Temperance's hand, pulling her in front of him. He didn't like having her at his back. If their captors came running, she would be the first one to be grabbed. At least this way, if that did occur, he could fight the two idiots off and give her time to make her escape.

When they reached the front door, he wrapped his hand around the iron handle and, with the utmost care, lifted the latch.

Cold rushed in and Temperance pressed back against his chest as a burst of wind whipped around them. James shivered as the icy bite of spring in the north country cut through the fine linen of his shirt. As pleased as he was that he had finally convinced Temperance to wear his jacket, he could not claim that he didn't miss its warmth.

Outside, clouds scuttled across the night sky until the moon was forced to play hide and seek, its light slipping in and out. James had not counted on the cloud cover, but there was little they could do about it now. Despite the inky blackness of night, James could feel the gravelly texture of the lane beneath his boots. It was enough to let him know they were on the right path.

The path to freedom. To safety.

To a much different future than the one he'd mapped out for himself before leaving for the Frontenac's party. Was it only a few nights ago that he'd indicated to Alex that he had no wish to marry his American cousin? That he would choose for himself a suitable English lass of proper breeding and class?

It seemed another lifetime ago.

James looked up. Based on the first hint of the sun's rays beginning to peek out over the horizon as it began its slow ascent, he estimated they had been walking for nearly two hours, keeping parallel with the road, though hidden in the copse of trees that lined the way. Thus far, there was no hint their captors had even noticed their unannounced departure, giving them a bit of a head start. One that could be quickly eradicated should their kidnappers come after them, as they had the benefit of the horses.

He cast a glance over his shoulder. Temperance had started to lag behind in the past quarter hour and he noticed a bit of a limp. She'd tripped over a half-buried tree root earlier and though she claimed to be fine, it had obviously been a lie.

He stopped and addressed her. "Temperance, please allow me to assist you." He had taken to referring to her by her given name. Partly because he liked the way it tasted on his tongue, warm and enticing, and partly because it brought the fire to her eyes, which was warm and enticing in a completely different way.

"I am perfectly capable of making my own way, my lord."

She had yet to give in and address him as James. A shame, really. He was quite interested in knowing how it sounded on her lips.

He put his hands on his hips. His fingers had lost feeling and grown stiff from the damp and cold. He'd tucked them under his arms for warmth but it had done little good. "You are slowing us down and your stubbornness in refusing assistance may well be what allows our captors to catch up to us. Is that what you want?"

"Forgive me if my legs are not as long as yours, nor have I

the advantage of wearing boots to protect my feet, but I am doing the best I can."

Was that tears he heard in her voice? He was well aware she had slept little last night. Her nervous tossing about had, in turn, kept him up as well, but he could not fault her restlessness. He too had continually run through everything that could go wrong should they be caught escaping.

James dropped his hands from his hips and walked toward her. A drizzle had made its way through the trees and her hair fell in damp, clumpy waves. He softened his voice when he spoke, her effort against all odds and her determination to keep going despite obvious pain, touched something deep inside of him.

"Forgive me. I know you are trying your best, I did not mean to suggest otherwise. But you have obviously injured yourself and I cannot bear to see you in pain. We are both tired and cold and growing wetter by the minute. If I carry you on my back, even for a short period, it will ease the pain on your ankle."

Temperance kept her gaze fixed on the middle of his chest and said nothing, though given the way her lips twisted to one side, he suspected she teetered on the edge of agreement. She simply needed a little nudge to get her there.

James placed a finger under her chin and lifted her gaze to meet his, offering an encouraging smile. "Come now, where is that sensible woman I have come to know, hm?"

Her shoulders sagged and a breath escaped, brushing against his hand and warming it briefly. "Very well. How shall we do this?"

James looked around then led her over to a stump. "I shall crouch a bit and you shall climb onto my back and hook your legs around my waist."

Her eyes grew round. "I will most certainly not do that."

"My dearest Temperance," James said, placing his hands

upon her shoulders. "We have shared a bed for several nights. We have entwined our limbs and fitted our bodies around each other—"

"To keep warm!" A flock of birds took flight as the words shot out of her mouth.

"Hush." The last thing he needed was her indignation bringing attention to them should their captors be near. "I understand it was out of necessity and so is this. It is the best, most efficient way for me to carry you."

"But—"

James waited. She was a levelheaded woman despite her unusual opinions. He had no qualms she would eventually see the sense in his suggestion.

Her shoulders slumped as the fight left her. God help him, but she looked wretched. If only he could wrap her in his arms and erase the misery emanating from every edge of her. Press his lips to hers and make her forget—make them both forget —their precarious circumstances.

The kiss they had shared previously still lingered in his mind and he could not deny the unyielding need to experience it again. Perhaps it was simply their current situation that had created such a response in him. A desire to lose himself in her. Which was nothing short of flat out nonsense.

Clearly, the blow to his head had left him far more addled than he'd believed.

Regardless, this was neither the time nor the place for such things as passionate kisses. There would be time enough for that later.

Once he convinced her to marry him to save herself.

Once upon a time, as a small child, before her life became all about propriety and etiquette and finding a husband of higher social status and breeding to elevate her family even further in Society, Temperance could remember a time when her eldest brother, Daniel, would carry her in the same manner James did now. He would run through the hallways of their stately home whinnying like a wild horse, letting her direct him where to go. As a young boy, he'd been fascinated with the idea of traveling to untamed areas, to seeking out new adventures and seeing the world. It was a need so ingrained in him that one day, after a particularly loud row with Father, Daniel had disappeared for good. Temperance had always wondered where he had gone; hurt that he hadn't said good-bye. Devastated that he had never written to let her know he was safe and happy. Had he finally found the adventure he sought? Did he miss his younger brother and sisters or think of them at all? Was he even alive?

"Are you doing well back there?"

James—as it had become increasingly difficult to think of him as Lord Ridgemont since the kiss—turned his head just enough so that his cheek brushed against hers where she looked over his shoulder.

"As well as can be expected. Do you need a rest?" Carrying her could not be an easy endeavor, especially given his injury, but if he was experiencing any ill effects from it, she could find no trace of such.

"No. We shall go a little farther. Surely we will come upon some form of civilization soon."

But she heard the worry in his voice. They had been traveling for hours, keeping to the woods, hurrying across the open terrain when the trees briefly gave way. There was no sign of their abductors giving chase as yet, but Temperance did not expect that to last. Knowing the bumbling idiots, they likely expected their captives to have gone the way they came. Hopefully it was several hours before they realized the error of this assumption. But even then, they would be traveling by horseback, or have taken the carriage, and their pace would be far swifter than the one she and James had been able to keep.

"I'm certain you're right," she said, unable to infuse into her tone a sense of certainty. They had gone too far without even a hint of civilization. How much longer could they carry on? And what if they didn't find shelter before night fell once more? She pushed the fearful thoughts from her mind as best she could.

They carried on for another hour before James slowed. "Perhaps we should stop for some sustenance."

They had horded the stale bread and cheese they'd been given for the past two days in preparation for their escape. It wasn't much—their captors were hardly the generous sort—but with the grumbling in her stomach, she was happy for what small amounts they had.

James crouched, allowing Temperance to slide down to the ground. The sensation of gliding against his body, the hard muscle and sturdy construction under his clothes, sent a thrill shooting through her. As if having her legs wrapped around his waist, his arms tucked beneath her legs to hold her place, for the past couple of hours had not been torturous enough.

Her legs buckled as they hit the ground and James reached out for her. "Steady. It will take a minute for the blood to flow back into your legs."

She gave him a feeble smile. Speaking to a man about her body parts was still a rather odd experience.

Sweat caused his linen shirt to cling to him in spots, a testament to the work it took to drag them both over the uneven ground. She needed to pull her own weight, literally and figuratively.

Temperance tested her ankle. It ached a little, but not as it had when she had originally turned it. Though her feet were cold and the strips of quilt wrapped around her shoes were filthy and tattered, she was determined to continue on under her own power.

"I think my ankle is much better. Thank you for the rest." She looked up at him and found him smiling down at her as if their situation were comical and not dire and frightening. She should be angry at his lack of seriousness about their circumstances but instead, her own smile tugged at the corners of her mouth. "What about this can you possibly find amusing?"

His smile grew and the warmth in her veins increased in direct proportion. "Did you think, at any point in time when we were waltzing at the Frontenac's ball, that this is where we would find ourselves just a few days later?"

A bubble of laughter worked its way up her throat and threatened to escape. She shouldn't let it. Their current situation was nothing to laugh about. They were in the middle of nowhere, likely being chased by two men determined to hold them hostage, or kill them, shivering in the cold and no idea when—or how—their plight would end. Their predicament was quite dangerous, their future uncertain.

And yet, she couldn't stop the laughter from coming. The more she thought about what he'd asked her, the more ridiculous their present situation seemed. Because this *wasn't* where she'd expected to be. At this point, she'd expected to be on her way to the school Miss Rosalind Caldwell had established with the help of several other women of import, ready to shape and mold the minds of young girls so that they might rise above their circumstances and have a better life.

Instead, she was standing in the middle of a forest trying desperately to find a safe place to shelter themselves and return home before their captors caught up to them and did heaven only knew what. She was cold and sore and frightened and her only companion was a man who, up until this point, she'd considered a pompous windbag whose sense of entitlement made her want to tear her hair out in frustration.

A man who had kissed her like no other man had before.

A man who was as handsome as sin.

A man who could make her laugh, even under the worst of circumstances.

Like now.

Her chest shook from the effort of trying to hold it in until she no longer could and the laughter erupted from her until tears filled her eyes and she could no more control it or stop it than she could the rising and setting of the sun. He joined in and by the end of it, when their senses regained footing and their bodies were exhausted and yet exhilarated from the effort.

"Sshhh..." James said, reaching out and pulling her against him, smothering what remained of her laughter against his chest. She could still feel his own rumbling in response as his cheek rested against her head, his arms holding her tight. Despite wearing only his linen shirt as protection against the damp, cool air, heat emanated from his body into hers and it was with great reluctance that she pulled away. She could not allow such intimacies. It was not proper and she did not want to give him the impression that she was softening on his insistence that they marry.

Because she wasn't softening. She had come close enough to marriage in the past to see it was not a palatable future.

Though in moments like this, when he held her and made her laugh despite having no reason to do so, a part of her wondered.

Imagined.

Questioned.

Was it possible not all men would behave with the same sense of entitlement and disregard for her feelings as Beauregard had?

She shook her head. No. Such thoughts could not be entertained. Perhaps James might be different, but what if he wasn't? She could not risk finding such a truth out when it was too late and she could not turn back.

Besides, she had already determined her path. Being head-mistress at Rosalind's school would allow her to use her mind, to do something good and worthwhile. It saved her from being forced to adhere to Society's expectations. How could such an inequitable state as marriage offer her any kind of happiness? She had not always thought this way, but now that she'd had her eyes opened to what she could expect, she had no desire to be made the fool again.

"We should continue on," she said.

James looked down at her, his gaze traveling across her face, memorizing it as if he understood her fierce determination would supersede his insistence. "Very well. We can eat our bread and cheese as we walk, if you're amenable to such."

She nodded. Yes, better to keep moving, to avoid moments like this that weakened her resolve and made her look at James not as the man she had assumed him to be, but instead as the man he was. A complex individual, whose most intriguing layers lay hidden beneath the facade of a gentleman, their edges smoothed over so that most people missed seeing them. Though once seen, could not be forgotten.

And those recalcitrant thoughts made resisting James's pull a Herculean feat.

Chapter Nine

S omething had happened back in the woods. What exactly that something was, James couldn't pinpoint, not with a name. But he felt it. Deep inside, something stirred as Temperance had doubled over, holding one hand against her stomach and the other over her mouth, laughing. He'd never seen her so free. So much...herself.

Perhaps that was it. In that moment, when her emotions overtook her, he had caught a rare glimpse of the woman she was at the core. Not the single-minded, mule-headed woman determined to never marry or live a conventional life. No, in that moment, lost in her laughter, he saw a woman of courage. Strength. Daring.

All of which were the same things that caused her to insist upon her own personal freedom. And, while James might have strong concerns with how she planned to achieve this freedom, he understood that should anyone try to rein those aspects of her personality in, they would be heartily challenged.

The thing of it was, however, it was those aspects of her

that he found the most intriguing. The most beguiling. The most seductive.

He'd never known a woman quite like her. And the more he came to know, the more he wanted to know, and the less put off he was by what he had once assumed were the foolish opinions of the uninformed.

James stopped suddenly, his musings interrupted by the vision just beyond the edge of the wood. Just as well. He had no business allowing his thoughts to wander in that direction. While he insisted they must marry, he was quickly learning that his insistence had little sway with his companion. Something to which he was not accustomed.

"Is that a cottage?"

"Indeed," James whispered, blinking just in case it was nothing more than a mirage brought on by fatigue and hunger. But if Temperance saw it too, then it must be there.

"Do you see anyone about?" Temperance moved closer to him.

"No. The place looks deserted." Not completely, though. The cottage was kept up, the pathways between it and the stables beyond worn down. The garden off to the side was well tended and the ivy and rose bushes were trimmed and ready to bloom. A proud rooster was perched atop the chicken coop, its sights trained upon them as if he suspected they might try to raid its interior and he would not stand for it.

The cheese and bread they'd consumed earlier had worn off and James had to admit, the idea of scrambled eggs made his stomach growl. A raid may be well worth the risk.

"Should we knock on the door? Or are we planning on standing at the edge of the wood for the remainder of the day?"

James glanced down and gave her a scowl. "I am assessing the situation."

"The situation is that no one appears to be home, but the

most expedient way to determine this for certain is to walk up and knock on the door."

"And if no one answers?"

"Then we go inside and make ourselves at home."

The idea horrified him. "Just break in like we have a right to be there?"

Temperance raised one dark eyebrow. "Aren't you the great Marquess of Ridgemont, lord of all you survey?"

"I am not lord of all I survey. And I find the idea of breaking into someone's home like a common criminal nothing short of appalling."

"Do you think we should wait out here braving the cold and drizzle and potential risk of being discovered until the owners return then?"

"It would be the proper thing to do."

"It would be the idiotic thing to do if they are absent for several days."

She had a point. They could not stand out here for days. She was shivering and exhausted and he was not too far behind her in that regard. "Very well. Come." He held out his arm to escort her from the woods to the homestead, an action that garnered a bit of a chuckle from Temperance that in turn resulted in a glare from him. "Gentlemanly behavior, regardless of the situation, Miss Lindwell, is never out of place."

His condemnation did little to erase the smile on her face at his expense. Instead, she curtsied as best she could in her quilted shoes and offered up a very polite, "Yes, my lord."

As they made their way across the road to the lane that led to the small, well-kept cottage, relief swept through James's body that they had reached this point. That he could offer her shelter—even if he had no right to it—and take them out of sight of their captors. It surprised him somewhat that they had not been caught. Then again, the fools who'd abducted them had not struck him as the most intelligent of men. Likely, they had kept going down the road that they had come up without considering the possibility their captives might have opted for another route. Whatever bungled reasoning the two kidnappers had used, he was glad for it. It had bought them some time to think how to get from where they were now, to where they needed to be.

And it gave him time to consider what must be done upon their return to London.

When no one answered his knock, James reached for the latch. The door opened easily enough, the interior much like the exterior—clean and neatly appointed. It was evident that whoever lived here had only recently departed and intended upon returning. It was also evident by the pervasive cold that it had been at least a day or two since the fires had been lit. Yet, wood was neatly stacked both by the woodstove and large hearth in the kitchen area and main room. Likely, another one would be found in the bedrooms farther down the hall as well.

"It's quite lovely," Temperance whispered as if they were in church and the quiet space deserved a certain kind of reverence.

Her praise surprised him. "I would think this a far cry from what you are used to."

"Such small quarters may be vastly different than what I am used to, but it does not mean I cannot appreciate it. There is something to be said about the closeness a family would share when the space they occupy is limited."

Sadness permeated her tone, surprising him. He'd spent his life in grand homes and did not feel as if he suffered from a lack of closeness due to the size. His father and mother were always present in his life and, upon his mother's untimely death from illness, his stepmother, who he'd also loved dearly and who'd provided him with the great gift of his youngest sister. They had been a small family, smaller still after his father and stepmother perished in a fire nearly a decade ago, but a grand home had not created a divide between them.

"Are you not close with your own family then?"

She had pulled ahead of him and looked back over her shoulder. "My sister and I are very close, of course. And my brothers...we were close once upon a time as well, though less so in recent years."

"What happened to change that?"

Temperance's gaze fell away and she became engrossed in the rudimentary painting of a vase that hung on the wall nearest her. "Life happened, I suppose. And my father's interpretation of how it should be lived."

"And what interpretation is that?"

She completed her perusal of the painting and continued on down the length of the main room to a hallway beyond. "My father places a high value on appearances and he expects his family to follow suit. Constance and Collin have always tried their best to curtail their behaviors to fit Father's expectations. Daniel refused, of course."

"And Temperance?"

She disappeared around the corner without answering and James found himself drawn to following her, reluctant to let the conversation go. He had a hunger to know more about her, to learn what made her the way she was—fiercely independent, insistent upon pushing at the boundaries others tried to impose upon her, bucking convention and tradition like a horse with a burr beneath its saddle.

He found her in the bedroom, opening the drawers of a large bureau. "What are you doing?"

She pointed at the contents of the open drawer. "Whoever owns this cottage will be returning. They've left their clothing behind."

He watched in horror as she rummaged through the articles

of clothing and pulled out a chemise, a pair of wool stockings, and other sundry items he chose not to pay particular attention to as to avoid unwanted thoughts rioting through his head.

"What in God's name are you doing?"

She turned from the bureau and made her way over to a nearby armoire. "If we are to continue on, we will need to outfit ourselves with proper attire."

While he could not fault her thinking, he could fault her actions as she brought out a dress and dumped it next to the underclothes.

"You cannot steal these people's clothing!" What kind of person did this? Granted, he'd heard stories of Americans and their odd sensibilities but this went beyond the pale. They were not thieves! At least he was not.

"James," she said, stressing his name in such a way it harkened back to when his mother was about to scold him for doing something foolish. "When our captors finally come to their senses and realize what direction we have gone, they will come after us. But they will be looking for a lord and lady wearing certain attire. If we continue to wear this—" She waved at her sodden gown. "—then we shall stick out like a parrot among pigeons."

"What exactly are you saying?"

She pointed at the navy wool dress she'd taken from the armoire. "We must become pigeons. We may send the clothing back with reimbursement for their use once we are safely back in London if it makes you feel better."

"It doesn't."

"Then feel free to continue waltzing about in your gentleman's attire, but you will do so on your own. I, for one, am not about to allow pride to put me back in the situation we have only just escaped from."

He loathed the idea of stealing from the home's occupants. It was obvious they did not have much, though what they did have, they took great care to keep clean and orderly.

"Fine. But on one condition."

She turned toward him with a cautious look. He didn't blame her. The last time he'd requested conditions, he'd just finished kissing her and the conditions given were in exchange for not doing so again. A bargain he now regretted making, as there had been any number of moments since when he would have loved nothing more than to kiss her. She had the most delectable mouth when it wasn't giving him grief.

"And what might that condition be?" she asked.

"That we stay here for the night to rest your ankle." And for him to rest his entire body. He did not wish to admit it aloud, but he ached from the effort of carrying her and it was clear he had not yet regained his full vigor. "It will be dark in a few hours and I cannot guarantee we will reach a village before then. If we stay, we can feed ourselves proper, get a good rest, and make a plan for tomorrow."

For once, Temperance did not argue. "Very well. Then I should like to change out of these sodden clothes and into something warm and dry."

James nodded. "I fear we should not light a fire. I know it is quite chilly in here, but I would not want to draw any undue attention this way."

"I suppose we should be used to such conditions by now."

"It will mean we shall have to—" He waved a hand toward the bed, struggling to find the proper words so she did not think he was trying to take advantage of their situation. "For warmth, of course. I shall be on my best behave—"

"You may relax, my lord. I agree with you on that account as well. I have no desire to freeze when we are so close to being free of our current circumstances."

That was rather easy. Almost too easy. He smiled. Was it possible that Miss Temperance Lindwell, despite all her objections to the contrary, might be developing the smallest hint of tender feelings toward him?

"Now, if you will excuse me, my lord. I would like to wash and change and I don't feel I need an audience for that particular event."

Then again, maybe not.

Hungry as she was, Temperance took her time peeling away her damp clothing piece by piece and redressing in her unaware hostess's more rudimentary wool dress and stockings and plain, rather unflattering underclothing. The woman was a few sizes larger than Temperance, and a couple of inches shorter, but she cared little. The dress was warm and dry and comfortable. Her mother would faint dead away if she ever witnessed her daughter's current attire, but there was something about the plainness of it that suited her. Unlike Constance, Temperance had never been the type for fancy flourishes or accouterments.

The only part of her own clothing she kept was her stays —the other woman's were far too large to fit her smaller frame —and her jewelry. The latter she had stuffed down her bodice after being thrown into the carriage, to prevent her captors from taking it. She had no particular attachment to the jewels, but thought if worse came to worse, she may be able to barter their way out of captivity if the ransom wasn't paid. For now, she slipped the baubles into one of the pockets sewn into the seam of the wool dress for safekeeping. They may need them still.

Once dressed, she tackled her hair. Most of her pins had been lost and the few left had been used to pick the lock on their door during their escape. A task that proved far more difficult than they had anticipated and caused her an untold amount of stress. Thankfully, James had refused to give up, something she was noticing was a running theme with him. Aside from her father and brother, Daniel, she did not think she had ever met a man so determined.

After she worked the tangles from her hair and pulled a brush through the long strands, she found a ribbon and tied the thick layers back. It was a simple, somewhat domestic look. Not what she was used to seeing and even though the mirror in the room was small and warped, the reflection that stared back at her was a girl plain of feature and dress.

Is this what she would look like as headmistress of Rosalind's school? It was an odd thought. Not one she had actively considered. She'd avoided thinking about that aspect of her plan as much as possible, simply focusing on everything she needed to do beforehand. Truth be told, the idea of being headmistress of a school for young ladies left her feeling a bit underwhelmed. Initially, it seemed the answer to her current dilemma, a way to avoid a marriage forced upon her by Father. But a future that meant the same thing day in and day out for year on end left her rather...unsettled. Was it truly independence if you gave up one choice only to tie yourself to another?

She pushed the question aside. She had little choice in the matter now. James was correct in one regard—whispers and innuendo would swirl about them upon their return to London. How could it not? Father would demand James do the right thing and offer for her and James, being far too much a gentleman for his own good, had every intention of doing so.

What would happen when she said no? Would the scandal be so great Rosalind would have no other choice but to rescind her offer of employment? And if that happened, what recourse was left to Temperance? Would Father make good on his threats and cast her out? It wasn't as if she would be the first of his children he'd turned his back on.

Still, there was this other part of her, the part she preferred not to give any credence to, that wondered what marriage to James would be like. He was a temperate man, not given to fits or rages. He listened to her when she spoke, though often he did not agree with what she said. Would it always be like that? Or would it be as it was with Beauregard? Where he enticed with the act of gentlemanly behaviors to win her over and then once her heart was engaged, his true self came through.

It had been James's own sister, Henrietta, who, shortly after her marriage to Lord Rothbury, had told her that a woman could tell a man's goodness by the way he kissed her. She had never given the claim much credence, until now.

She touched her lips, staring at her reflection. James's kiss had been deep and exhilarating. It was what she imagined one would feel like after over-imbibing in spirits, though without the nasty headache and queasy stomach she'd witnessed her brothers suffer. Beauregard's had been nothing like that. They had been almost chaste. Tepid at best. She hadn't given the matter any thought back then, now she wondered if she should have. Had that been a lack of interest on his part? If so, then James did not suffer the same malady.

Her stomach fluttered.

If marriage meant she could experience such a kiss on a daily basis, perhaps the institution did have at least a few merits to recommend it.

She glared at her reflection. Thinking like that would get her nowhere.

Temperance spun on her newly booted heel—the one item of clothing that actually fit her properly—and marched from the room, leaving thoughts of James and his kisses behind in the room they would share later.

"There you are." James smiled at her, his gaze traveling over her like a warm caress. "You look much...cleaner."

Her ego dampened. Cleaner? How flattering. Not that she was looking for him to flatter, because she wasn't. She did not care one whit what he thought of how she looked. Truly.

"Thank you. I feel much better," she answered, her words brisk as she pressed her hands against the navy wool. She needed to corral her thoughts in a more sensible direction. She could not afford such foolish daydreams. She had allowed that once and it had led her to the edge of disaster. "Were you able to find something to eat?"

"Indeed I was." James moved away from the table and waved an arm toward the spread. Bread and cheese and a plate of salted pork. "The bread is a bit stale, but it should suffice. I also found some oats that we can have in the morning before we set out again."

Temperance's stomach growled in response but her mind pushed aside the thought of moving on. For now, for this one moment in time, she wanted to do nothing more than enjoy a brief hint of domesticity. To partake in the simple act of having a meal with a man who had proven to be far more layered and complicated than she had originally estimated. And, if she were being honest, a man she found more and more difficult to dislike with each passing hour.

"Come." He offered her his arm and, without thinking, she slid her hand through it, relishing in the warmth of his skin and the subtle shifting of muscle beneath the homespun shirt he'd donned. It was the only change in his clothing from when they arrived, unlike she who had changed everything right down to her unmentionables.

"Was there nothing for you to wear?"

"Ah yes, well, it appears the gentleman of the house and I are of a different size. The trousers were quite large in the waist and far too short in the leg. As my own clothing are still serviceable and my boots in proper condition, though Gregory will likely disagree, I have opted to keep them."

"I feel quite dowdy in comparison," she said, as he pulled out a chair at the table built from planked wood that had been worn smooth.

"You could not be dowdy if you tried. I think you look exquisite."

"And I think you are still suffering from the blow you took to the head."

A smile flashed across James's face, changing his expression instantly. "Not so. Blue is a lovely color on you. I've always thought so."

"Flatterer."

He continued smile as he took a seat next to where she sat at the head of the table, instead of at the other end as she had expected. There was an unexpected intimacy to sitting within arm's reach of him. How odd to discover such a thing. Was it simply that her emotions were heightened by their current situation? Or was she, heaven forbid, growing attached to his lordship?

Temperance shoved a piece of cheese into her mouth, heedless of manners. Anything to rid the foolish thought of becoming anything to James Harrow, Seventh Marquess of Ridgemont. She had set her course and refused to be deterred. To tie them both to a marriage neither of them wanted. No matter how handsome his lordship was, or how well he could kiss.

And he could kiss quite well. So well, that she would not mind experiencing such one more time before she started her new life. A sweet memory to carry with her that she could draw upon if she became lonely or feared she had missed out on a part of life other women took for granted.

"You must have been quite hungry."

James amused tone cut off her foolish thoughts and she

turned to see him staring at her, eyebrows raised in delight. Temperance glanced down at her hand that held a second chunk of cheese and the large portion of pork balanced on the end of her fork, ready to be delivered to her mouth that was already filled with the first piece of cheese.

Heat infused her cheeks and she set both things down, embarrassed at her lack of manners, especially in front of someone who probably lived and breathed them as if they were second nature. Clearly, such was not the case with her. Further proof to him, no doubt, what heathens the Americans were.

"Yes. Well. I suppose I am," she said, speaking around the food in her mouth only to realize that, too, was not well done. She swallowed but the food stuck in her throat, causing her to choke as it went down the wrong way.

"Are you quite all right?"

She tried to answer, but the words could not get past the blockage and it took all she had to catch her breath which also appeared to be stuck somewhere behind the errant piece of cheese.

"Bloody hell," James said, pushing back the bench he sat upon and pulling her chair away from the table.

Temperance tried to wave him off, but he ignored her as he wrapped one arm around her waist, balanced her near his hip, and began pounding on her back with the force of a sledge-hammer. After several hits, the cheese shifted and she coughed, air rushing into her lungs as her body went limp.

James caught her up in his arms as Temperance bandied between coughing and breathing. Her eyes watered and she was quite certain her nose was running. If James had any question over the veracity of his belief that Americans lacked the grace of their English counterparts, she had likely just solidified the impression.

"Set me down." Her voice rasped when she spoke and she

used the sleeve of her borrowed dress to swipe the tears and who knew what else away from her face.

With gentle precision, James did as she asked though his arm remained around her waist and held her close. Too close. "Are you certain you are recovered?"

She nodded and cleared her throat. "From everything but the embarrassment."

One side of his mouth quirked upward. "Well, at least your humor has remained unaffected by the ordeal. Would you like to sit?"

"Please." Anything to put a little distance between the intoxicating pull of having him hold her against him. She hated this weakness. Hated how his nearness made her body do things she had no control over. The longing it created in parts of her she dared not think about. Her mother claimed such things were sinful and dangerous. Temperance wasn't sure about the first, but she fully agreed with the latter.

James Harrow was, indeed, a very dangerous man.

Chapter Ten

Once James had settled Temperance back in her chair, he pushed a glass of water toward her. "Sip slowly to wash the food down."

She did as he said, giving no argument despite feeling like a child. A stupid, foolish, clumsy child. After several sips, the drink had worked and she set the glass down.

"Thank you."

"You're quite welcome. I'd hate to think I had gotten you this far only to lose you to a piece of cheese."

She raised her eyebrows. Had she heard him right? "That you got me this far? I am quite certain I got myself this far, sir."

James leaned an elbow on the table and rested his head against his fisted hand, clearly unconcerned by her umbrage at his assessment of her part in their escape. "Is that so? Did you carry yourself half the way then?"

Her lips tightened. The worst part about arguing with someone was when you knew they were right but your pride refused to allow you to admit it, whilst your intelligence indicated you did not have a leg to stand on.

"Stop scowling at me," James said, his voice quiet and enchanting, lulling the anger from her body. "I saved your life. You have to be nice to me now."

"I do not."

"It would be bad manners not to."

"If I recall, you've already indicated that we Americans wouldn't know good manners if they came up and clobbered us over the head."

"I'm quite certain I didn't say it like that."

"It was inferred in your tone."

"I have a tone?"

"Yes. A rather haughty one at that." Although the tone he was using currently sounded nothing like that. In fact, the one he used now lured her in, cast a spell over her until she could not remember exactly why they were arguing. Things became fuzzy around the edges until the only thing that existed was the man sitting next to her, his enticing smile, and warm blue eyes that sparkled like water kissed by the sun.

As if reading her thoughts, his smile broadened. "Do you recall when I agreed not to kiss you again unless you requested it?"

She nodded, all the words she had ever known having flown from her head at his intense gaze and seductive voice.

"I would be most appreciative if you would request that I do so now."

She swallowed but sat mutely, staring at him. Need, want, and desire crawled through her and reached areas they had never gone before. She squirmed in her chair in an attempt to alleviate the sensation. An attempt that failed.

He reached over and took her hand, staring at their fingers as they interlaced together. "Might you do that, ask me to kiss you?"

She nodded again. How familiar his touch had become to her in just a few days.

A small smile played about his lips. Lips she could not tear her gaze away from. Previous experience told her they were the gateway to sin. Yet another part of her, a part that had remained resolutely silent until she had met this man sitting in front of her, demanded she open that gateway and learn all the secrets that lay behind its locked doors.

James pulled her hand toward him and placed his lips against her knuckles. "Ask me." His words whispered against her skin.

She could not form the words. Her heart pounded in her chest and blood roared in her ears. She might be dying. She could not be certain. She squeezed his hand and pulled him forward, but he was too heavy and instead the motion pulled her out of her chair toward him. She let momentum take her, let him lead her onto his lap. He let go of her hand and slid his around her waist, low enough to skim her hip. His gaze never left hers, however, and in it, she could see the same desire building inside of him.

She did not need to say the words. She did not need to wait for him to make good on her request. She could simply take the lead. *She* could kiss *him*. Was that not what being a woman of independent thought meant? That she could decide for herself when and what she did. And if it pleased her, then why would she not do it? There was no harm in a kiss and oh, my, but his kiss did please her.

She leaned forward and pressed her mouth to his. His lips were warm and welcoming, curved into a smile she could feel sneaking inside of her and filling her with an explicit joy she could barely contain. It took but a flash before the passion she'd experienced in their first kiss flashed and burned and overtook every barrier she'd put up to keep James at arm's length.

Why was such a thing so impossible to maintain?

But she knew. His touch was like the most intoxicating

elixir, whether it was his hand or his mouth or his whole body, fully clothed and pressed against her in the dark of night. Even his breath upon her skin when deep with sleep was enough to make her most private areas ache with longing. Much as they did now.

What would happen if she gave into that longing? Would she forever ruin the plans she had carefully put in place? As his hand slid around her neck and pulled at the ribbon in her hair until it gave way, she wasn't sure she cared. Not in this moment, at least. Maybe later. Later, she could determine what must be done, or not done. In this moment, all she wanted was to release the desire stirring within her. To know what her mother had always referred to with distaste as the *carnal pleasures of the flesh*. The very phrase had always struck her as positively wicked.

Tantalizing.

James's hand, as it traveled around to brush against her breast and gently cup it, proved her assessment had been true. She broke their kiss, her head falling back as his mouth teased the sensitive skin on her neck.

"I want more," she said, barely cognoscente of the words coming out of her.

"We cannot," he said and a flash of anger seared inside of her. How could he bring her to the brink of such ecstasy and leave her there to wither? To never know what came next? Because surely, whatever came after was even more delicious than what she experienced now.

"We must." She shifted, burying her fingers into his thick hair and pressing her hip against the hardness that had developed in his trousers.

He released a long, low groan. "Do not tempt me more than you already do, Temperance. My will is weak in that regard but I am determined that I shall not ruin you."

"You will ruin me if you leave me unsatisfied." She understood the basics of the act between a man and woman—although this part of the explanation she currently experienced had been left out of the lesson. And she couldn't quite fathom how the two married together. Mother had always indicated the act itself was a duty to be suffered through. But this didn't feel like suffering. This felt, oh, this felt wonderful! And she wanted more. Even as her mind threatened caution, her body pushed such warnings aside in favor of exploring and learning and finally knowing.

She turned and straddled him like the most brazen wanton, leaning in to kiss the curve of his ear, then whispered against it. "Besides, if you claim we must marry, what does it matter?"

James's breath caught as she pulled his earlobe between her teeth and his fingers dug through the layers of her skirts to grip her hips and pull her tighter against him. "You have refused to marry me, or have you forgotten?"

"Then convince me the merits of such a union." It was a horrible lie, but she pushed aside the guilt that came as she spoke the words. She was filled with need and abandon and cared little for such things as truth or right or wrong. She wanted this. She needed it. Needed him. Whatever came come morning light, she would deal with then. "Please, James."

She wasn't certain which part of her plea was the part that convinced him, nor did she care as he stood, bringing her with him, and carried her into the bedroom at the end of the hall-way, their meal forgotten as they sought sustenance of another kind.

To suggest she was scared over what she was about to do would be a fair assessment. But it wasn't the kind of fear she'd experienced when her abductors grabbed her without warning, or when James crumpled to the ground and they had threatened to kill him. No, this was a different sort of beast. It was threaded through with exhilaration and expectation. The fear was the unknown. She did not know quite what to expect, what to do, or what to say. Or what would come after. That James obviously did was more of a hindrance than a help to some respect. It put her at a disadvantage and she did not care for being at such. The last time she found herself at a disadvantage where a man was concerned—

Well, that did not matter now, did it?

The bed in the small room at the end of the hall, while basic and smaller in size than what she was used to, was still quite comfortable as James laid her gently upon it then joined her, his body covering hers as he lavished kisses upon her neck and chest and jawline and that most sensitive spot just behind her ear. His attentions made it difficult to catch her breath, to think of what *she* should be doing, for surely she wasn't meant to simply lay there. But it was impossible to respond in kind, as she was never quite certain where he was going to move to next and she didn't thinking conking heads would help. Especially given his recent experiences in that regard.

When he returned to her mouth, however, she answered her own question, giving as much as she got. Taking James's lead, she slid the tip of her tongue against his, nibbled at his bottom lip, and kissed him fully with a fervor she had not known she possessed. The more they kissed and his hands roamed her body, the more she wished to be rid of the wool dress she had only just donned and feel the weight and breadth of his hands upon her bare skin.

It was a startling realization to think this man, who until recently was the epitome of everything she found wrong with the English culture, had now come to mean so much to her. That somewhere in the past several days they had forged a friendship, despite their differences, that went beyond simply being attracted to him because he cut a handsome figure. This was more. Deeper. It both amazed and frightened her, but she had never been one to give into fear. Fear no longer had a part in her life.

Yet, somehow, James Harrow, Seventh Marquess of Ridgemont, did.

What that meant, Temperance could not say. At least not now, while James undid the front of her dress until it fell open, revealing her stays and the simple chemise beneath. His nimble fingers quickly unlaced her stays and his hand slid beneath the soft cotton fabric and cupped her breast, his thumb brushing over her nipple. Shock ricocheted through her at the sensation that filled her and her hips lifted and pressed against James of their own volition, the ache within her increasing until she feared it might drive her mad.

"Did you like that?" He whispered the question against her newly exposed skin.

"Yes," she breathed. *Oh, yes.*

His mouth moved closer to where his thumb had been only seconds before. He kissed her once more. "And this? Do you like this?"

She nodded, words becoming increasingly difficult to form as she attempted to corral the sensations barreling through her.

He glanced up at her without moving and for the first time she noted how thick and dark his short lashes where, framing the mischievous glint in his blue eyes so that even that had a physical effect on her. Without removing his gaze from hers, he moved just far enough so that his mouth hovered over her nipple, the tip of his tongue reaching out to brush against it.

A low moan involuntarily escaped her and her hands fisted into the quilt beneath her. Then his entire mouth replaced his tongue and she found a piece of heaven that she never wanted to leave.

Eventually, he moved on, but no matter where he placed

his hands or his mouth, it set her body aflame in ways she had never expected a body could be. One part of her feared she would burn to nothing more than cinders and the other part welcomed the fire. Embraced the heat. Relished in the decadence as he peeled each article of her clothes away, and then his own until they lay bare skin to skin.

And that...well that was the most glorious thing in this world or anything beyond it.

James explored every inch of her, his hands roaming down the front of her thighs then up the back of the to cup her bottom and pull her close. His own need pressed into her, urgent and demanding but he did not push, did not attempt to coerce her before she was ready. His attention to her body made her squirm with want until she could stand it no more.

"James, please," she whispered, unsure of exactly what to say beyond begging for release from the ache, the deep longing he'd created within her.

His hand drifted across her stomach, low and tantalizing. "Yes? Is there something more you'd like me to do?"

Temperance's breath caught as his fingers dipped lower, touching her most private place and causing the ache to increase until she lifted her hips to meet his touch. "Yes. I want more."

"Anything specific?"

She could hear the humor in his tone but the way his fingers teased and taunted left her unable to reply beyond letting out a low, guttural moan. When words failed her, she responded in kind and reached between them, wrapping her hand around his hardness.

His breath caught and he fell against her. "Sweet Mother Mary!"

"What I would like," she said, her breath coming in short bursts as she tried to regain some control. "Is for you to stop teasing me and make this ache go away."

"But I like to tease you."

She slid her hand down the length of his cock—good heavens, how was this to fit inside of her? He let out a curse and grabbed her wrist, pulling it away as if her touch had caused him pain, yet the laughter that followed, strangled as it might be, indicated pain was not what he had felt.

"You are an uncommon woman, Miss Lindwell. And I would be most pleased to attend to this ache you claim to have."

James moved until his body hovered over her. Nudging apart her knees, he settled between them.

"This may hurt a bit at first."

"Do your worst," she said. She cared not. If it relieved her of this ache, she would weather the storm.

"Oh, no. I think not." James captured her mouth with his in a searing kiss that only served to make her want him more and did little to give her relief. "I think instead, I shall do my very best."

And he did. Oh, my, but he did. As he'd warned, it did hurt a little, though not so much that she wished him to stop and after a moment of his careful ministrations, she had all but forgotten it. The feel of him moving within her, the way their bodies fused together like the most decadent kind of waltz was like nothing she had ever experienced. She could have danced with him all night long, but the longing inside of her built until suddenly everything within her felt as if she had toppled over the edge of something and, for the briefest moment, knew what it was like to fly before slowly floating to land safely back to where she was.

And where she was, was tangled about the man who had brought her such bliss, their bodies slick with sweat, their breath coming in gasps and their hearts beating in tandem.

James turned his head to kiss her neck. "Are you all right? Did I hurt you?"

"No. Indeed, that was quite...quite..." She shook her head. She had no words for what that was.

James lifted himself to his elbows and smiled down at her. "Have I left you speechless again? Well, now that I know the secret—"

She swatted at his chest, unable to be angry at his jest. "You are the most irritating of men. Has anyone ever told you such before?"

"Never. I am, however, often told that I am quite reasonable and pleasant to be around."

"I do not believe it."

"Really? Because you did appear quite pleased only a moment ago."

Temperance smiled. "Perhaps I have forgotten."

"Should I remind you then?"

Temperance's body tingled with anticipation. "Indeed, I believe a refresher may be in order, if you would be so kind."

"Indeed." James smiled and tossed the blankets up to cover his head.

"What are you doing?"

The heavy quilt covering their bodies muffled his response.

"James, whatever are you—oh!" Temperance's body arched as his mouth delivered the most intimate kiss and the fire he had doused only moments before burned anew and suddenly she no longer cared to hear the answer and gave herself over to the passion James Harrow, Seventh Marquess of Ridgemont, pompous aristocrat and epitome of everything she railed against, delivered upon her.

Despite everything that had happened to them in the past several days, this she would not regret. Not for as long as she lived.

J ames rolled onto his side to face her, his mussed hair and several days' growth of beard giving him a disheveled, rakish appearance that made parts of her stir once more.

"So," He smiled and arched one eyebrow. "Have I convinced you that marriage is not the horrible institution you have made it out to be?"

"Hm?" Temperance avoided his gaze. If she looked into those eyes, she would only become lost again and then heaven only knew what she would agree to. His ability to distract her from her plans proved most disconcerting. But no more so than the implicit lie her body told as she relished what he'd done to her, knowing he would believe her acquiescence meant she'd agreed to his earlier proposal. How could she not, after all? For now, she was truly, at least in the eyes of Society, ruined beyond redemption.

But now that her wits had returned, the familiar doubt crept back in. What did she really know about James? As a member of the aristocracy, he had expectations of what he required from a marriage. He firmly believed the English way of doing things was the right way. How could she possibly marry a man who viewed her as little more than a brood mare he expected to deliver him of an heir and a spare? To look pretty and be submissive and carry on as if he were lord and master and she nothing more than a servant meant to do his bidding.

That was the world he lived in. And from her experience of men, it seemed to be the world they all lived in. But such was not a world she fit into. She could not be quiet and subservient. She had a mind of her own and held a deep need to do more with her life than be an adornment on someone's arm when it suited them and shoved into the background when it didn't.

There had to be more to life than that. There simply had to be. Didn't there?

James brows dipped downward, creating deep creases between them. "Bloody hell."

The words whispered out of him and Temperance held her breath, biting at her bottom lip as she waited for the realization to hit him fully.

"You have no intention of marrying me, do you? You never did."

Was it possible for a woman to feel like a cad? Because she did. A cad of the worst sort. But in the end, she was doing him a service. It wasn't as if he truly wanted to marry her, after all. He only offered out of a sense of duty. Honor.

Perhaps if she'd possessed a little more of both, she might have withstood his charms and her own longings and they wouldn't be in this situation. But she didn't. It was not a very bolstering realization to discover such a thing about yourself.

"Do not take it personally, James. I told you that marriage does not fit into my plans. And, aside from this—" She waved her hand between their naked bodies. "I see no benefit in marriage for me."

"No benefit?" He sputtered the words out then rolled onto his back, only to roll back again a few seconds later. "*This*, as you so eloquently refer to it as, can have consequences. It may already have done so."

"I assume you are referring to the possibility of getting me with child?"

"Yes. As we speak you may be carrying the next Marquess of Ridgemont."

Temperance smiled at him. "I don't believe the process works that fast." She paused, her fingers resting near her abdomen, doubt creeping in. "Does it?"

Temperance's uncertainty was echoed in James's expression. "I...I'm not sure." He shook his head. "Regardless of how long it takes things to, uh, take root and, um, flourish, the fact remains that you may well be carrying my heir in your womb and that is not something I take lightly. I will not have a child of mine raised a bastard, especially not my heir."

Temperance's anger flared. "But if it were not your heir? If it was nothing more than a girl, would you be a little less perturbed by the idea?"

James pushed up on his elbow and glared down at her. "No! Regardless of whether a girl or boy, I would want the child to bear my name and enjoy the security and benefits that came with that."

"And what of the children that do not have such an advantage?"

Confusion riddled his expression. "I beg your pardon?"

She seized upon the topic. It had nothing to do with anything, but Temperance needed to distract him, to give herself time to determine what all of this meant and what best to do about it. It was too much, too soon to contend with. She needed time and room to think. Something she could not do with James hovering over her, demanding she agree to his dictates.

"What of the children who are born to parents who cannot give them a lofty name, who do not have the advantages wealth and title bring? Who will ensure they have a good and proper life? Who will care for them?"

James shook his head. "What in the bloody hell are you talking about? How should I know?"

Temperance poked him in the chest. "And that right there, *my lord,* is everything that is wrong with the world. This is why I feel it so important that someone take up the charge for these children. That they be given an opportunity to better their circumstances. Someone must care enough to do something."

"And you think that someone must be you?"

There was something in his tone that irked her, a sense that she was being foolish. Or that he knew better. In that one phrase, he encapsulated everything she feared. That she would be expected to be less than what she was. Less than what she could be. Because it brushed against his ideal of what a wife was meant for.

"Why not me? I benefited greatly from my own education and now I wish to use it to help others. Clearly, this is not something I can accomplished if shackled to a husband who does not share my beliefs and thinks to order me about as if I were nothing more than a piece of property with no thoughts or opinions of my own."

"I did not say—"

She cut him off. Even if he hadn't said it in those exact words, the inference was clear. He had his beliefs and she had hers and, much as she had feelings for this man, whatever they were, she could not stop being herself. She could not live a life that did not suit with a man who did not respect her abilities or intelligence.

"You have said enough, James. You are who you are. And I am who I am. Our beliefs and politics are completely different, which makes us ill suited. And that is why I will not marry you."

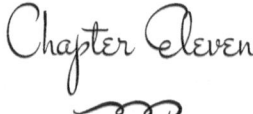

Chapter Eleven

J ames rolled over onto his back and rubbed a hand down
his face.

Where had this night gone so wrong? They had
been enjoying a passionate tryst. He'd experienced a level
of connection to Temperance, both physically and emotion-
ally he had never felt before with anyone, not even with Ruth.
And now, suddenly, she wanted to debate the politics of
society with him as if that was far more important than what
had just happened between them?

Because something *had* happened. Something had definitely happened.

At least it had for him. In the span of time it took for him to
carry her from the table to the bed, slowly undress her and enjoy
the wonders of her body, initiate her into the pleasures that can
be found between a man and woman, something had changed.

His feelings for her went far deeper than the physical act
they'd enjoyed. He wanted to marry this woman—not just out
of a sense of duty because he had taken her innocence, but
because...because...

Bloody hell, he didn't know why!

She was irritating and headstrong and annoyingly independent. She was stubborn and beautiful and intoxicatingly argumentative. She took far too much enjoyment in making him question everything he had been raised to believe about men and women and duty and honor and his way of life. And in such questioning, she made him reflect and wonder and think perhaps, in some regards, she made valid points that were worth exploring.

But beyond that, beyond all her thoughts and beliefs and arguments, what it boiled down to in the end was that he could not imagine returning to London and walking away, leaving her to her family, never to see her again. Or worse, seeing her again with another man. Or even worse still, to watch as her parents cast her out, making her a pariah, all her hopes and dreams dashed by her own actions and short-sightedness.

What would become of her then? Miss Caldwell's school would never succeed if they hired a fallen woman of ill repute as its headmistress and Rosalind Caldwell was too bright not to know that. Who would take Temperance in? Ensure her safety? She had brothers, yes. But they were back in New York, were they not? And to hear Alex tell it, there had been some type of scandal with respect to her former fiancé. That was what brought her to London in the first place. Likely, there was nothing there for her to return to that would not mirror what she faced here, in London.

Would she marry him then? Out of a sense of desperation? Would he want her to under those circumstances?

He closed his eyes and squeezed the bridge of his nose.

Yes. God help him. He would marry her even under those circumstances because he could not fathom the idea of leaving her unprotected. It was hardly as if she would be the first woman he loved unconditionally that did not return his affections in that regard.

Love?

His hand fell away and he stared into the fading darkness as it gave way to the first hints of sunrise. They had made love throughout the night. Slept. Wakened. Made love again before she set him back in his place.

Love.

He let the word drift about in his mind as he blinked at the thin, spidery crack in the ceiling plaster above him. Did he love her? It seemed rather quick for that, but as he searched his heart, the word settled around him with ease. Had their dire circumstances caused a heightened awareness, a need to brush aside a more measured, thoughtful advance?

He did not know. He didn't know much of anything at the moment other than the fact that this woman who had completely captivated him, now refused to marry him because —near as he could tell—he had failed to correct the world's woes.

"You have not said anything," Temperance whispered.

James continued to stare at the ceiling. He did not want to look at her. At her mussed up hair, or the radiance of their lovemaking blushed upon her cheeks, or the glow in her dark eyes that did not, quite obviously, harbor the same tender feelings for him as he held for her.

"I cannot think of anything to say, I'm afraid."

Perhaps he could admit what a fool he was for falling once more for a woman who would never return his ardent feelings. But her rejection of his marriage proposal was painful enough. He did not need to add further insult to her injurious words. He did not need to walk down that particular road again. He knew how it ended. In heartbreak and misery.

What he needed to do was to get out of this bed. Get away from her and these tangled passions that served neither of them any good. He needed to focus on getting her to safety. On shoving down his feelings for her so that they did not experience a repeat of what had occurred this night. If she was not with child, he could not risk making it so.

Though the idea of her carrying his child, bearing a babe with dark hair and dark eyes was enough to cause his groin to stir and his heart to swell. Or was it the other way around? God help him, he was so confused he could not say which was which!

"James?" Temperance reached out and placed her hand on his arm, the warmth of her touch seeping into him, drawing him back, making him forget what he was about. What she was about.

No!

He pushed himself up and swung his legs over the edge of the bed, moving beyond her reach. "I will find us something to eat and then we should be on our way as soon as possible. We do not want to risk having our captors catching up with us. The sooner we return to London the better."

James grabbed his clothing from where he had tossed it the night before and stalked from the room before he gave in to his baser instincts. The ones that told him to crawl back into bed with her, to open his heart even further. To try and change her mind. But Temperance Lindwell had a will of her own and a strong one at that. She would not be swayed by any heartfelt plea on his part. The only thing he would do was risk breaking his own heart beyond repair. He'd already done that once and still bore the scars. He had no desire to go a second round in the ring with that particular opponent.

Temperance watched James's bare backside disappear through the door, sorry to see it go. Sorry that their parting was far different from their coming together. How strange to think on what had occurred between them.

She had made love to the Marquess of Ridgemont as if it were the most natural thing in the world to have transpired. The strangest part of all was that...well, it had been the most natural thing. She'd had no hesitation. No sense that it was something being put upon her or that she must endure. Why, to hear Mother paint the picture, when the time came she would be best to lie back and let her mind drift somewhere more pleasant until the business at hand was finished.

But Temperance couldn't think of anywhere more pleasant than what she had shared with James last night. Nowhere else she would have wanted to be. It had been the most wonderful of experiences and she could not wait to do it again. And again.

Except...

She sighed and stared at the empty doorway he'd disappeared through, his anger and frustration with her, and her refusal of his proposal, abundantly clear. It wasn't as if the idea of spending her days with James was a horrible one, much to her surprise. Despite the circumstances of the past several days, she had found an unexpected joy in having James as her companion. His presence calmed her, kept most of the fear at bay. She'd felt protected and safe despite the unpredictability of the situation. She had never doubted for a moment that between the two of them, they would find a way out of this.

And they had, despite the obstacles. Despite the odds.

James had been her rock and she did not doubt for a moment that had it been called for, he would have protected her with his very life. That was the kind of man he was. Strong and kind and bullheaded and wonderful.

If she was inclined to marry, she could think of no better man than he to call husband.

But...

Temperance buried her head into the pillow as fear welled up inside of her. Fear that her heart clouded her judgment. Fear that her feelings for James made her blind to the other side that men possessed. The side that led them to treat the women in their lives as an afterthought. A possession. Was that not how her father treated her mother? Was that not what Beauregard had expected from her? She could not live like that. That much she knew without a doubt.

And what did she know about being a marchioness? The very idea was horribly daunting. All those rules and restrictions. The expectations and potential for folly. She'd be a disaster for sure. Heavens, she had not even been able to traverse New York Society without causing an uproar. How would she ever manage to navigate the British aristocracy, let alone become a part of it?

As if they would ever accept her.

She was an American, after all.

Why James couldn't see that was beyond her. The man wore blinders in that regard. And because of that, she must be the one who did not. She had to keep a level head. To see things as they were and not how they wished them to be.

Temperance sat up and let her legs dangle over the edge of the bed, the cold morning air raising gooseflesh over her skin. Her borrowed clothing was scattered about, a testament to their lovemaking. She stood and picked up the pieces one by one, getting re-dressed as she went. She was putting the bed back to order when James came rushing back into the room like a madman. He ran to the armoire and shoved it out from the corner of the wall then grabbed her ruined gown and slippers, balling them up and tucking them under his arm.

"What are you doing?"

"Ssh!" The sound came harsh and immediate.

James grabbed her arm and pulled her toward him, then spun her around and shoved her behind the armoire before following and pulling it back into place. The space was cramped, his body pushed against hers so that her back pressed against the wall behind her.

"James, what in the name of heaven are you about?"

He placed a hand over her mouth. There was barely room to move in the restricted space. James's words rushed out in a whisper, brushing against her cheek, his mouth very near her ear. "Ferris and Niles are riding up. I saw them from the window."

Fear stabbed through her. Despite the possibility of this happening, Temperance had hoped the two men would make good on their claim to make a run for it before they were caught. But perhaps the lure of the ransom had proven too strong.

"Do you think—"

She didn't have time to finish. A loud bang echoed through the cottage, followed by several more. Then silence. Temperance couldn't breathe and had James's body not been pressed into hers, her knees would have given out and sent her to the floor. They were so close to freedom. So close to finding their way home.

The creak of the front door opening made her breath catch. James's heart pounded against her, or was that her own? She could not tell where one of them left off and the other began.

She turned her head to better face him and mouthed the words, *the food.* They had become so overwhelmed with each other, with need and want and a hundred other things that they had never finished their meal from the night before. At one point through the night, James had slipped back to the kitchen and brought them a snack in bed, but the remains of the meal had been left on the table, a dead giveaway that someone was here.

He shook his head and pressed his lips against her temple. She wasn't sure what that meant. Had he cleared the food away when he saw them coming? Or had he started setting out their next meal and not had time to clear that? Footsteps and muffled male voices filtered down the hallway, sliding into the bedroom like an evil specter, bringing with it the portent of death and destruction.

James's arm tightened around her. Temperance held her breath, afraid to breathe as the floorboards in the bedroom groaned under the weight of uninvited guests. Every muscle in James's body went rigid. Temperance began to pray with such fervor Reverend Marston would never believe she was the same girl he had seen each Sunday in church, daydreaming instead of listening to his sermons.

"Ain't no sign they was here." Niles.

"Hm." Ferris sounded less convinced. "They must've come this way. Don't make sense. If they'd gone the other way, we woulda found them by now."

"Maybe they didn't want to stop. Dunville is jus' an hour's ride. Maybe they figured they'd be safer there."

Ferris scoffed. "You're a bloody idiot. You know that? They ain't from these parts. They's don' know where the damned town is, ya fool."

"They would if they kept walkin'."

Ferris didn't answer, but in her head, Temperance could picture the glare Niles would have received for his cheeky answer. "Let's go."

"You think maybe we can see if there's some food in here? I'm a mite hungry."

"Shut up, idiot. If they made it to Bromley, it's over. We show up there, we're dead men. They'll have us swinging by the neck on his lordship's order before we can make it to the center of town."

Niles snorted. "He can't give that order. We still get a trial."

"You feckin' fool!" The sound of something being smacked reverberated through the room.

"Ow!"

"What kind o' trial do you think that'll be, huh? Our word against a lord and lady's? We might as well dig our graves now an' crawl straight into them. Ain't no court in the land goin' ta believe a word we say. Now, you want to take your chances, you go right ahead. Me? I'm headin' north. Got me a cousin in Ludlow. Might be he'll take me in for a bit."

The floor creaked again and retreating footsteps faded bit by bit.

"Bloody wanker," Niles muttered then after a moment, he too, quit the room. Beyond the beating of her heart, Temperance heard the front door open and a few moments after that the steady beat of horses' hooves disappeared into the distance.

"Is it safe?" she whispered. Her fingers trembled despite how tightly she had wound them into front of James's shirt.

He nodded and tightened his hold on her, burying his face into her hair. Temperance melted into his embrace, the need to hold onto something—no, someone—who represented a safe place, was strong enough to shove her pride aside.

"I need you."

His plea, simple yet edged with desperation, flooded through her, meshing with her own. She nodded, knowing what he meant. It wasn't just emotional. It was physical. Overpoweringly so. As if they both needed something tangible. Something they could feel and taste and touch to prove they had skirted danger, death, once more.

James pushed the armoire out of the way with his foot and pulled her out from the corner that had hid them. They fell upon the bed, mouths locked together, hands searching and pulling. They did not dispense with clothing. There was no time. The need too immediate, too intense. Far beyond Temperance's experience to even quantify. It was pure, almost animalistic, in nature. They pushed aside what clothing they needed to and came together in a rush of heat and celebration. She locked her legs tightly around James's hips as he filled her, moving with swift, hard movements that brought her to the brink before sending them both over it, tumbling and falling and flying as their bodies went rigid with pleasure, then slack with relief. Their hearts beat hard and fast and their breath dampened the skin. It was several moments before either of them could speak, but it was James who broke the silence first.

"Forgive me."

Temperance wrapped her arms more tightly around his back where she still held him against her, unwilling to let him go. "No. Don't. There is nothing to forgive. I...I needed it as much as you did."

She kissed his temple, filled with tenderness for this man who continued to go above and beyond for her. She had no words for what she felt. Gratitude did not begin to express what was in her heart. But what was in her heart frightened her too much to allow a deep examination. She feared if she looked too closely, she would fall into it, like Alice toppling down the rabbit hole.

James lifted himself onto his elbow and stared down at her, his expression unreadable. What did he see when he looked at her? Did he bear witness to her confusion? To her uncertainty? Her fears? She did not want to have feelings for this man. She did not want to allow her heart to get the better of her and set her up for pain and misery when nothing turned out as she wished it to.

She would not do that to herself.

She would not do that to him.

His finger traced the edge of her bottom lip, his gaze fixed on it as if it were the most fascinating thing he'd ever seen. For a fleeting second, she thought he might kiss her. Hoped he would.

Then something changed. His expression altered, became distant, and heavy with disappointment. Without a word, he pulled away. Stood up. Fixed the front of his trousers as if the searing passion they had just experienced had never happened.

Unsure of this sudden change, Temperance pushed herself into a sitting position and reached down to straighten her own skirts.

She waited for the inevitable insistence that they must marry and her heart teetered on the edge, threatening to overpower her better sense. She wasn't fool enough to ignore the fact that should Society whisper their assumptions about what might have happened between them during their captivity, her reputation would be ruined. And if that happened, her plans of becoming headmistress of Miss Caldwell's school would crumble. What would she do then?

Would marrying James not be a better option?

But could a marriage made out of necessity have any hope for happiness? Likely not.

But his insistence upon marriage did not come.

"I will find us something to eat." James avoided her gaze, almost as if he were speaking to himself. "We should give them an hour to travel in the other direction before we head to the village. From the sounds of it, we aren't that far away. If we keep a good pace, we will likely reach it before sundown."

Temperance nodded, then, since James wasn't looking at her and couldn't see her response, added, "Yes. I agree."

But it didn't matter, because he had already left the room. Left her.

Chapter Twelve

Alex had often accused James of being a glutton for punishment, a description he had summarily rejected. A rejection he now must reconsider. Clearly, his friend had had the right of it. What other explanation could there be for what had just transpired between he and Temperance?

Insanity?

He stopped cutting through the stale loaf of bread the owners of the cottage had left behind. Perhaps that was it. Perhaps he had lost his mind. He did feel a bit crazy. His emotions had tangled themselves six ways to Sunday where Temperance was concerned and he didn't know where to begin to disentangle them.

Nor did he want to.

That was where the glutton for punishment kicked in.

Because he had to extricate his emotions. If he did not, it would be Ruth all over again. He wasn't sure his heart would survive that a second time.

The problem was, he believed in marriage. Held it in high esteem. He had witnessed time and again the power it held, how it enriched the lives of those who embraced it. His parents had loved each other deeply. His father had been fortunate enough to find that kind of love twice in his lifetime. Family had been everything to him. So much so, he'd given his life to save his wife and daughter. He hadn't been successful in the first respect, but he'd saved Henrietta and for that, James would be forever thankful.

Because that is what you did when you loved someone. You gave them everything you had. You protected and you revered and worshiped and you remained ever grateful for their presence in your life.

The only problem with that was, when it did not turn out as you hoped, when those feelings were not reciprocated, the pain was so great it almost destroyed you.

As James had learned the hard way.

He was no fool. He was well versed in how his heart worked. It fell hard and fast and gave very little warning beforehand. When he had met Ruth, she had been newly presented and attending her second ball. He'd taken one look at her and been entranced. He'd had one conversation with her and been head over heels. It took all of three weeks before he'd determined he wanted her to be his marchioness. Beautiful and vulnerable, flirtatious yet fragile. He would spend his life protecting her and taking care of her. Making her eyes light up and her smile never falter.

But it hadn't turned out that way, had it?

No. It hadn't.

Instead, she had chosen Alex, and James, wishing to see Ruth happy above all else, had stepped aside. Alex was the better man, after all. More charming, more daring. A future duke. And James had wished to see them both happy.

And for the first little while, Ruth had been happy. Until the worst happened and their first son died. Something broke inside of both of them then. Something James could not help either repair.

He bit back the memory. Ruth was gone. He could not change that. But Temperance was here. And as much as he wanted to believe his growing feelings were nothing more than a temporary aberration, he knew they weren't. Perhaps they had been heightened by the dangerous circumstances they'd found themselves in, lending an urgency that caused them to grow much quicker than normal, but, in the end, they were what they were.

And what they were was a disaster.

James set two pieces of salted pork onto their plates and wrapped the rest up, along with some cheese, in a linen cloth to take with them. He'd found some oats and did his best to boil them each a hearty bowl for breakfast, hoping he had done it right.

While he waited for Temperance to join him, James looked out the window then at his reflection in the glass. He'd been a much younger man back when he'd fallen in love with Ruth. Foolishly thinking he possessed the ability to make someone who didn't want him happy.

But he was not that man any more. He would not hand over his heart to a woman who did not want it. There was nothing to be achieved there but heartbreak and he'd had enough of that to last him a lifetime.

James waited dutifully for Temperance to join him before breaking his fast, though having her sitting across from him, silent as the grave, sending furtive looks in his direction, did nothing for his digestion. The simple fare sat in his stomach like a heavy weight.

"We should leave within the hour," he said, breaking the uncomfortable silence between them. How quickly he had become accustomed to their easy banter. To her quick quips, even when at his expense, and her sharp observations. They'd had little to do during their incarceration in the tiny room but talk and her ability to converse on any number of topics surprised him. She was, indeed, very bright.

Bright enough to know her own mind. And her own heart.

He needed to resign himself to the fact she would not marry him. Not unless she found herself with child and even then, he suspected he might still have a fight on his hands. She did not want him. Not as a husband, at least. A lover, perhaps, which baffled. He'd never met an unmarried woman of good reputation that preferred to be a mistress, rather than a wife.

But he wasn't the kind of man who could willingly take part in such an arrangement. Perhaps, when they reached London, he could spin a tale that would mitigate any hint of scandal wafting their way. The chances were slim, but not impossible if he rallied the right people behind them. People of high standing who had experienced their own dalliance with ruination and come out the other end of it. Hawksmoor, perhaps, would be an obvious choice. Lord and Lady Black-bourne, clearly. Lord Huntsleigh and, if he could sway her, his great-aunt, Lady Dalridge.

He would do what he could for Temperance then he would walk away. He would not linger as he had before with Ruth. He would not relive the pain day in and day out, cutting his heart to shreds because he was too stubborn and idiotic to let go. Surely, the pain of loss would ebb, dissipating with the same swiftness as it had appeared.

He could not deny he would miss her when she was gone. He hated the truth of that fact, but there it was. Plain, simple and irrefutable. He would miss her. She'd made a sizeable impact upon him in the intense days they'd shared. But, hopefully, once they both returned to their real lives, the intensity of those feelings would abate. Sanity would return and this entire episode would become nothing more than a hazy memory.

But in order to achieve said haziness, to mitigate the hurt of losing something he never really had, he must distance himself from her with all due haste. Cut off the silly feelings she evoked within him and treat her with the same indifference he had throughout the past few Seasons as her parents peddled her and her sister to the highest bidder.

It was for the best. And it would begin now.

"What are you doing?" Temperance watched as James picked up his pocket watch and a letter he had penned, setting both inside a deep bowl in the center of the kitchen table for safekeeping.

James had barely spoken a word to her since leaving the bedroom after their furtive coupling, the change in him distinct and puzzling. One would have thought he'd be pleased that she'd refused to hold him accountable to the antiquated idea of marrying her when he did not need to.

"It is payment for the food, clothes, and lodging," he said, avoiding her gaze as if she was Medusa and one quick glance might turn him to stone. "I cannot take from those who have so little as if it was my right. Despite what you think, I do not walk about believing I am entitled to things I am not."

His voice held a hard edge to it that left Temperance mute. His fingers, that had brought her to such joyous heights, touched the engraved cover of the watch one last time before he folded them into his palm. Pain etched into the fine lines at the corner of his eyes and across his mouth that he had sealed shut. Then he turned away and walked past her, careful not to touch her despite the narrow passageway through to the main room where he'd left his jacket. She had taken a heavy, hand-knit shawl from the armoire, thankful the lady owned several and would not be left without, so that James, too, would have something warm to wear as they made their way to the village.

She waved a hand at the bowl even though he could not see her do so. "But it belonged to your father, and his before him. You said it was your most prized possession."

Had she not caught him reaching for it whenever he became stressed or worried? Oh, he hadn't said as much to her about feeling so, but she could tell. See it in his face. It was as if the skin across his cheekbones grew taut and his lips pulled into a tight line. During those times, his hand reached into his pocket. He would pull out the watch and rub his thumb along the engraving, as if it was a talisman that could ward off evil.

Maybe it was. They were here after all and had managed to outrun and outwit their captors.

She could not believe James now thought to give the watch up given the importance he placed on the keepsake that had been given to him by the father he had loved and admired. What it must have been like to be raised by a man who inspired such reverence.

He did not answer her claim and so Temperance walked partway down the short hallway to the main room. "James?"

He faced her as he buttoned the jacket, but made no effort to meet her gaze.

"It is the right thing to do." His voice, though quiet, was resolute.

"But—"

He cut her off. "If you are ready, we should leave. I do not know how far this village is for certain and I wish to reach it before daylight wanes."

She shook her head, resigned to this new reaction he had to her. "Fine. Your gloves are in the bedroom. You should bring them with you. It looks chilly outside."

James nodded and once out of sight, Temperance walked to the table and stared at the watch. Yes, it was but a watch and, yes, it would more than compensate their unknowing hosts for the food and clothing they had taken. But it wasn't just a watch to James. It was an important link to the father he had loved and lost. How could he let it go so easily?

But it wasn't easy, was it? She could see the strain of it cut into every movement he made, the hard ridge of his shoulders, the sense of loss rife in his blue eyes that usually gleamed with a hints of laughter and intelligence and the inescapable honor that led him to make such a decision in the first place.

Yet, it was she who had taken the most. She who would walk out of this cottage with someone else's clothes on her back. She couldn't let James suffer on her behalf. Despite what he said, it wasn't the right thing to do and the guilt would nag her to her dying day if she allowed it.

With a quick peek over her shoulder, Temperance reached into her pocket and pulled out the jewels her father claimed to have spent a small fortune on. No paste jewelry for his daughters—oh, no! He wanted his wealth on full display for all to see. But the baubles meant nothing to her. She wore them about her neck like a noose that would tighten at any moment.

She dropped them into the bowl and picked up James's watch, slipping it safely into her pocket. There was no point telling him what she'd done. His honor would never allow such a thing. He'd see it as his responsibility to take care of her and make retribution for the things taken. She disagreed. Besides, her jewels were likely worth far more than the watch on a monetary level. But from a heart level, the watch would be irreplaceable.

Once they reached London, she would give it back to him. Recompense for her refusal to marry him, which he apparently took great umbrage to, given the way he was giving her the cut direct. Likely, he would also take offense to the fact she'd robbed him of doing the right thing where his watch was concerned as well, but hopefully, having the watch back in his own possession would soften the blow of that one.

It was the least she could do for all he had done for her.

———

T he walk to the village took three hours. Three long, silent hours as James maintained a distance of two strides between them the entire way. He'd spoken barely a word and the ones he had were never coupled with anything resembling eye contact. They amounted to curt warnings, "Watch for the root," and "Don't step there."

By the time they reached the village, Temperance was thankful for other people milling about so that she might engage in polite conversation with someone who did not view her as...as...well, she did not know what James viewed her as, given he had not bothered to tell her. He'd simply turned a cold shoulder and stopped speaking to her. She'd tried repeatedly to engage him in conversation but the most she was able to pull from him was an onerous grunt and, on occasion, a haughty stare down his long straight nose.

It was a harsh reminder of why she'd thought him a pompous lord who considered himself her better. She would do well to remember that about him. Except...

She sighed.

Except that now she had seen the other side. The private side to the man walking in front of her as if she didn't exist. The side that was warm and funny and engaging. The side that did not shy away from a debate of ideals and opinions just because she was a woman. The side that, on occasion, agreed that some of her views, at least, had merit.

That man had surprised her. That man had made her love—

She stumbled. Stopped. Blinked.

No. Not that. Not love.

She'd promised herself after Beauregard she would not be trapped into such folly again. Besides, one did not fall in love with someone over a matter of days. It took time. Months. Three at least. One had to learn the essence of the other person before they could make a determination regarding suitability and whether or not to engage their heart. Why, it had taken four months of courtship before she'd decide to give Beauregard her heart.

She scowled. Perhaps had she waited another four, she'd have discovered what a complete cad he was and saved herself the embarrassment and scandal that followed after discovering him in the stables rutting like an animal with a footman and the dairymaid!

"Is the village not to your liking?"

Temperance glanced up at James as they stood at the edge of what appeared to be the main street. "I beg your pardon?"

She wasn't sure what astonished her more—that he thought she had reason to dislike the village, or the fact that he spoke more than three words to her.

"You huffed with derision, as if what you saw disgusted you."

She had huffed? Temperance settled her features into what she hoped was an unreadable expression. It wasn't the sight of the village that had disgusted her. It was the scene inside her head, the memory of Beauregard in the throes of his debauchery, his pale bottom bouncing—

Temperance cleared her throat and gave her head a shake. "The village looks lovely. It is nice to have reached something resembling civilization once more. Now what shall we do?"

Chapter Thirteen

"**N**ow we throw ourselves upon their mercy," James said. He didn't look at her. It was better that way. He didn't need the reminder of how lovely she looked, even in her homespun dress of navy and mismatched wool shawl. Her hair trailed down her back, a long wave tied back by one ribbon. How was it such simplicity could be so starkly beautiful?

And why was it he could not seem to resist its lure? *Her* lure?

The sooner they reached London, the better, and the quickest way to make that happen was to find someone who could get them there. He'd already determined he could not introduce himself as the Marquess of Ridgemont. With his oversize borrowed shirt, scruffy growth of whisker and disheveled hair, he appeared no more a lord than any other farmer plucked off the street. Granted, the Hessians might give it away, but scuffed as they were now, would someone from the lower classes even recognize their value?

Odd how something that seemed so important to his set was completely inconsequential to those who had to toil for a living. Was this what Temperance had meant when she indicated he was out of touch with the reality of the common man? Perhaps she was right. Perhaps he should make an effort to learn. If he was to argue points and politics in the House of Lords, should he not at least know how it would affect those with less say in the matter?

He shook his head as he made his way through the slop and muck of the main road. There were several villagers about tending to their business that gave them sidelong glances. One lady, in particular, stopped in her tracks as if strangers were not something often encountered in these parts. Given the out of the way nature of the place, James shouldn't be surprised.

A glance up and down the street did not look promising as far as finding lodgings that might accommodate them. Ahead of him, the sign read MacGibbons' Goods and Services. It was as good a place to start as any.

James waited for Temperance to catch up before he pushed the door open, a bell tinkling above his head, as he ushered her inside. At the sound of the bell, an older gentleman came out from a backroom to greet them, stopping short.

"G'day, suh. Might I help ye?" The man's accent was thick and heavy and James had to struggle to understand him.

"Indeed." He straightened and cleared his throat, motioning toward Temperance. "My wife and I were making our way from up north back to London when we were unfortunately set upon by highwaymen."

"Aye, ye don't say. Weel, that be a keen way ta' start yer day, aye?"

James blinked. The man appeared completely unmoved by his claim of victimization. Did this happen a lot in these parts? "Yes, well. Uh, such as the case may be, they took everything save the clothes on our backs. We have spent the past two days walking and are in desperate need of assistance. Are you Mr.

MacGibbons per chance?" There was no point going any further if the man did not own the establishment. James needed to speak to the man in charge.

"Aye." The man drew out his answer as his gaze slid past James to where Temperance lingered somewhere behind him. "Are ye unharmed, miss?"

"Yes, sir. Thank you for asking."

"Ye talk strange."

"I'm from America."

MacGibbons grunted, though there was no telling from the sound what he actually thought of Temperance's origin. "Ye be a wee bit far from 'ome, lassie."

"Yes, indeed I am."

James straightened and moved to block the man's view of Temperance and recapture his attention. "Mr. MacGibbons, my wife and I require lodging for the night, a hearty meal and assistance in returning to London. Might you be able to help us in this regard? I assure you that I can send reimbursement for any cost incurred once I reach London."

"Hm."

Was that a yes or a no? James squinted at MacGibbons and attempted to take the man's measure. He was perhaps in his sixth decade and short, though solidly built like a weathered old tree trunk that had withstood more storms than most. His face, the parts not covered with a grizzled gray beard, was etched with deep lines and a pair of light blue eyes, sharp with intensity. Likely, the man missed little.

Did he know James lied when referring to Temperance as his wife? Was it so apparent they were completely unsuited that even referring to her as such to a stranger was not convincing enough to pass muster?

"Mr. MacGibbons," Temperance said, coming to stand at James's side and slip her hand through his arm. "We are, of course, most aggrieved to throw ourselves at your mercy. We do not wish to impose in anyway and would be most grateful for any help you can give. I only wish to return home, nothing more."

I, she said. Not *we.* James gritted his teeth. Message received.

"Weel, lassie, we Scots are no in the 'abit of leavin' a lady in distress. There be a small room above stairs ye can use. Now," the older man's bushy brows lifted. "Would ye prefer I put yer 'usband 'ere in the stables?"

Was that humor that twinkled in the old man's eyes? Whatever it was, James was not about to allow Temperance to stay anywhere without his protection. He could not guarantee the two idiots that had abducted them in the first place might not rethink their plan to head north to safety. He was not leaving her side until he delivered her safely to her father.

"Mrs. Bromley and I will remain together, sir, and I thank you for your generous hospitality."

"Aye." The man's eyes continued to shine with humor. What, exactly, he found so funny James could not say. He was not accustomed to being laughed at by those of lower status. "Me and the lady of the 'ouse will dine at sunset, my lord." Mr. MacGibbons executed a short bow.

"I am not a lord," James said. Bloody hell, was it that obvious? He glanced down at Temperance who was pressing her lips tight, clearly amused. "I am Mr. James Bromley. Barrister. My wife and I were returning from a visit with her family in Boroughbridge."

"Aye, Boroughbridge, you say? Thought your missus was American?"

Devil take it! "She is. That is, her father is. Her mother is from Boroughbridge originally and it was her family that we paid a visit."

"No' the best time of year ta be travelin' north."

"Clearly."

"Don' see much highwaymen up this way either."

James pulled his mouth into a tight line. He really was not very good at this lying business.

"Mr. MacGibbons," Temperance said, her hand sliding away from James's arms as she stepped forward. "Forgive us for trying to lie to you. It would be fair to say my parents did not give us their blessing to marry. They had hoped I might attach myself to a titled gentleman, a baron perhaps."

A baron? He was bloody well higher ranked than a baron! What the deuce was she about?

"But I could not consider anyone else but Mr. Bromley and as such, we decided to elope. Unfortunately, we have never been far from the city. In returning to London, we trusted a couple of unsavory gentleman who promised to convey us there. Instead, they relieved us of our belongings and left us stranded in the middle of nowhere. Thereby forcing us to be dependent upon the kindness of others."

James stared at Temperance, momentarily rendered speechless with how easily the lie tripped off her tongue, fully supplied with everything required to convince MacGibbons of its authenticity. A confession of James's previous lie, clumsily told, heart-wrenching familial conflict, star-crossed lovers who trusted the wrong people only to meet with calamity, and finally, the determination of youth to overcome it all, if only they could win over the assistance of others to help them do so. All of this delivered in swift seconds without stumbling and told in such a sincere manner even he was convinced! James didn't know whether to applaud her ability or be duly frightened by it.

"Aye, weel, I guess that sounds a wee bit closer to the truth. Come ta the back at sunset and we'll fill your bellies. For now, up the stairs ye go. I expect ye'll be wantin' ta rest for a wee bit. I'll have the missus bring ye a cold lunch to tie you over."

Temperance offered the man a genuine smile, the kind

he'd been privy to before he'd left her alone in the bedroom after taking her without benefit of preamble, his actions fueled by fear and relief and the need to connect with her, to know she was fine and alive and unharmed. That they had escaped death one more time.

"Thank you so much, Mr. MacGibbons. How will we ever repay you?"

James's muscles tightened. He had nothing left to repay the man with. He'd left his watch back at the cottage, an action that rested heavy on his heart. He only hoped his father would have understood.

"Aye, no need. Off with ye then," MacGibbons waved his arm toward the staircase at the back of the shop.

As they made their way up the staircase, James did his best to avoid staring at the way Temperance's hips swayed beneath the dress she wore. To avoid thinking of how the curve of her hips had felt beneath his hands as he'd sunk into her, finding a place he could only describe as home.

It was a disturbing thought. Not one he wanted any part of. Despite his best argument toward marriage, she remained diametrically opposed and it did not appear anything he said or did was going to sway her in his direction. Perhaps he should take this as a good sign. They had, after all, come together under upsetting circumstances, their bond forged under duress and the threat of death. Surely, anything that developed under such circumstances could not last once order was restored. Why, once they came to their senses, likely they would realize they did not have any feelings for each other whatsoever. That Temperance had come to her senses much sooner than he, however, did smart something awful.

And yet, despite such reasoning, James could not shake this insatiable need to protect her, even if it was from her own misguided opinions. The fact remained that he had compromised her. Thoroughly. Repeatedly. He'd relieved her of her innocence and that was not a responsibility he took lightly. She deserved his protection from any fallout incurred from that. If whispers and rumors circulated, if she discovered she carried his child, he would marry her without hesitation. There would be no other option.

The question was—how would he convince her of this? How did he make her see that they were better together than apart? That what had happened between them at the cottage was, perhaps, the beginning of something wonderful and amazing? That marriage, when done right, was a wonderful and amazing thing?

"It's quite...small."

James pulled himself from his thoughts and looked around the room's interior. It was small compared to what he was used to, certainly, but it was clean and nicely appointed with the necessary items.

"It will do."

Temperance glanced at him over her shoulder with a strange look and it was only then he realized she had been referring to the bed, not the room in general. A rather narrow bed, at that. There would certainly be no avoiding each other under the covers this night.

"Perhaps you might sleep on the floor," she suggested, offering up an encouraging smile.

James looked down at the planked flooring, hard and uncompromising beneath his feet then at the bed, soft and welcoming. "Perhaps you might instead."

Temperance sucked in an indignant breath. "That's hardly a lordly suggestion to make."

"I am not a lord," he reminded her, unable to stop the smile that pulled at the corners of his mouth. Why was it so difficult to keep his distance from her? To keep himself from responding to every nuance and mood and expression?

"Is that so?"

"Indeed. I am but a barrister." He bowed deeply. "Mr. James Bromley, at your service ma'am."

"You're impossible." But her lovely smile softened the admonishment.

James lifted one brow. "And you, my dear, are a consummate liar. I shall have to think twice about anything you tell me from here on in."

"We all have our own special skillset. Now, about the bed—"

James shook his head. "We have shared a bed for the past week, surely one more night will not matter. There is no sense one of us sleeping on the floor."

"Especially if that someone is you?"

"Especially then."

S upper with the MacGibbons proved an interesting affair. Where the mister was gruff and keenly observant, the missus was warm and lively. The cadence of their voices held a musical air to it that rolled off the tongue in a way that Temperance found most pleasing. They asked her about America and told them of their three children—two sons and a daughter. The daughter had gone and married herself to an Englishman, a baronet at that, while one son was a blacksmith and the other a landholder near the border where he raised sheep and such.

Temperance wasn't entirely sure what the *such* amounted to, but it hardly mattered. She enjoyed her time with the MacGibbons. It helped keep her mind off the night to come.

How was she to sleep in such close quarters with James on that narrow bed, and not allow her thoughts to travel places they should not go? His manner toward her had softened somewhat, vacillating between moments where he kept his distance, to moments where he forgot himself and said something to make her smile. It was in those moments, a deep keening for him opened up inside of her and she found it difficult to push thoughts of their time together to the back of her mind.

But dinner ended soon enough, with the MacGibbons informing them they would transport them to the next village over. From there, a coach could be procured to take them to London.

"I shall ensure reimbursement is sent to you promptly," James promised.

MacGibbons nodded. "Aye, you seem a man of your word. I 'ave no doubt ye'll keep it."

As Temperance made her way up the narrow staircase to the room and the small bed, nerves created a fluttering in her stomach. A fluttering that felt a little too much like hope for her liking.

Chapter Fourteen

"You may take the bed," James offered, as they entered the room.

Temperance turned on her heel, his suggestion surprising her given his adamancy of earlier that there was no reason for them not to share the bed.

"Don't be silly. The floor is hard and uncomfortable, you said so yourself. Besides, you'll be too cold." As would she without the comfort and warmth his body provided, but she left that part out. Stick with the practical. She did not want to give him the impression she had changed her mind on what would happen between them when they reached London.

Because she hadn't. Couldn't. No matter the unwanted notions flitting through her head. Foolish daydreams of sitting by a fire curled into each other's arms late into an evening, discussing all manner of topics. Or the more tantalizing images of being wrapped in each other's arms in other rooms of the house, discovering pleasures she had thus far not been privy to. Though now that she was, she could not help feel a deep reluctance at giving them up.

Giving *him* up.

Oh bother! Why was this so difficult?

When she turned around to face the man who now occupied far too many of her thoughts, she found his gaze moving between the floor and the bed.

"Perhaps it would suffice if I slept atop the blankets and you under. It is not ideal but should help to preserve..." His voice trailed off as he rolled his hand in the air, as if that somehow filled in the missing words.

"Preserve what?" She tried not to smile, but it was difficult. His statement had completely sidestepped the obvious. "What could possibly be left to preserve, James? Certainly not my innocence."

The passion they had shared had made short work of that and likely, her reputation would not withstand the whispers that came from having spent this much time alone in his company. Despite her insistence that such would not be the case, she wasn't an idiot. She had seen over the past few Seasons how damaging even a hint of scandal could be on a young lady's future prospects. And it was no secret that the ton waited with bated breath for the moment one of the *American girls* fell from grace.

But Temperance wasn't willing to hand over her life, or force James to do the same, based on something as foolish as a whisper. It wasn't fair to either of them to allow their futures to be held for ransom because of someone else's supposition of what may or may not have happened.

"Actually, I was thinking more of my sanity," he muttered.

"Is there much left worth saving?"

He shot her a dark look. "Unlikely."

She smiled at him. Heaven help her but he was handsome when he was put out like this, struggling to do the right thing when she had no doubt what he really wanted to do was the wrong thing. And, oh, how much she wanted him to do wrong. Just once more. Come tomorrow, they would be on their way back to London. Back to lives that had nothing to do with each other. He would go about his business as lord of the manor doing whatever it was he did. Eventually, he would find himself a proper wife who would give him a proper heir.

And she...well, she would do the best she could with what remained of her reputation. If Rosalind would no longer be able to hire her as headmistress, then perhaps she would return to New York and find a position there as a governess, outside the city proper where no one knew of her past and therefore would not judge her harshly. It wasn't ideal, and the more she thought about it, the less appealing the idea sounded. Yes, she had wished for independence, but how independent would she be under such circumstances? It wasn't as if she could come and go as she pleased. She'd be a servant, forced to curtail her life to someone else's dictates.

How different was that from marriage?

The question echoed in her mind and pressed down upon her like a weight on her chest. She had been so busy trying to avoid being forced into an institution she no longer believed in, that she hadn't considered the few alternatives left available to her were likely no better.

And if that was the case—then what was she to do?

"I've lost you."

James's voice startled her from her thoughts. "Hm?"

"You went off inside your head somewhere. Where do you go when you do that?" He drew closer, his voice quiet. Speculative. His head tilted to one side as if she were a specimen worthy of investigation.

"I—I don't know." No one had ever asked her that before. Not even Constance, who had once suggested that her thoughts were likely the only thing that were her own and she wouldn't want to take that away from her.

"You don't know what you were thinking?"

"I—I—" Oh, bother! "I suppose I was thinking what I would do when I returned to London."

"And what answers did you come up with?"

None. The weight on her chest continued to press down. She struggled to find an answer that might suffice. "Maybe travel. I hear Italy's lovely."

"It is." He took a step closer.

"Or perhaps return to New York."

"I suppose that is always an option."

Not much of one, but she kept that thought to herself.

He stopped in front of her and she was forced to look up lest she have a conversation with his chin. Though it was a nice chin. Square and strong and rough with stubble, having not met a razor in many days. How many had it been now? Five? Six? It seemed so much longer since they'd been grabbed and callously tossed into a carriage against their will. Yet, in some respects, the time seemed to have passed in the blink of an eye. And soon it would be over.

She would miss him. Far more than she wished to. "Our misadventure is almost at an end."

He smiled. How rare that had been for the past twenty-four hours and how madly she had missed its frequency. "Is that what we're calling it? A misadventure?"

"I thought I would err on the side of positivity." She smiled back at him. It was difficult not to, especially when his eyes sparkled and that hint of mischief had returned to glint brightly in their depths. "It wasn't all bad, after all."

"No?"

She shook her head, slowly, his smile holding the power to mesmerize.

"And what parts were not so bad?"

Heat burned up her neck and bloomed in her cheeks. What did she say to that? The truth. "The parts with you in them."

"I see. Yes. I suppose I wasn't too bad in the way of company, save for the times I was unconscious."

"Oh no, those were my favorites."

Laughter burst out of him and for the first time since they'd first made love she witnessed joy lighting his features, pushing back the worry and upset that had come before and after.

"You are an interesting woman, Temperance Lindwell. I must admit, you have surprised me."

"Have I?"

"Indeed."

This news should not delight her so mightily, but, oh, it did. "I am pleased to hear that. You have turned out to be nowhere near as pompous as I once thought. I regret slapping you now. It was a horrible display of bad behavior on my part."

James reached out and tucked a loose curl behind her ear sending tendrils of pleasure spiraling through her as his finger brushed the sensitive shell. "Likely I deserved it."

"Likely."

He smiled, but just as quickly the motion halted then disappeared and he took a step back, away from her. The speculative expression that he'd worn only seconds before receded until it disappeared entirely as if a curtain had fallen behind his eyes. "Well, we should get to bed. We have a long trip ahead of us tomorrow."

The sudden change in his manner left her off kilter. What had just happened? Where had the warm and engaging man with the seductive smile and dancing eyes gone?

She stared at him. His movements were brisk, efficient as he pulled down the blankets from the bed on one side and settled himself on the other, using the quilt folded at the end of the bed as a cover. He left every stitch of clothing on, including his boots.

"Yes," she said, her voice lacking the same level of distance as his had. "Of course. But I feel I should set your mind at ease."

"About what?"

She cleared her throat. Heavens, how did one broach such a thing? It had been embarrassing enough raising the matter with Mrs. MacGibbons so she might procure the necessary materials.

She stared straight ahead at the wall a few feet away. She could not look James in the eye when speaking of such private matters. Which seemed a little silly given everything else she had shared with him of a private nature.

"About any concern you may have had that I might be with child. As it turns out, I am not."

Silence reigned and Temperance itched to turn around and see his reaction but she couldn't bring herself to do it. After a long moment, he finally responded.

"I see. Is one able to tell so...uh, soon afterward?"

Temperance blinked. She had always been led to understand if when a woman's courses arrived that was an indication the man's seed had not taken. But given the short period of time between when they had made love and when her courses arrived...good heavens, she really didn't know for certain. There had never been reason for her to know before now. But still, likely the same principle would apply. Wouldn't it?

"Yes, of course," she said, forcing a certainty into her tone that she did not fully possess. She guessed time would tell on that one, but for now she would go with what she knew and alleviate any worry he may have had in that regard.

James remained silent a moment, then, "Given your refusal to marry me, I suppose that is the best outcome for the situation."

His response should not have hurt as much as it did. James did nothing more than speak the truth of the situation. And yet...yet, that he no longer pushed the idea of marriage and had not since her last decree that she had no intention of marrying him was rather telling.

He had not truly wanted to marry her.

And why would he? Up until this unfortunate incident that had thrown them together, they'd been little more than distant acquaintances that had barely spoken more than a handful of words to each other. The idea that he would *want* to marry her was ludicrous. He had only been doing what he'd done every day since this ordeal had begun—protecting her.

"Yes." Temperance swallowed the foolish lump that had formed in her throat. "Indeed, it is for the best."

"Very well then."

Because the idea of them marrying *was* the height of absurdity. They came from different worlds. They wanted different things. They held different opinions. It made no sense that a marriage between them would be happy or rewarding. Obviously, he had come to the same conclusion, hence his easy agreement on the matter now that the threat of a child was no longer an issue.

Honestly, had she been hoping he'd be disappointed? Try to convince her one last time? And what if he did? It wasn't as if she'd jump into his arms and accept whole-heartedly.

Would she?

No! No. Of course not. No. This was the absolute best outcome they could hope for. It was what she had wanted. Clearly what they both had wanted.

And yet...it was just that...

A small sigh escaped her. Well.

"Good night then, Temperance."

"Yes. Right. Of course. Good night, James."

It was better this way. Wasn't it?

She was no longer sure of the answer.

L ying beside a woman on such a small bed made it impossible not to touch her. Although, if he were being honest with himself, James would admit that the bed could have spanned the entire width of the room and likely, he would have gravitated toward wherever she lay. He would have wrapped his arms around her and curled his body against hers. Much as he did this night.

It should have made for a fitful sleep. They were finally safe from their abductors and had procured a way home. They had come out of their ordeal unscathed. He had kept her safe, protected her.

Ruined her.

James took a deep breath, the slight movement disturbing Temperance's sleep enough that she snuggled closer into him, her bottom pressing against his burgeoning erection. He swallowed. The blankets he'd placed between them offered little respite in that matter. Every little movement she made only heightened his awareness of her. The way the waves of her hair slipped over her shoulder to tickle his chest where his shirt opened. The way she nestled into him as if he were a safe place of comfort and ease.

She had come to trust him. To see past her idea of *what* he was and instead see the man who resided beneath the title and affluence. And she liked him, which seemed the strangest thing of all, given how they had left things on the dance floor of the Frontenac's ballroom.

What would have happened if he hadn't chided her into responding with a slap? Would they have found a common ground? Set aside their differences to look beyond their own prejudices? He couldn't say. London during the Season— London at any time, really—was not the kind of place where that sort of thing happened on a regular basis. Everyone, everything, had a place and Society did not care for it when anything or anyone stepped outside of their allotted space.

Perhaps Temperance was right in that regard. Perhaps that was something that needed to be addressed. Look at Lord Hawksmoor, after all. Had he not married a servant and elevated her to a lady? And had Lady Rebecca not married a common man in Mr. Marcus Bowen? Both of them had reached outside of their constricting circles to find happiness and both had attained much success in this regard.

And Society relented, albeit with some reservation. The constructs of their world had not come tumbling down. Life went on just fine.

What would happen if, God forbid, he married an American heiress? A bold speaking, frighteningly intelligent one at that? He had overcome his initial hesitation and prejudice toward Temperance. Was it not possible Society would as well? She had, after all, saved one of their own. Certainly, that would work in her favor, would it not?

The truth of the matter was, his survival had been in her hands in the beginning of this misadventure and she had behaved remarkably. She had stepped up to the challenge and kept him safe and alive. As much as his ego shuddered at the idea that he'd been left in such a state, his heart swelled that she had taken the initiative and protected him. Without thinking. Without debate. Without hesitation.

If only she would employ the same level of bravery and embrace the idea of marrying him. But she had made it clear she viewed marriage—especially marriage to a lord—as being trapped inside a gilded cage, her wings clipped, with freedom always remaining just beyond her reach.

What was it that caused her to think this way? And what words did he need to employ to discover the true reasons that had turned her so far away from the notion of becoming someone's wife? Should he simply ask her? Should he embrace the same manner of plain speaking she used to discover the answer?

Or should he leave well enough alone? Stop badgering her to do something she'd made clear she wanted no part in? His pride demanded the latter. But his heart—his stupid, misguided, foolish heart—it did not know when to stop. It did not know when to retreat before it incurred grievous injury.

James released a long breath and looked over Temperance's shoulder to the window beyond. The sun had started its accent over the horizon. They would begin their journey home today and come tomorrow, return to their separate lives.

What would become of her then?

What would become of him?

The trip home proved long and arduous, not because of the roads, but more so due to the uncomfortable silence that had descended upon them. Temperance had not argued with James when he made the unilateral decision that they would ride through, stopping for fresh horses when necessary, then continuing on. It was as if he could not put this ordeal behind him soon enough.

Or put her behind him soon enough. With the utter lack of conversation between them, it was difficult to tell which held the greater appeal. Perhaps both, closely linked as they were. After all, this ordeal had resulted directly because of her. James had merely paid the price for inserting himself into the process. By trying to play the hero.

As if she had deserved such treatment from him after slapping his cheek on the dance floor. She regretted her rash action now. The man she had slapped was not the man she'd come to know. Less a pompous lord and more the knight in shining armor. Not that she had been looking for a knight in shining armor. Though finding one had certainly had its benefits.

"We should be home soon," James said, his gaze fixed out the window rather than on her. It had been that way since they'd started their trip home, this avoidance. The absence of his attention created a deep sadness inside of her. "Before morning light, I suspect."

"I suppose they will be quite surprised to see us."

They had not sent word ahead, determining it safer that way in the event there were more individuals involved in the initial abduction than they were aware. James did not want to alert them of their impending arrival in case they decided to make a second, more successful, attempt. Or silence any witnesses to the crime.

"Yes, I suspect so. You should try to get some sleep."

She didn't answer. How could she sleep? Her stomach was in knots, a mixture of relief that they had survived, and fear of what awaited her once she returned home to Father and his expectations. Society and its gossip. Her future and the widening gap between what she had thought she wanted and the realization that such freedom came with a price.

They lapsed into silence once more. The interior of the carriage was a mixture of light and dark. Weak beams from the moon found its way through the windows and splashed across their profiles, while the small flame from the lantern that hung in the far corner danced seductively with the shadows.

Temperance leaned heavily into the cushioned squabs of the carriage. With each turn of the wheels, they drew closer to London, closer to whatever awaited her at the other end. Ruination? Acceptance? Curiosity? Gossip? Likely, she could count on Constance and a few friends to stand by her. Lady Rothbury, James's younger sister, had always been kind to her. Rosalind was unlikely to turn away even if she couldn't hire her as headmistress for the school. Lady Hawksmoor, perhaps, as she was rarely swayed by the gossip of others, finding such things trite and unnecessary.

"Are you worried about how you will be received?" James asked.

How easily he read her. "Perhaps a little. Although, this is not the first scandal I've weathered."

His eyebrows lifted and suddenly she had his full attention. "I assume you are referring to your broken engagement."

Temperance narrowed her gaze. He had alluded to knowing of her past before, but how much did he really know? The specifics had not been spoken of to anyone outside of the family. Mother had been too appalled and Father too incensed that, despite the circumstances, she had refused to overlook her fiancé's predilections and marry him regardless, simply because he was a Montgomery and such an attachment was not to be looked upon lightly.

"Yes. That is what I refer to."

"And what did occur, exactly? I would not think breaking off an engagement worthy of such a reaction. Unless, of course, there were extenuating circumstances." James leaned forward in his seat slightly and his brows rose a little higher. "Were there extenuating circumstances?"

Perhaps she should suggest it was none of his business. It was a painful topic and not one she cared to discuss. But this was the most animation she'd seen out of him since their departure and she was reluctant to let it go. She had missed their discourse, far more than was healthy.

"I'm afraid my former intended's family did not take well to my abrupt change of heart on the matter of marrying their eldest son. They took it as an affront, as he was lauded as the most eligible of gentlemen. They thought I assumed I was better than he."

"And was that the reason for this change of heart?"

"No."

This time only one eyebrow arched and a glint of curiosity gleamed in his eyes. "Then what was the reason?"

Temperance pursed her lips. Divulging the truth meant admitting aloud that her intended had possessed no interest in her as a woman. That, in the end, all she was to him was a placeholder. Someone meant to fill a role and nothing more. She could have been anyone. It mattered little to him, so long as she had the proper breeding, largest dowry and came from a respected family. The truth of which had hurt her grievously, because she had not felt that way at all. She had loved Beauregard. Foolishly and blindly and without restriction. He'd charmed her to the core and she'd believed he shared her feelings.

She had been wrong.

And now she had allowed this conversation to reach a point where she'd engaged James's curiosity and it was doubtful he would let her off with anything less than the truth.

"If I tell you, then you must reciprocate."

"Reciprocate? In what way?"

Temperance adjusted in her seat. "You must have a tale of heartbreak, do you not?" She was certain he did. Something always lingered just on the edge of his smile, something she recognized as kindred.

He hesitated and within that hesitation, the truth revealed itself. His heart had been broken. It pained her that someone had done that to him. She almost regretted asking, but curiosity and the need to know more about this man kept her from retracting the suggestion that they share their heartbreak.

He nodded slowly. "Very well, then. Tell me your story. What horrible deed did your former fiancé perpetrate to sour your opinion of love and marriage?"

Heat burned up her neck and into her cheeks. She loathed telling anyone what had happened. A part of her still wondered if it had been her fault. Perhaps if she had been more feminine, more...something...then it might not have happened.

She looked down at her hands, unable to hold his gaze. "If you must know, I stumbled upon my fiancé indulging in a ménage-a-trois in the stables."

"Hm."

Not quite the response she had expected. She glanced up. James sat back in his seat and appeared to give the matter some thought. "I've never found much interest in trying to please two women at once."

"Yes, well—" Temperance cleared her throat, the image of what she had seen burned into her mind's eye. "There was only one woman involved and unfortunately my former fiancé appeared more interested in pleasing the other gentleman, so..."

"Oh."

"Yes, well, I suppose that was my reaction as well to some extent. Regardless, after one has witnessed such an event, it casts a pall on the future one imagined they might have with this person."

"Yes, I can see how that would be the case."

"His family, however, was less understanding. They took my refusal of marriage as an affront and, given their standing in Society was more established than ours, made sure to do everything they could to ruin us. Father's business began to suffer; invitations to parties and events dried up. Then Collin's fiancée decided she could not marry into a family whose reputation and standing had dipped so low her association with us was no longer advantageous. It quite broke his heart, I think," Temperance said, her voice trailing off. The weight of guilt still rested heavy upon her conscience. It was one thing that she suffered, but to see the result of her decision hurt her brother in such a way had been unbearable. Love, she had learned, was a very capricious thing. It came and went on a whim and cared little for what destruction it left behind.

"And so your family came to London, figuring if they could attach their name to a title or two it would resurrect the standing they had lost."

"Very astute of you."

James smiled and scratched at the scruff of beard that had grown in along his jawline, the rasp of his fingers against the whiskers filling the silence. "You're not the first family to attempt such a coup. And if you return to New York now, without benefit of having achieved this goal, how will you be received?"

Temperance's shoulders sagged. "Likely, I wouldn't be received at all."

"It appears you sit between the proverbial rock and hard place then. Is this broken engagement the only reason you do not wish to marry? Not all men are like your former fiancé, you know."

She could not argue with his statement in that regard. Because in the end, it wasn't so much about the type of man Beauregard had turned out to be as it was about her own inability to recognize such. In hindsight, there had been signs. He had not been interested in her, not in the way she was with him. It had always been she who'd had to request a kiss from him. A forward move, but she'd been so in love and they were to be married, what was the harm in an innocent kiss or two? But when he had given in and kissed her, the sensation had left her...disappointed. It had lacked the passion she felt in her heart. His kisses had been swift and lukewarm. But with no experience to draw upon, Temperance had assumed the whole kissing thing had been overrated. That she had allowed Constance's romantic novels to build it into something it wasn't.

She knew now, the novels had been right. At least if one

kissed a man who wished to kiss you back thoroughly and completely.

But a kiss wasn't enough to build a life on.

She had learned that lesson the hard way.

Love made you blind. It hoodwinked and bedazzled you until you fooled yourself into disregarding all the signs. It allowed your heart to make excuses, until you were rudely awakened by reality. Such foolishness had brought her to the brink of having Beauregard place a band of gold onto her finger and watching as it turned into a shackle of misery. She had escaped such a fate once, before it was too late, but what if she hadn't? What if next time, she wasn't so lucky?

How did one see through the veil love created to what was beyond and keep from stepping into a future you couldn't escape?

"Temperance?"

She sighed and looked across the space that separated them. He wanted to know and perhaps, after all they had been through, he deserved to.

"I had once thought Beauregard loved me as much as I had him. That he respected my intelligence and supported my goals to use my standing to help make the world a little better. To ensure those that had less were given an opportunity to become more. I think that's important, don't you?"

"I suppose it is definitely something to consider."

She let out a small laugh. It wasn't a complete agreement, but it was definitely a bit of movement in the right direction on his lordship's behalf.

"Anyway, as it turned out, he cared little. About me, my thoughts, my goals. None of it. He was marrying me because a marriage between our families was advantageous. It looked good to others and would keep at bay anyone questioning his true...inclinations. It had nothing to do with me or him or my feelings or any future I had envisioned. He could have been marrying anyone. All he truly needed was someone to help create the image he wished others to see. I will not put myself in that situation again where the future I had hoped for is of no value to the person I share it with."

"I see."

"Do you? Let's face it, as a man—a titled gentleman, at that—the world is yours to conquer. Likely, you have never been told no. Never had something you wanted refused you."

James's expression darkened, as if a storm had slid between them, bringing with it the crackle of lightning and threat of driving rain. "Is that what you believe?"

"Tell me I'm wrong."

Silence, thick and heavy, hung between them.

"You are as wrong as one can be."

"How so?"

James remained silent a moment longer before speaking. "You are hardly the first person to experience heartbreak."

"And what was yours?"

"I fell in love with my best friend's wife."

"Lord Rothbury?" Her distant cousin had been married years previous but she knew little about it other than the fact that the first Lady Rothbury had died, leaving the future duke a widower with a small daughter to raise.

"Yes. You see, he and I fell in love with the same woman. In the end, she chose him and I..." He shrugged, leaving Temperance to fill in what he didn't say. It was easy enough to do, knowing what she knew of him now.

"And you stepped aside because you wished more for their happiness than your own."

James looked away from her and out the window. "It was the only thing to do."

"Was it?"

His gaze shot back to her. "What else would you have suggested? That I alienate the man who was like a brother to me? That I force Ruth to love me instead of Alex? Such a thing is not possible. One's heart makes its own choices. Mine chose her. Hers chose Alex. There was nothing to be done about it but to step aside."

"And did Lord Rothbury love her as much as you did?"

James hesitated and Temperance watched the struggle that played out in his expression. "In his own way, as best he could. In the beginning, at least. Things changed after their son died. Alex shut down. He could not console Ruth and so..." Another shrug.

"And so you did."

"I tried, but ultimately she sought solace elsewhere."

Temperance's heart ached. It was clear the pain this past hurt still caused James. How it haunted him, even after all these years. He must have loved her deeply. "You didn't give up on her though, did you? You were determined to save her from herself."

"I thought to save them both."

"But you failed." And that was it. *That* was the pain she saw. Not the heartbreak of unrequited love, but the inability to save the woman he loved from her own broken heart. He had set aside his own wants and needs in the hopes of repairing hers, but he had been unable to do so. He had not been enough.

How well she knew that feeling.

James returned his gaze to the window. When he spoke, pain quieted his voice until Temperance had to struggle to hear him over the creak of the wheels and springs as they bounced along. "Ruth went down a dark path I could not retrieve her from, and it resulted in her death. She took up with another man and—" He shook his head. "I did what I could, but it was not enough."

"I'm sorry, James."

He did not answer and eventually, they lapsed into silence

once more, the only sound the noise of their carriage as it bumped along the rutted road that led them home. At some point, she had dozed off. When she awoke, the lantern had been extinguished.

Another hour passed before the city loomed in the distance, its shadowy silhouette of familiar structures growing larger with each passing moment. Soon they would be swallowed up, pulled in until they became a part of it once more. Before morning broke across the sky to chase the shadows away, Temperance would arrive at her parents' doorstep, her future as murky as the fog that hung low over the city, slithering along its roads and alleyways.

"You're frowning. Are you not looking forward to arriving home?"

She looked over toward James, half of his face cast in darkness, while moonlight pooled through the window to alight upon the other half. The effect was striking and her body remained heated even after she had looked away. Would this longing for him dissipate with time? Or was she doomed to suffer it each time she laid eyes upon him?

"No, it is not that...I suppose..." She stopped and shook her head.

"You suppose what?"

Temperance shrugged. She was thrilled at having escaped their ordeal, relieved beyond belief. But—

"I suppose, at the end of the day, I do not think of London as home."

"You think of New York as home, then?"

She was about to nod then stopped, because that didn't feel right either. Not any more. New York had forsaken her, turned its back because she had dared stand up and declare she would not accept a marriage that was less than what she had wanted.

"No, I'm not sure I do. Perhaps I am unsettled because I

no longer feel I have a home. A place to call my own where I can simply be who I am without worrying of someone else's opinion of it. My situation is much different than yours. Your family has likely lived in the same place for generation upon generation. Your roots run deep."

"On the contrary. I do not think of any particular place as home."

"Because you have so many you can't choose?" She meant to chide him and received a raised eyebrow in response to her jest.

"Because I have always considered home to be the people I am with, not the place I am at. Structures, places, these are all temporary things easily destroyed or taken away. When you live in the heart of a person, however, that does not go away. It is somewhere you may always return to."

His word, eloquent and honest, struck a chord deep within her. Had she not had the opportunity to learn James's true worth over the past week, perhaps his response would have startled her more, but it didn't. This lord, this seventh generation marquess, this man who had risked everything to save her life nearly at the expense of his own, had proven time and again where he placed his true value. What was important to him. It was not his title, or his reputation, or the lands he held.

It was honor. It was truth. It was love.

Temperance opened her mouth, but the chance to say something, anything, to repair the distance that had crept between them, was stolen away by time, by her inability to know the right words to say. Or, to her dismay, the bravery to overcome her fear that by speaking those words, she gave herself over to a future she could not control.

The surface beneath the carriage changed to the familiar bump of cobbled streets. Civilization. The tactile reminder that their journey had come to an end and they would now go their separate ways. Sadness tangled around her, making her limbs heavy and her heart ache.

James leaned forward to look out the window, relief evident in his tone when he spoke. "We should arrive at your residence within the hour."

And he would be rid of her. Rid of the responsibility of seeing her safe. Rid of the necessity of risking his life to save hers. Free of marrying a woman he did not love and able to find someone he could, as he had the late Lady Rothbury.

While Temperance would be left with the agony of realizing too late what a wonderful man this Marquess of Ridgemont was, and how easily she could have loved him and quite possibly been happy to call him husband.

Chapter Fifteen

"I cannot believe what has happened to you. Mother and Father were beside themselves!" Constance wrapped her arms around Temperance as if she were afraid if she let go, her twin would disappear once more.

Temperance patted her sister on the back before slowly extracting herself from the embrace. "I am fine, Constance. Truly, I am. Ja—Lord Ridgemont ensured no harm came to me. He was surprisingly gallant in that regard."

Her sister smiled. "What a shock that must have been to you."

"Fine. Have your fun. I admit I was quite mistaken in my estimation of his lordship. And I have apologized to him for this."

"And did he accept your heartfelt apology?"

"Of course. He is a gentleman, after all."

"And did he *behave* a gentleman?" Constance's blonde eyebrows arched upward and a knowing gleam brightened her light blue eyes.

"Of course!" Temperance let the claim, wrapped with a hint of indignation, roll off her tongue. She was determined to hold fast to the story they had told. That nothing inappropriate had transpired between them, nor did their captors subject Temperance to any abuse. She was as untouched as she had been before the incident took place.

Such balderdash!

And given the skeptical way Constance's gaze bored through her, her sister knew it.

"I am not so certain I could be trapped in a room with such a virile and handsome man, fearing for my very life, without giving in to the need for a certain amount of...comfort."

"Constance!" Temperance could not believe her sweet, innocent sister would say such a thing! Clearly, she had been reading those silly romantic novels again.

"What? I may be an innocent, Temp, but I am not an idiot. Besides, I saw the way Lord Ridgemont looked at you while Mother and Father were abrading him with questions."

"How he was looking at me? Whatever do you mean?" Heat spiraled from her belly up to neck and cheeks with swift purpose.

"Like a changed man. His gaze spoke of things that go unsaid. There was a depth to it. A sadness, as if in leaving you here, he left a piece of himself behind. It was a far different look than the one you shared as you danced at the Frontenac's ball, that is for certain."

Constance had always been the more observant of the two of them, and it was an aspect of her that Temperance had always enjoyed. Until now.

"That is foolish. Likely the look you saw was his lordship happy to be rid of me." Why, when he left, he'd barely done more than execute a brief bow in her direction and a quick wish for her happy future.

Constance sat on the edge of the bed and folded her hands in her lap, an enigmatic smile settling upon her lips. Most who met the sisters thought of Temperance as the smarter of the two with her penchant for books and knowledge and her plethora of opinions on any number of subjects. But the truth of it was, Constance's intelligence when it came to reading people and seeing through the facades they wore in public put her miles ahead of Temperance. Perhaps had Temperance possessed even an ounce of Constance's astuteness in this regard, she would have recognized James was a wonderful man, honest and honorable and dedicated to his family. Perhaps she would not have railed against him as hard as she had and they would have struck up a proper friendship.

Maybe even more.

She shook the thought from her head. No. She had made her decision in that regard long ago. Her heart was not to be trusted with something as important as the decision of marriage. It lacked the sensible nature required for such a life-altering event. Her heart had a bad habit of rushing into things without considering all the variables, and ending up being trampled and crushed by the reality of the situation.

Temperance turned her attention to her reflection in the vanity mirror and picked up her brush, running it through her freshly washed hair, releasing the scent of rosebuds so that it wafted around her.

The reality was that James had no interest in marrying her. They had allowed themselves to become caught up in the moment, nothing more. And she would not punish his honorable nature by forcing him into a marriage he did not truly want.

How horrible a life would that be to know the person you were with was only there out of a sense of duty? That wouldn't be fair to either of them. Likely James would spend his days castigating himself for acting rashly and shackling himself to a woman who was so far removed from what he knew or wanted. And she would know this. Know that he did not love her and she...well, she would likely be unable to keep her heart from loving him.

Such an unbalanced partnership would be doomed to failure.

And that would be a far worse fate than anything Society could throw at her.

Temperance looked at her sister through the reflection in the vanity. Constance had not moved from where she sat, nor had her expression changed as she watched her older sister.

Finally, Temperance could stand it no longer. "You might as well say it. I know you're going to sit there until you do."

"You love him."

Temperance sputtered. That wasn't exactly what she thought her sister would blurt out. "I beg your pardon, I most certainly do not!"

Constance's smile grew. "Of course you do. We both know it. And you know you cannot lie to me. You love him."

Temperance averted her gaze away from her sister and back to her own reflection, studying the lines of her face in an attempt to discover which part of her had given it away. There was no use in denying it. It was as Constance said. She could not lie to her sister.

"It will pass," she whispered.

"Will it?"

"Of course." She had loved Beauregard, after all, and those feelings had died, mortally wounded by the vision of him seeking his pleasure with the footman and dairymaid. Not to mention the callous way he had treated her after she ended their engagement. As if she had been the one at fault.

"Then you have no plans on seeing him again?"

Temperance paid particular attention to the curl at the end of a long hank of hair draped over her shoulder, applying the brush to it with a fervor it likely did not deserve. "I suspect we shall see each other at parties and such. It will be unavoidable, unless I find myself shunned—"

"I do not think it will come to that, Temp."

Temperance set the brush down and turned on the short stool to face her sister. "I applaud your optimism, Constance, but let's face it, I have just spent several days alone with a gentleman and despite all assurances that all propriety was maintained, the gossips will have their way. We both know the lords and ladies of le bon ton have been praying for some scandal to pin on the upstart Americans. This is their chance and I doubt they will pass it up."

"If they do, I am certain Lord Ridgemont will come to your defense. Father is insistent that he offer for you to save your reputation from being damaged."

"And I am insistent that he does not. Besides, Society cares little for me. I can only hope there will be but a few days gossip and then they will forget about me and move onto something else. That their need to protect one of their own from marrying our kind will be stronger than their need to embarrass me."

"And you do not wish for Lord Ridgemont to offer? To save you any embarrassment or ridicule?"

"He did offer and I refused him." Temperance ignored Constance's gasp, continuing on before her sister could inquire further on the matter. "His lordship has done quite enough. I will not allow him to sacrifice himself for the sake of my reputation. In the end, the whole thing will come to naught."

Nor would she consign herself to marrying a man who would never feel for her what he had for his first love.

Again, the enigmatic smile spread across Constance's face as she stood and walked toward Temperance, leaning down to place a quick kiss on her sister's cheek and whisper in her ear.

"Which goes to prove my first point, that you are in love with him."

Before she could deny the claim—as if it would do her any good—Constance stood and quit the room, leaving Temperance alone. Confusion swarmed her heart and mind. Had she done the right thing? And if so, why did it feel as if she had made a horrible mistake that was too late to rectify?

She turned back around to stare at her reflection. How long would it take before her feelings settled and she felt herself again?

Or had the feelings James had awakened in her left her forever changed?

"We scoured the bloody city and its outskirts for you," Alex said. "That they had spirited you so far away, never occurred."

"Well," Henrietta inserted, casting her husband a look James recognized all too well, "Lord Hawksmoor *did* suggest if it were he who had perpetrated such a crime, he would have—"

Alex glared over at his wife, but her sweet smile melted his irritation's potency in quick order until his old friend relented and returned her smile. "Very well. I will concede Hawk did suggest such a thing, but the rest of us believed they would have kept you closer at hand to receive swift news of the ransom payment."

James had had little time to spend with his family over the past twenty-four hours since he'd arrived home. Much of it had been spent answering Mr. Lindwell's pointed questions and veiled accusations the previous night and well into the late morning hours. Following that, James had spent the rest of the day with the authorities giving them every scrap of information he could think of, in the hopes they would find the two men responsible before they disappeared into the wilds of northern England or beyond, never to be seen again. They'd already apprehended the man who'd stayed behind to deliver the ransom note and act as the go-between. He'd sung like a bird in the hopes it would go well for him, though whether that helped his cause remained to be seen.

By the time James had finally arrived back at Harrow House, he'd had enough time for a brief reunion with his sister, great-aunt, and Alex before falling into a deep, dreamless sleep that lasted well through the day. Though when he awoke, he felt no better. Something was missing.

Someone was missing. Someone he'd reached for before full wakefulness reminded him he would no longer find her curled against him, her warmth and scent wrapping around him like the warmest of blankets.

"I'm afraid our abductors were not overly intelligent men, so expecting a well laid out plan was overreaching on your part. Regardless," James said, looking down at the gurgling face of his nephew, letting the babe wrap tiny hands around his finger. "All is well that ends well, and both Miss Lindwell and myself have been returned none the worse for wear."

Unless one counted the ravages that had assaulted his insides. Those would take some time to heal. How long, however, was anyone's guess.

"And you're certain you are fine?"

James looked up at his sister. She knew him too well and had a sixth sense when it came to sensing his moods. Even as a young girl, on the day Alex had married Ruth, it was Hen who had refused to leave his side, as if sensing a part of him was broken and needed mending.

She hadn't been wrong. But sometimes there are broken things that cannot be repaired. James had the sinking sense whatever had happened between him and Temperance was one of those things.

"Yes," he lied. "Quite certain. A bit of a headache still, but the doctor promises that shall fade soon enough." If only the memories of holding Temperance against him, the feel of her skin sliding against his would remove itself in time as well. But he suspected that would not be the case.

"And how did you find your imprisonment with the opinionated Miss Temperance Lindwell," Alex asked.

"It was very...enlightening."

Alex laughed and slapped his knee, garnering a wide-eyed glance from his infant son. "I am certain of that. I should warn you, however, that despite her very vocal protestations that there is no need for you to marry, her father has approached mine over the matter."

Apprehension crept up James's spine. "And why does Lindwell wish to discuss the matter with the duke?"

Alex leaned back in his chair and stretched his legs out. "Do you even need to ask? His only purpose in coming to London was to marry his daughters off to titled lords so he might return to New York and use this coup to re-establish his place in Society. A place, I might add, that was lost due to his eldest daughter's breaking her engagement with a man touted to be the favored son of New York Society."

A man who had broken Temperance's heart and destroyed her ability to trust.

"And you think he will push to have me offer for her?"

Alex shrugged. "Are you surprised? The man is a mercenary when it comes to climbing the social ladder. He is determined to return to New York a king, or at the very least, a few steps removed from one."

"You could do worse than marrying Miss Lindwell," Henrietta suggested.

"Doubtful," Alex said.

"Alex!" Hen swatted her husband's arm then turned her attention back to James. "Temperance is a lovely girl. Quite brilliant, really, if somewhat forthright. I happen to find her very interesting. She does not shy away from things."

"No, indeed she does not," James whispered, an unwanted vision of her atop him, lost in the throes of passion, inserted itself in his mind's eye. He gave his head a shake to dispel the memory.

"I have to say, brother dear, I'm surprised you did not offer for her. That is unlike you."

James looked over at his sister. "I did."

Her eyebrows lifted. "And she refused you?"

"Yes. Repeatedly. And quite vehemently, I might add. She has no interest in marrying me. Or any English lord, for that matter."

"That's preposterous," Alex said. "What else is she going to do?"

"Knowing Miss Lindwell, I suspect she will do whatever she wants." James brought his nephew's hand to his mouth to put a kiss upon the tiny fingers, receiving a giggle for his efforts.

"Then she shall miss out on spending her life with a very wonderful man and for that I feel quite sorry for her," Hen said.

"I thank you for your kind words, my dear, but I think you have a biased opinion of my virtues," James said, standing up to hand his nephew off to his sister. "Well, I think I shall retire for the evening."

Hen hugged her son to her and stood to give James a quick kiss on the cheek. "Of course. You have been through quite the ordeal and I suspect it will take you a few days to fully recuperate. Would you like me to have Mrs. Bromley send up some tea and biscuits?"

James smiled at the housekeeper's name. He hoped she

would not have minded his misappropriation of it during their adventures. "No, thank you. I think I will be well asleep before it ever arrived."

James hugged his sister, careful not to crush his nephew cradled in her arms, before turning to leave and seek sanctuary in his bedchamber.

"Good night, old chap," Alex said, clapping him on the shoulder as he passed. James was well out of the room before his friend spoke again, his comment drifting down the hallway to catch up to him. "He does not seem himself, Hen. Are you certain he is fine?"

James didn't wait to hear his sister's answer. He didn't need to. The answer was written across his heart, embedded into the traitorous organ with each beat.

No, he was not fine. He was a very long ride away from fine.

The problem was, he didn't know how to find his way back. His compass had become distorted and every path he found, led back to the one thing that had caused him to become so lost in the first place.

In essence, he'd become trapped inside an endless circle of his own making and could find no break within it to set himself free.

Chapter Sixteen

"It must feel a bit surreal being back in the thick of things," Constance said as they stood on the edge of the ballroom at Lord Willanthorpe's fete in honor of his stepson's birthday. The newly anointed marquess hoped to find Lord Plimpton a suitable bride of good fortune, though given his tendency toward spitting when he spoke, his questionable intelligence—or lack thereof—and propensity toward a rotundness his short stature could not carry about without waddling, they had their work cut out for them.

At least in Society's estimation. Then again, Temperance gave little credence to what Society thought. She and James had been back in London for a fortnight and it was clear her ordeal had left an indelible blemish on her reputation. Not that anyone had said anything about it to her face, other than to express their horror that such a thing had happened, but it was clear whispers and rumors abounded.

"Temp?"

"Hm? Oh, yes," Temperance said, having forgotten to answer her sister's question. "Yes, I suppose it is. Very surreal."

"Well, I'm sure you will be back in the swing of things

before you know it." Constance patted her hand, but Temperance did not share her sister's optimism. She had already spoken with Rosalind Caldwell, only to be informed that she could not confirm employment at this time. Perhaps once the rumors died down.

"You know I despise such nonsense, Temperance, but I have to think of what is best for the school. If the parents keep their children away, despite how narrow-minded the reasons, we will have no school for you to run, will we?"

Temperance did not fault Rosalind for the decision. Had she been in her position, likely she would have done the same. But that didn't lessen the sting of it. Becoming headmistress of the school was the only avenue left to her, the only hope she had of putting an end to this endless loop of parties and teas and what not. Her escape from the stares and whispers that followed her now wherever she went. Women would slide her sly looks as if they could see the stain of James's handprints where he had touched her. Men would openly stare, a speculative gleam in their eyes.

And James—where was he? He had been conspicuously absent from every event she'd attended since they'd returned to London, but she had been certain he would not turn down Lord Willanthorpe's invitation. Temperance tried pretending James's absence went unnoticed, that it didn't matter, but it did. Heaven help her, but she missed his presence. Longed for it.

Was he holed up at Harrow House after sending his great-aunt, Lady Dalridge, to their home to do his dirty work? Father had been intent on wringing a proposal from James, but after a brief meeting with Lady Dalridge, he quickly changed his mind. Now, much to Temperance's horror, he had set his sights on Lord Willanthorpe's stepson, Lord Plimpton. And his lordship was actually considering it! Rumor had it, the man loved money and loathed his stepson.

If he could broker a deal with Father that gave him the former while ridding him of the latter, he would consider it a boon.

Temperance shuddered at the thought. Lord Plimpton was a harmless individual, but lacking in both wit and intelligence. She'd jump into the Atlantic and swim to America before she ever agreed to marry a man who could not hold up his end of a debate.

"You're scowling," Constance said.

Temperance's scowl deepened. "You would too if Father was contemplating your marriage to Lord Simpleton."

"It's Plimpton."

"An honest mistake. Did you know he does not even attend the sessions in the House of Lords? How can one have such an opportunity and squander it? He could make great change." She sighed as she watched the gentleman in question trample upon the toes of Miss Godfrey. "Then again, perhaps he'd do more harm than good. Why, he cannot even manage a simple step without causing grievous injury to his partner. Imagine what havoc he could wreck on national policies. I shudder to contemplate."

Constance stifled a giggle behind her gloved hand. "You are awful, Temp."

"So is the idea of marrying such a man."

Temperance let out a long breath and scanned the room once more. It was a sizeable crush of people but nowhere among them did she spy James's dark head and piercing blue gaze. It was as if he had vanished. Was he even still in London?

Not that there was anyone to ask. If she even dared hint at the question likely the rumors would swirl to new heights and she'd become more of a pariah than she already was. Why, if it wasn't for Lady Dalridge's grudging support—clearly part of whatever agreement she and Father had reached—invitations would have dried up and blown away on the first wind.

Temperance almost wished they had. Almost. Only the

faint hope she might run into James kept her from feigning illness and staying home. Though, now that that faint hope had been dashed by his absence, she did feel rather ill.

For some reason, people were staring at her more than usual tonight. They were not being overly covert about it either.

"Do I have something on my face?" She had nabbed a few sweets earlier, much to Mother's consternation, but nervousness made her hungry.

"No," Constance said, looking at her face before her gaze traveled to two ladies to their right, their names once given but long forgotten. She lowered her voice when she spoke again. "Is it just my imagination or—"

"No. It is not. Why are they staring at me?"

The whispers rolled toward her as if on a wave, beginning in the distance until they lapped at her feet. The air had shifted, filled with a heightened awareness. Something had changed. Temperance's ears buzzed until the sound drowned out the music. Even a few of the couples waltzing closer to the edge of the ballroom floor had slowed and begun to look around. Had they heard it too?

But Temperance didn't need to look around. The way her skin came alive and the butterflies battered her insides, she already knew what was coming. Or rather who. And in a moment, she had her confirmation as his dark head bobbed in the crowd where he stopped and greeted ladies, bending over their offered hands in his usual gentlemanly manner.

"Oh," Constance breathed. "Well."

Temperance could feel her sister's gaze, the studied way she had of looking at her, but she couldn't look away from James's slow approach. Was he intentionally coming her way? Or did he even know she was here?

But then he looked up, his gaze meeting hers and she had her answer. He did know. He was coming this way.

He heart picked up speed.

"Should we leave?" Constance asked.

Temperance gave a small shake of her head. She didn't want to look away, afraid if she did, James might evaporate into the ether and she'd be left with the realization that it had all been a dream. A vision crafted by her own desires. Desires she had done her best to repress over the last fortnight with little success.

How she longed to be held in his arms once more. To feel the heat of his skin against hers. To revel in the hard, sinewy muscle, the way it rippled across his stomach and burgeoned at his shoulders. The taste of him still lingered on her tongue from their last kiss and her heart still sang from his last heated stare.

Was he slowing down?

She pulled her brow downward. He was. He'd stopped to speak to a young woman. Temperance stood on tiptoe to see whom it was.

"Lady Charlotte Overton," Constance supplied.

Temperance started and let her heels touch the floor once more.

Lord Willanthorpe's niece. The young woman had recently come out of mourning following her father's death. She was quite lovely with her pale skin and rosy cheeks, dark hair framing a round, almost angelic face. In short, Lady Charlotte was everything James should want in a wife.

Perhaps everything James *did* want in a wife. Pretty, proper, English, and a lady. Familiar with the ins and outs of Society, likely quite biddable and perfectly happy being so. In short, the complete opposite of everything Temperance was.

Jealousy spiked inside of her as James lifted Lady Charlotte's hand to his lips and brushed his lips against her knuckles, bringing a hard glare from Lord Willanthorpe who stood next to her. Or perhaps that was his normal expression. Temperance had never seen the man look any other way.

"I understand the new Marquess of Willanthorpe is most anxious to have Lady Charlotte married by the end of the Season."

"Then why does he not marry her to his stepson? They are of no familial relation. It would kill two birds with one stone. I've heard Lady Charlotte's father took a page from the late Lord Blackbourne's book and left everything unentailed to her, and that her dowry itself, is quite sizeable. If it is money his lordship wants, it would seem an easy solution."

Constance waved her fan in front of her face. "Mother told me Lady Charlotte's father made certain stipulations in his will with respect the dowry, strictly forbidding her marriage to Lord Plimpton. Clearly, he expected Lord Willanthorpe to think as you did and take the easy way out."

Temperance wasn't keen on the idea of having her thoughts on equal standing as Lord Willanthorpe's.

"Do you think they are considering James?"

Constance gave her a knowing look at the unintended slip. "Do you mean Lord Ridgemont? Why yes, one would expect it. He is, after all, the most eligible bachelor of the Season and Lady Dalridge said she has high hopes that he will choose a wife before Season's end."

"Truly?" Temperance's heart lurched at the news. It was to be expected, of course, but that fact didn't help the truth of it settle anywhere comfortable. Why would he not hold out for love? Was it that he still kindled a flame for the one he'd lost and no one else would ever measure up, leaving him with only duty?

Constance interrupted her thoughts. "Of course. Now that Lady Rothbury is comfortably settled, the countess has turned her attention to her great-nephew and is very determined in her efforts. She is quite partial to Lady Charlotte, I hear. And the sizeable dowry likely does not hurt, though Lord Ridgemont is hardly lacking in that area."

Lord Ridgemont was not lacking in *any* area, but Temperance kept those thoughts to herself.

"You are a fountain of information, aren't you?" she muttered. None of the information her sister imparted, however, made her feel any better about this evening. Or about watching James as he smiled and conversed with Lady Charlotte as though she were the only woman in the room.

If it was a sizeable dowry James was after, he could have agreed with Father's insistence that he marry his daughter. Likely her dowry would give Lady Charlotte's a run for its money, so to speak. What Temperance didn't have, however, was the pedigree. There was no *Lady* preceding her name. No family that went back several generations. No worthwhile connections unless one counted a rather tenuous one with the Duke of Franklyn, though even that was once or twice removed. Likely, her parents had already milked that one dry given the way the duke avoided them and his duchess rarely ever found her way to their receiving room.

From her vantage point, James appeared quite taken with the lady, though it was difficult to be certain as he did pride himself on being a gentleman and Temperance could attest that even when he did not particularly like a lady, he was always polite and gave the impression that she had his full attention. At least, that was how he'd made her feel. And given the way Lady Charlotte blushed—and quite prettily, at that—she was not immune to his charms either.

What if Lady Charlotte was the one who might heal James's wounded heart? If she was, then Temperance should be happy for such a union. Shouldn't she? Yes. Of course, she should.

And yet, she wasn't. Instead, the idea of the two of them

together left a bit of a hole in her heart that she did not know how to fill.

"I think I'd like to visit the powder room," Temperance said, the words whispering out of her. She could not watch the two of them any longer.

"Come," Constance said, pulling on her arm without questioning. She and her sister had always been that way. Understanding each other in a way that was mostly unspoken and yet never incorrect. It was both a blessing and a curse. A blessing, because there was always someone there who understood how you felt. A curse, because there was always that one person you could never hide your true feelings from.

And Temperance wanted to hide them, at least until she had time to fully understand them. She had done her best over the past fortnight to set aside what had happened between her and James. To ignore the whispers of impropriety that wafted about as people gossiped over what may have happened during their captivity.

If they only knew the truth of her wickedly wanton behavior. And of how little she regretted what she did. What kind of woman did that make her? Certainly not the kind suited to a proper marriage.

Was it any wonder James had given up trying to convince her when she gave her final refusal to his proposal? He did not truly want to marry her. He had simply been doing what he always did—the proper thing in the hopes of protecting her from scandal. Duty was the driving force behind everything he did. And it was the thing that had helped keep them both alive, her unharmed, and aided in their eventual escape. And that dedication to her well-being did not deserve to be rewarded with a lifetime married to someone he did not wish to be married to.

Constance led Temperance into the ladies' powder room, but if she hoped to avoid the gossip, she had come to the wrong place. The room was overflowing with ladies giggling and whispering, all of which came to a striking halt the moment it was realized who had arrived.

Temperance had never experienced such piercing scrutiny and despite the self-preservation that urged her to turn and run, she was not the type to do so. She instead straightened her spine and pulled her shoulders back then made her way into the room, to an empty vanity near the back. Next to her, Constance tensed, but she did not falter, nor abandon ship.

Silence continued to permeate the room until Temperance took a seat on the cushioned stool fiddled with a recalcitrant curl for lack of anything better to do.

"I'm sorry, Temp. I had no idea it would be so crowded in here," her sister whispered, taking the seat next to her.

"It is of no matter. I suppose I should get used to such scrutiny until they grow bored and move onto someone else." Perhaps if James proposed to Lady Charlotte, it would give them all something else to gossip about.

Her stomach clenched. Oh bother, that did not help at all.

"Did you hear?"

It took Temperance a moment to realize a young lady whose name escaped her had directed the question at her. Lady Betsey...? Or was it Agnes...?

"Did I hear what?"

"Lord Ridgemont had decided he shall choose a bride before the end of the Season. Did you know of this?"

The words battered against her, echoing the rumors Constance had informed her of moments earlier. These words, however, were not delivered with the same softness as her sister's. They held a caustic edge, a prying stare. They assaulted her heart and threatened to break through the barriers she'd thought she'd shored up.

Temperance turned in her seat, arranging her skirts around her. "I can't imagine why I would have heard."

The young lady—Patricia! That was it—came closer, her round eyes growing narrow as a pert smile played about her mouth. She looked like a cat that was about to swallow the canary.

"He did not discuss such things with you during your...*adventure*?"

"I would hardly consider being abducted an adventure. But perhaps you should try it sometime and let me know if you don't agree with me." The woman lacked the sense God gave a mule. Who in their right mind would think being taken to parts unknown against your will, the threat of death hanging over your head, was a bloody adventure?

"You know," Lady Patricia said, and her eyes widened once more until Temperance worried they might pop out of her head altogether, "Some say it wasn't an abduction at all. I have heard that your father staged the entire event to force his lord-ship to offer for you, but that he refused to be forced into such a marriage through trickery."

Next to her, Constance bristled with indignation. "That is the most preposterous thing I have ever heard! And a complete lie. Father would never do such a thing."

Lady Patricia shrugged, neither accepting nor denying Constance's claims. "But don't you find it odd that he didn't offer for you? After all, you were alone for several days. Anything could have happened—"

"Nothing did," Temperance stated, forcing the lie out of her mouth with as much legitimacy as she could muster.

"Truly? That is not what I've heard. And certainly not what other people believe."

"I cannot help what others are prone to believe," Temperance bit out, her anger simmering to the point of boiling over. "But Lord Ridgemont was the consummate gentleman."

Lady Patricia waved a hand in the air as if to dismiss Temperance's claim. "Regardless, the suggestion of such impropriety—for lack of a better word—will be enough to keep any other man of consequence from making you an offer, even Lord Plimpton."

"I care little about what some man plans on doing or not doing. I do not set my future based on the whims of others. I have better ways of spending my time."

Lady Patricia stared at her as if Temperance had claimed she intended to disrobe and run through the ballroom in nothing more than her stockings and stays. "I don't understand."

"No, I don't expect you would. You've been raised to believe the only value you hold is based on what some man tells you it is, and you do not possess the gumption to change that way of thinking." Temperance stood and Constance quickly joined her. "You will go blindly toward whatever man chooses to make you his bride and spend the rest of your miserable, uneventful life doing his bidding as if you had no mind of your own. I think such a life will suit you quite well, as you don't strike me as a particularly intelligent sort and would be better off letting others make your decisions for you. I, on the other hand, have no intention of living such a shallow half-life. Now, if you will excuse me, I am quite certain there is somewhere more interesting for me to be other than standing here conversing with the likes of you."

Temperance strode from the room, leaving Lady Patricia sputtering in her wake. Constance's arm slipped through hers as they opened the door and walked through at what Temperance hoped was a sedate pace. She refused to run away, no matter how much the other lady's words had wounded.

As the door shut behind her, she heard Lady Patricia harrumph her final words on the subject. "Well, what kind of behavior do you expect from an *American*."

The group murmured their agreement but Temperance paid it no heed. If this is what they thought of her, so be it. She had no desire to join their group. Lady Patricia and her syco-phants only served to reinstate her original beliefs that London Society was not her cup of tea and it never would be. Despite any feelings she held for James, or how the discovery of who he really was had begun to turn her head and her thoughts in another direction.

No, she had been correct in her original assessment. These people would never accept her as one of their own. She would always be an outsider. Always be looked upon as the *American*, as if such were a dirty word.

Refusing James's proposal had been the right thing to do. Knowing him, he would spend his life trying to protect her from the hurtful opinions of others, and beat himself up over his continual failure to do so. She was not like them. She would never be like them, nor did she want to be. She enjoyed having opinions and thoughts and she fully believed when one was in a position to make the world a better place, it was incumbent upon them to do so.

As much as the dream of spending her life with a man as wonderful as James had intruded on this belief and turned her head, causing her to wonder if there was not more than one way to achieve such, it was clear she must set such nonsense aside. She and James were not meant to be. He had moved on.

And so must she.

Chapter Seventeen

"I should think it would not be too difficult to find yourself a bride," Lord Huntsleigh claimed, waving a hand toward James. "You're not completely hideous."

James arched one eyebrow but before he could find an appropriate response to the earl's rather damning praise, Alex, who had invited the man and his friends to join their table at White's, weighed in.

"Not completely, and what shortcomings he has in that respect are easily compensated for with his annual income. Provided he agrees to keep the room dark at night, he shouldn't scare off his chosen bride."

"Gentlemen," Lord Hawksmoor said, holding his snifter up as if to inspect the brandy within it. "I think you are over-looking a rather obvious flaw in your considerations."

The Earl of Blackbourne's dark, brooding appearance disappeared with the flash of a smile. "Hawk has the truth of it. Clearly it is not his looks that are his most egregious failing, but rather his horrid choice in cravats."

James scowled and lifted a hand to his neck. "I beg your

pardon, but I have flawless tastes in my cravats, thank you very much." Or rather, Gregory did. James rarely bothered with such things.

Huntsleigh smirked. Blackbourne snorted. Alex and Hawk shook their heads as if he were a poor, misguided soul in desperate need of their assistance and advice in the manner of finding a bride, simply based on the fact that they had all overcome their own list of shortcomings to find success in that matter.

But, despite the good-natured teasing from his companions, it was Mr. Marcus Bowen who set his drink down upon the table and spoke in his clear and quiet way. And in doing so, came closer to the truth than all the rest.

"I suspect Ridgemont's list of preferred brides is a short one."

Alex looked at the man as if he'd lost his mind. "Whatever are you about, man? There is any number of unmarried women we might place on the list for him to consider."

"Any number that *we* might place on the list," Mr. Bowen corrected, his dark gaze even and unreadable. "But only one that Ridgemont would put there. Is that not the case?"

Hawksmoor had once claimed that Marcus Bowen held some magical power that enabled him to read people's minds, as there was no other explanation for the unfailing accuracy of his observations. James had always considered such a claim to be pure poppycock, but now he wondered if perhaps Hawk's claim held some validity after all.

"I think Bowen has the right of it," Lord Glenmor said, leaning forward. "He would not be dragging his feet in proposing to Lady Charlotte otherwise."

Huntsleigh, too, leaned forward in his seat, a grin cutting across his face and his golden eyebrows arching upward. "Indeed, do tell who it is that has so captured your attention.

That will make this go much easier if we can narrow our focus."

James had no idea what *we* Huntsleigh referred to, or when his marital status had become anyone's business but his own.

Silence fell over the men as all eyes landed upon him. James squirmed in his seat and gave his brandy his full attention, turning the glass slowly on the table. Heat burned up his neck beneath his cravat.

"Oh, bloody hell," Blackbourne said. "You will have to tell us Bowen, as clearly Ridgemont is as in the dark regarding the lady's name as we are."

James met Mr. Bowen's gaze. He would not speak her name. Could not. To do so would be to admit his failure to rid himself of the unwelcomed effect she'd had on his heart and mind. But Mr. Bowen knew. James could see it in the hint of sympathy found in the slight upturn at the corner of his mouth.

James sighed and gave a slight nod.

"Miss Temperance Lindwell," Bowen said, the name delivered quietly so as not to reach beyond their table. Just as well, as the effect of speaking her name had rendered the rest of his cohorts silent. Dumbstruck, if the expressions on their collective faces were any indication.

"A-ha!" Glenmor slapped the table. "Capital choice. I like her. I don't care if she is American."

"You like everyone, Ben." Blackbourne shot over to his brother-in-law, though the comment held a warmth Blackbourne reserved only for those closest to him.

Alex shook his head as if Mr. Bowen had spoken an unfamiliar language he could not make heads or tails of. "What the deuce, James? One of the Lindwells? And Temperance, at that? I would have thought a week in the lady's company would have been enough to swear you off her forever. Why, she all but cold-cocked you on the dance floor at Frontenac's party!"

James cleared his throat and lifted his brandy to his lips, wishing there was more left in the glass. He took a sip then muttered to his rapt audience. "Yes, well, I may have had a hand in pushing her in that direction."

Huntsleigh, always the most good-natured of the bunch, laughed uproariously and smacked the arm of his chair with such delight you'd have thought he'd paired the two of them together all along.

"Well, this is an interesting development." Blackbourne appeared equally as pleased by the idea as Huntsleigh and Glenmor, though his pleasure was delivered in a far more understated way with raised brows and a slight twitch of the lips. Hawksmoor's expression could only be described as ironically amused, while Alex...well, Alex continued to sit there, mouth agape, stupefied and horror-stricken in equal measure.

Mr. Bowen, for his part, gave no indication one way or the other as to his thoughts on the matter. Nothing unusual there. As able as Mr. Bowen was to read others, reading him required a language most did not speak.

James set his glass back onto the table and kept his focus on its dwindling contents. "As it turns out—" He stopped. How did he explain it to them? He couldn't even explain it to himself. There were so many things about Temperance to recommend her, but many of those, for the sake of her reputation, could not be mentioned here.

"Yes?" Hawk prompted. "You were saying? As it turns out, what?"

James cleared his throat again. If he didn't know better, Hawk was enjoying this far more than he should. Then again, he'd fallen for Mr. Bowen's housekeeper and caused quite the uproar when he married her, so, perhaps he was hoping to have someone else jump into the same pool as he, and deflect some of said uproar.

Then again, people expected The Hawk to behave outside the bounds of Society's expectations. James, on the other hand...well, he had always been the most proper of gentlemen, hadn't he?

"As it turns out," he continued. "Miss Lindwell is an intelligent and engaging companion. Had it not been for her quick thinking during our misadventure, it is quite possible things would have turned out much worse than they had. She even managed to save my life after I was rendered unconscious and our captors thought killing me was the best course of action."

Alex tilted his head to one side. "Is that it?"

Indignation rose in James. "Is that it? I hardly think saving my life is a small matter."

"She saved your life?" Huntsleigh's smile softened somewhat and he sat back in his chair and gave a firm nod. "Well then, that settles it, doesn't it?"

"In what possible way does that settle anything?" Alex asked.

Mr. Bowen looked across the table at the future Duke of Franklyn. "Who among us here has not been saved by the woman we now call our wife?"

Murmurs and nods echoed around the table, until even Alex groaned in defeat, because the truth was, Mr. Bowen had the right of it, and every man sitting at the table knew it.

Alex turned to James. "If this is true, then why the devil did you not take Lindwell up on his insistence that you marry her when you had the chance? Why did you allow Lady Dalridge to convince him not to seek recompense? No one would have looked askance if you had agreed to marry her then. It would have been looked upon as the gallant thing, albeit unfortunate. Now it will look as if you *want* to marry her."

The only problem James saw with Alex's suggestion was the uncomfortable truth that he *did* want to marry her. The first time he'd proposed, it had been because he deemed it necessary to protect her reputation. But each time after that, it became less and less about necessity and more and more out of want. Something about the idea simply...fit. He couldn't explain it, not in words. He only knew that when he issued the proposal he had been certain he would never regret it.

But Temperance had not shared his certainty. She envisioned a life with him akin to wearing a garment that did not fit. One that would chafe and restrict and be a misery to wear. What other choice did he have but to let her go? And where did that leave him now?

James fisted his hand then opened it, staring down at his palm. He'd once been told you could read your future in the lines found there, but if that was true, it was a skill he did not possess.

"Rothbury makes a good point," Glenmor said. "Why did you not take the opportunity when it presented itself?"

"I did not want to press her into a situation she did not want."

"What woman does not want marriage?" Alex asked.

"This one," James told him, unable to help the smile that twitched the corners of his mouth. Despite her feelings and the reasons for them, he could not help but applaud her strength, her ability to stand up for the choices she had made, even if he believed the choice to be misguided and a product of past hurts. Even if it kept him from having what he most wanted. "She finds the idea of being some man's property an antiquated and undesirable future. She wishes to be free to make her own decisions, to affect change in the world and make it a better place."

"That's absurd," Alex said. "I always knew Americans had

some strange ideas, but surely she must know that a woman cannot change the world."

"Can they not?" Mr. Bowen asked. "Have they not already changed us? Altered our way of thinking and the manner in which we make our decisions?"

"Well, yes," Alex stuttered. "But...it's just that...Society will not allow it. She'll be ruined. Destroyed. She'll have far more power to make changes as the Marchioness of Ridgemont than as an unmarried woman, not to mention an American with whispers of scandal nipping at her heels."

"Then I guess we shall simply have to convince her of that, won't we," Blackbourne said.

James choked on his drink. "I beg your pardon?" When had winning over Temperance to his way of thinking become a group effort? She had made up her mind. And her mind was resolute. It could not be changed.

"We shall convince her that marrying you is in her best interests," Huntsleigh said. "Oh, I do love a little matchmaking. It makes for a far more interesting Season."

"Here, here," Glenmor said, lifting his glass in the air.

"Anything to make a Season in London more palatable is good in my books," Hawksmoor answered with a shrug, lifting his glass to join the other two.

"To love then, gentlemen," Mr. Bowen said, adding his glass. The rest followed suit, even Alex, though it took a nudge from Huntsleigh as, clearly, he was still trying to overcome the news that his best friend had fallen madly in love with his American cousin.

James shook his head. These men had no idea what they were up against. "She's very stubborn in her opinions," he warned.

"My good man," Blackbourne said, setting his glass back on the table and leaning forward, a wide grin on his face. "If there is one thing we are well versed in, it is stubborn women with strong opinions. Now, relax and leave it to us."

"Lord Plimpton is a completely respectable gentleman, titled and willing to offer for you despite the whispers currently circling with respect to your reputation," Father said, his voice rising with each word spoken.

Temperance refused to back down. She would not marry the man; she didn't care what whispers circled around her or what title he held. She could not imagine a more horrible fate than to marry a man she did not know and definitely did not love. The only thing that could possibly make it worse would be if James married Lady Charlotte, forcing Temperance to spend the rest of her days watching the two of them prance about happy as...as... well, she didn't know what, but she didn't want to see it. Thinking about it was torturous enough.

She turned to her father. "I expect Lord Plimpton has as much say in this supposed offering as I do. It is his stepfather that is pushing the marriage and we both know it. And while I concede that Lord Plimpton is not as horrible a man as his stepfather, he allows his Lord Willanthorpe to lead him about by the nose without argument. Such a man will never stand up for me, or for any of my needs or beliefs. I will not marry him and that is final."

"Then you leave me no other option, Temperance. I will give you a fortnight to reconsider your choice. If you do not change your mind with respect to marrying Lord Plimpton by that time, I shall have no other recourse but to make good on my earlier promise and cut you off financially. I will have no other association with you."

"Just as you did Daniel?"

Her mother, who had sat quietly in their parlor as she and

Father battled back and forth, sucked in a breath at the mention of their eldest son, but made no move to contradict her husband.

This wasn't the first time her father had used the threat of cutting off one of his children. And when it came down to pulling the trigger, he'd held firm to his word. Daniel had refused to join Father's business. He had longed for adventure. For freedom to be his own man, forge his own path. Upon receiving his refusal, Father had cut him off. Turned his back on Daniel as if he'd never existed.

Temperance understood the desire for freedom. She was more like her oldest brother than her parents realized. Or perhaps they did realize and that was why they tried to hold on so tightly. They did not want to lose another one. But their suffocating grip, their insistence of having things the way they wanted, regardless of the cost, was the one thing that had made Daniel leave. But as a man, he'd been free to do so. To make his way in the world.

What would she do, if it came to that? Where would she go? The school was no longer an option. At least not while the rumors of what might have happened between her and James were still being whispered behind fluttering fans and gloved hands. Returning to New York wasn't an option either. Nothing awaited her there save the remnants of the scandal her broken engagement had caused. And likely Father would punish Collin, should he take her in.

The very harsh reality of her situation weighed down upon her. She was wedged between an unwanted marriage and...what? Poverty? Living on the street like a pauper? When Father turned his back, he did so completely. Daniel could attest to that, if only she knew where her brother was.

"I have made my decision," Father said, the words cutting through the room. "Two weeks, Temperance. No more."

She swallowed. What would she do now?

After her father quit the room, Temperance sat quietly staring down at her hands. Could she hire herself out as a governess? Would that even be possible with the hint of scandal that wafted around her? A maid? What did she know of the work they did? Perhaps she could find another school that might take her on for room and board?

"Your brother is in New York," her mother whispered.

Temperance looked up, having forgotten her mother was still in the room. "Yes, I know." Collin had taken over running the businesses while Father was in London hoping to repair the family's reputation.

Mother shook her head and reached into her pocket. She pulled out a letter and held it toward Temperance. "No. Not Collin. Daniel."

"What?" Temperance slowly reached for the letter. She opened the folded vellum and read the contents, written by Collin as told to him by his older brother. "Daniel has been in Canada?"

"Yes, some place called Halifax." Her mother worried her hands, her concern for her firstborn evident in the lines on her face. How difficult it must have been for her when her husband banished Daniel from their family, as if he were expendable. As if they all were, if they did not do his bidding. How telling that she'd had no recourse to countermand his decision. Was that not Temperance's biggest fear?

"Where is Halifax?"

"In Nova Scotia, on the Atlantic coast, but Collin says he plans to purchase land and raise sheep, of all things." Her mother waved a hand in the air as if to dismiss the idea as utter nonsense.

Temperance could not help but smile. Daniel had always been enterprising and did not shy from hard work as their father often accused. He'd simply wished to work hard toward what he wanted to do. She continued to read the letter. Her brother planned on coming to England, to investigate the venture. To determine the viability of selling premium wool to textile plants at home and abroad, hence the reason for his visit to New York, and his hope that Collin would agree to invest.

"Collin says he'll be in New York until June, then he'll return to Halifax?" Oh, how she longed to see her brother once more. It had been years and she missed him dearly.

Mother nodded. "Yes."

June. It was already mid-April. If Halifax was on the ocean, surely it had a port of some sort. Temperance had enough pin money saved she could easily buy passage on the next ship across the Atlantic. In fact, she believed Lord Huntsleigh's family had a large interest in a fleet of ships. Perhaps she could speak to him—discreetly, of course—and see what could be arranged.

Daniel would take her in, of that she had no doubt. They'd always shared a special bond and before he'd left, he'd promised one day he would come back for her should she ever need him.

Well, now she needed him.

Would Constance come with her? A heaviness weighed upon Temperance's heart. Not likely. Constance was not the adventurous sort. Her sister and Collin had always been the peacemakers of the family and as such, she would stay behind and do Father's bidding. She would marry a man of his choosing and consign herself to that life whether it made her happy or not. And if it did not, she would keep it to herself. That was just her way.

It broke Temperance's heart to think of the misery that awaited her sweet-tempered sister. Could she possibly convince her to take a risk and come home with her? To travel to this place called Halifax and join Daniel in his venture? To embrace freedom and map out their own life?

She had to at least try. But first, she would speak to Lord

Huntsleigh. They were attending Lord Potterfield's party this evening. Hopefully his lordship would be in attendance and agree to speak to her. If he could offer her assistance, she would send word to Collin and Daniel of her plans and set about convincing Constance to join her.

"May I keep the letter, Mother?"

Her mother nodded. "Your father has not seen it. Likely that is for the best. You know how he can be when it comes to your brother."

Indeed she did. It was all too similar to the way she had just been treated. With stubbornness and ultimatums.

"Thank you, Mother." Temperance rose and leaned in to kiss her mother on the cheek before she went in search of Constance, holding close to the hope she could convince her sister to join her on the ship that would send her across the ocean to a new and better life.

A life where she could reinvent herself and leave her wounded heart behind, buried with the memory of a special man that could never be hers.

It was for the best.

This life was never meant to be hers. She'd known it from the beginning, but she'd allowed her heart to gallop off into dreamland, thinking that maybe, just maybe...

She shook her head as she took the steps to the third floor. Foolishness. Despite James's offer to marry her, once he was presented with a way out to avoid such a fate, he'd taken it and moved on. Rumors abounded that a proposal to Lady Charlotte Overton would soon be in the offing. And who could blame him? After the heartbreak he'd suffered with the late Lady Rothbury, did he not deserve happiness? And Lady Charlotte was a lovely girl, though clearly struggling under the thumb of her uncle. A marriage proposal from James would be just the thing to rescue her from such a fate, and James certainly did have a penchant for rescuing damsels in distress.

What would he do if he knew the distress she now faced?

Temperance pushed open the door to Constance's bedchamber with more force than necessary, as if she could sweep the recalcitrant thought away.

She did not need James to save her. She held tight to the letter in her hand. She would save herself.

Chapter Eighteen

"Ladies Blackbourne and Glenmor?"

Temperance stared at the cards Horace had handed to her on the silver salver. She had come in search of Horace to post a letter to Collin, to inform him of her plans. She'd already approached Constance about the idea, but her twin was far less enthused about the notion of escaping London than Temperance. She rather fancied the lords and ladies and held out hope she might fall madly in love with a gentleman and live happily ever after. It was a nice dream. A dream Temperance admitted still lingered inside of her, much as she wished to banish it in favor of a more sensible choice.

Regardless of Constance's wish to remain, there was nothing left in London for Temperance. If she wished to have any kind of life, she must start anew somewhere else. And she must not tarry, as Father's deadline loomed closer with each passing day.

Lord Plimpton was a simple man, a harmless one, but the idea of allowing anyone to have access to her body, to do the things to her James had done with such thoughtfulness and skill was beyond comprehension.

She simply could not fathom the idea.

"Miss?"

Temperance looked up at the butler who interrupted her wayward thoughts, the thick vellum calling cards held between her fingers. Surely, there was some mistake. Why would the Countess of Blackbourne pay her a call? She never had before. Nor had Lady Glenmor.

"And you're quite certain they wish to see me?"

Horace gave her a look. That particular look he liked to give any time his *American* employers asked what he clearly considered an uninformed and foolish question. "Indeed. Quite certain, miss."

"And you have seen them to the receiving room, then?"

Another look.

"Indeed." Horace drew the word out, lacing as much sarcasm into the two syllables allotted him as was humanly possible. Because what else would he do? It wasn't as if he'd leave the two countesses standing in the front hall.

"Then please have tea and biscuits sent—" She stopped because, well, the *look*. "Yes, of course, you already have. Very well, Horace. Thank you."

Temperance waited until Horace left her alone in the hallway before she pursed her lips in frustration. Of all the days for Mother to be under the weather, she had to choose this one. Likely if she knew who waited in their receiving room with only her eldest daughter to manage the visit, she'd throw an apoplectic fit. Mother had little faith in Temperance's willingness or ability to curry the favor of the aristocracy.

Granted, given her past behavior, she couldn't fault Mother for her opinions. Still, with Constance visiting Lady

Walkerton newly returned from her honeymoon, Temperance was the only one who could receive the ladies.

She pressed her hands against the deep blue of her dress, straightening the skirt before marching down the hall to see what this was all about.

Temperance entered the room, forcing a pleasant smile. "Lady Blackbourne, how lovely to see you. And you, as well, Lady Glenmor. To what do I owe this unexpected pleasure?"

Not that either of the ladies needed to explain to Temperance what brought them to her receiving room, and likely it was rude of her to even question their arrival, but curiosity got the better of her.

Lady Blackbourne smiled at Temperance, the warmth of the expression taking her by surprise. "We wished to see for ourselves that you were well after your ordeal. Lady Hawksmoor sends her well wishes and regrets. She had wanted to join us but was feeling poorly."

"Nothing serious, I hope?"

Lady Glenmor laughed, a deep, rich sound. "Nothing that won't remedy itself in about six months I would think."

"Ah." A baby. Temperance tried to imagine Lord Hawksmoor as a father. Now that would be something to see. Then again, there had been a marked difference in him since his recent marriage. "Well, please give her my heartfelt congratulations."

Lady Glenmor took a sip of the tea Horace had seen fit to send to the room before he tracked down Temperance to notify her of the visitors. Despite the man's barely disguised contempt of his employers, he was quite adept at his job.

"I suspect you can tell her yourself soon enough. I doubt she will stay hidden away from friends and family."

"I'm not sure I rank as either."

"Nonsense," Lady Blackbourne said. "Madalene considers

you a particular friend. I think having come from outside the ton, she feels a particular kinship with you. As does Lady Rothbury. You are, after all, related to her husband's side of the family."

"Distantly," Temperance reminded her. "And to enough degree it is a tenuous connection at best."

Lady Glenmor laughed, the motion transforming her normally serious expression into one of brightness and levity. "Good heavens, Miss Lindwell. One would think you didn't want us here. I do hope that is not the case. I promise, we come for the best of reasons."

"To see that I am well?"

"Yes. It was a frightful ordeal you suffered. We were all very worried, for both you and Lord Ridgemont."

"But mostly James."

Lady Blackbourne raised one blonde eyebrow sharply at the use of James's given name. "My goodness, Ridgemont was right. You do speak your mind quite freely."

But if this put the lady out, Temperance could find no indication of it in her open and engaging smile. Regret immediately filled her. "Forgive me. I am being a terrible hostess. You shall wish you'd never come at all if I keep this up."

"Nonsense," Lady Glenmor said. She placed her teacup into its saucer and set both on the small table between them. "Abigail and I both know all too well how cruel some members of Society can be. And I know they have not always been kind to you and your family. Now, with this latest tribulation, it only fans the fires. The ton does like its gossip."

Her last statement came delivered with a wry twist of the lips. Temperance could not help but like Lady Glenmor's straightforward and sensible manner. Under different circumstances, she had no doubt they would have been great friends.

"Which is one of the two reasons we are here," Lady Blackbourne said.

Temperance shook her head. "I'm afraid I don't—"

"Please, call me Abigail. All my friends do."

The lady's quick inclusion of Temperance into this group, when she really had no cause to, reached inside and touched a spot on her heart. She had done her best to ignore the lingering loneliness that came when her former friends gave her the cut direct after she ended her association with Beauregard. Now, here were two ladies she could not help but hold in high esteem, offering an olive branch, of sorts.

It embarrassed Temperance how badly, and how quickly, she reached out to grab it. "Very well, then. Abigail."

"And you must call me Judith. Enough of all this ceremony. It becomes so tedious at times."

"Now, to the reason we are here." Abigail leaned forward, her hands poised on her knees. She was smaller than Temperance, yet something about her gave off an aura of strength, as if her bones were made of the strongest iron.

"And that reason would be?" Temperance took a sip of her own tea before it grew cold.

"Convincing you to marry our dear friend, Lord Ridgemont."

Temperance choked on her tea, causing Judith to stand and reach over to remove the cup from her hands before she upended its contents onto her lap.

Judith laughed. "Heavens, one would think the thought had never crossed your mind."

She cleared her throat but her words still croaked out. "It hadn't."

"Temperance Lindwell," Judith said, standing up straight and taking full advantage of her height. "You are a horrible liar. I cannot imagine there is any way that you did not consider such a thing. His lordship is a formidable man, but also warm and lovely. I think it would be most difficult for a lady to spend time with him and not fall in love."

"You didn't," Temperance countered, having been told by

Judith's cousin, Lady Walkerton, that her guest had come to London as paid companion to Lady Rothbury, living in the same house as James.

"Yes, well," Judith sat down once more and smiled. "My heart was fully occupied by another, I'm afraid. Otherwise, I expect I would have been quite smitten."

"I assure you, I am not smitten." What she was went far deeper than that.

"Don't be silly," Judith said in that no-nonsense tone she had.

"I am not being silly. And regardless, I am not planning on staying in London." Oh, bother! She did not mean to blurt that out.

"Not staying? Is your family returning to America?" Abigail leaned forward. "I had not heard this news."

"No, not my family," Temperance admitted. "Just me. I am hoping to take passage on one of Lord Ellesmere's ships to join my brother. He's settling in Nova Scotia—"

Abigail's face scrunched up in confusion. "Nova what?"

"Scotia," Judith said, turning to her sister-in-law. "It is in Canada."

"Yes," Temperance said. "My eldest brother is planning on settling there. I thought I might join him. I wish to get away from Society, to be honest. Escape from their silly whispers and gossip and high-minded ideas about what women should do and be."

"And that is what you truly want?"

"Yes, of course it is." In part. She had no use for the ton's way of using gossip as a weapon, slinging it about with no regard for the damage their words caused.

But even as the admission slipped out, another want pushed its way to the forefront, tormenting her with its titillating possibilities. The dream of a future that found her curled up by a fire discussing all matter of things with James.

Of nights wrapped in his arms, their bodies tangled in passion. Of growing old with a man who was both lover and friend and equal.

She shook her head in an attempt to dislodge the silly dream. She'd held a dream similar to that once before, though that dream had been steeped in the innocence of youth and inexperience. But its end had taught her the reality of life. The fact that dreams had no bearing on the day to day, and that men would do as they wished, and a lady's heart had no part in the equation.

No, such marriages proliferated Society, be it London or New York, and did not allow for happiness. Or love. And definitely not equality.

Yet, such reasoning faltered as she sat across from the two ladies that had come to pay a call. Neither of them appeared restricted or unhappy. And as she had seen both of them with their respective husbands, she could attest that it was not a look of ownership Lords Blackbourne and Glenmor bestowed upon their wives, but rather love and devotion.

But, surely, that was an anomaly.

Wasn't it?

Temperance shook her head. It mattered not. James had made up his mind. He'd allowed her to refuse his offer of marriage and then turned his attentions toward another. Likely, by now he'd set aside any thoughts he had about her and the time they'd spent together.

Abigail released a short, sharp breath. "Oh, fiddlesticks. That is disappointing. Hen was so looking forward to calling you sister."

"Well, I suppose Lady Rothbury will have to settle for Lady Charlotte instead," Temperance said.

Another sigh from Abigail as she sat back into the sofa, all proper posture forgotten. "Yes, I suppose."

"You do not approve of Lady Charlotte?"

Abigail waved a hand. "Oh, she's a lovely lady, truly she is. But her uncle is an absolute ogre. I do not trust him one whit, nor do I like the idea of our friends sharing that particular association. Can we not convince you to stay? To at least consider the possibility of—"

"No." Temperance said, cutting off the idea before it had time to take root. One heartbreak in a lifetime was enough. "I am firm in my decision."

She had to be. James had made up his mind and allowed Temperance hers. This was what she had wanted. The freedom to make her own choices. And she had chosen to let James live the life he was born to, while she moved away from London to start anew.

Nothing remained here for her but a forced marriage to Lord Plimpton and watching James fall in love with a woman far more suited for him than she.

"Very well, then," Abigail sighed. "But at least promise me you will attend my party later this week."

Temperance shook her head. "I beg your pardon?"

Abigail released a small laugh. "Oh, I know it is short notice, but I have decided to turn a small affair into a big one."

Lady Glenmor smiled warmly at her companion. "My sister-in-law has a habit of impromptu decisions. But we do hope you and your family will attend. You will, won't you?"

A tingle of anticipation tripped down Temperance's spine. Likely James would be there. It would allow her a chance to say good-bye, one last time. And to give him something she'd been holding onto for far too long.

"Yes. Of course. I would be honored to attend your party."

"Leave London? Whatever are you talking about?" James set his glass down on the table in the games room of Sheridan House and stared first at Lord Huntsleigh, then Glenmor, then the rest of the men circled around the table. Surely, they were mistaken. What they said made no sense.

He had told the group repeatedly that the idea of convincing Temperance to marry him was doomed to failure, but clearly, when Lords Blackbourne, Huntsleigh, Glenmor, Hawksmoor, and Mr. Bowen got an idea into their collective heads, there was no talking them out of it. To make matters worse, the gentlemen had taken to calling themselves the *Lords of Love*. Although, to their credit, Mr. Bowen and Hawksmoor had winced and cringed respectively when Huntsleigh had applied the moniker. Yet they had still managed to recruit the assistance of the very proper Lord Walkerton, recently returned from his extended honeymoon to Italy, who thought it would be *great fun*.

Great fun? How one could consider setting themselves up to be summarily rejected for the umpteenth time to be *fun* stepped beyond his ability to comprehend. Only Alex had remained steadfast in his refusal to take part in the other lords' matchmaking mania.

Not that it mattered. As now it appeared Temperance was throwing a permanent wrench in their plans by leaving London altogether.

He shouldn't be surprised she would resort to such drastic measures.

Lady Charlotte had made it clear to him that Lindwell and her uncle, Lord Willanthorpe, planned on pawning the latter's stepson off onto Temperance. The thought of her marrying such a simpleton as Lord Plimpton had made the requirement for a stiff drink essential, leading him to the games room in the first place. Now that he was here, the matter only became worse. She was leaving London.

That was not something a glass or two of brandy could wash away.

"She specifically asked me if any of the Ellesmere fleet would be sailing to Nova Scotia in the next two weeks," Huntsleigh said, expanding on his initial information.

James shook his head. "Nova Scotia? That makes no sense. Her family is from New York." Clearly, they were mistaken in both their information and their interpretation of what it meant.

Glenmor and Huntsleigh exchanged a look. The kind of look that told James he was the one mistaken and whatever they were about to tell him, he was not going to like. At all.

"What is it?"

Glenmor twisted his mouth to one side. "After Miss Lindwell questioned Huntsleigh about the ship, we sent Abby and Judith over to pay a call."

"You sent Ladies Blackbourne and Glenmor to the Lindwells?" He shook his head at the expression that must have rested upon Mrs. Lindwell's face when the two Count-esses arrived on her doorstep.

"Well..." Blackbourne shrugged. "More like we couldn't keep Abby away. Judith went along to ensure she didn't give away our plan or stick her foot in her mouth."

James leaned forward. "And what plan might that be?"

"Getting the two of you together, of course," Hawksmoor answered. "Have you not been listening?"

James sat back and shook his head. "The lot of you needs to give up in that regard. It is clear such is not going to happen. Especially now with her plans to leave!"

Hawk shot him a hard look. "And why wouldn't she plan to leave? Do you think she wishes to stay only to be forced into a marriage with Plimpton? Nice enough man, I grant you, but dumb as a post, I'm afraid."

James shuddered at the thought. "Of course not." A woman of Temperance's intelligence and liveliness would never consign herself to such a fate. Why, if he stared such a fate down, he'd do anything he must to escape—

"Ah, I see the dawning of realization," Mr. Bowen said, speaking for the first time since James had sat down.

"Bloody hell." She really was leaving.

Glenmor nodded. "Exactly."

"Has she purchased a ticket?"

"I do not know for certain," Huntsleigh said.

"Well, isn't there a passenger manifest or something?" Panic rose in his throat. Temperance was not the type to sit idle while others tried to force her life down a path she did not wish to take. Hadn't he learned that the hard way?

"Of course, but—"

"Well, check it man!"

Heads of nearby gentlemen turned their way but James cared little. His world had shifted and part of it threatened to fall away. He should have acted sooner. He should have done something. Anything! Instead, he'd brooded about and bided his time, part of him hoping she would come to her senses. Or that the feelings she evoked within him would fade. Neither of those things had happened. He loved her now as much as he had when they had been abducted and forced together. And Temperance had not come to her senses.

"I did check it," Huntsleigh said, bringing James's attention back to the present. "The only lone female traveling on *The Caelie* is a Mrs. Bromley."

Bromley? "Bloody hell."

"What is it?" Mr. Bowen asked.

James closed his eyes and pinched the bridge of his nose. "That's her."

Blackbourne looked confused. "Are you certain?"

James nodded and pressed harder. "That is the name I used when we reached the village. We..." He cleared his throat. "We posed as a married couple to avoid any sense of impropriety."

Huntsleigh let out a bark of laughter and slapped the arm of his chair as if James had just told him the most amusing of tales. When James finally opened his eyes, he found the men smiling broadly at him, even Mr. Bowen.

"Well, I hope it worked as well for you as it did me," Huntsleigh said.

"Clearly it did not as Miss Lindwell is planning a trip across the ocean to escape me."

"Not you," Hawksmoor pointed out. "Plimpton. Perhaps if she was given another option, she might stay."

"I did give her another option. Repeatedly," he reminded them. "She did not care to take it and has obviously not changed her mind in that regard. She despises London and the aristocracy and wants nothing to do with any of us. Clearly."

Mr. Bowen shook his head. "Good God, Ridgemont. Do you always give up so easily in matters of the heart? Have you never considered the idea that you may need to woo her? Or did you simply expect your title would be enough to convince her what a good husband you'd be?"

The gentleman's pointed observation knocked the wind out of him. The truth had a way of doing that to a man. When faced with fighting for love, he *had* always backed away. He had not fought for Ruth's affection, nor had he mounted any true resistance when Temperance made it clear she thought matrimony akin to servitude. He told himself it was for the best. That he did not wish to badger them into a relationship they did not wish to be a part of. But was that the whole truth?

Or was the real truth that he had been a coward? That he

had deemed the pain of rejection too high a price to pay? At the time, he'd thought so. But now, he wasn't so sure. What if he had fought harder? Argued his case better? It wouldn't have saved Ruth. She'd already given her heart to another.

But now he'd been given a second chance and he'd mucked it up in stellar fashion. Of course, Temperance had rejected him. And why wouldn't she? She feared being ignored, treated as an inferior. Then he had gone and lorded his superiority over her during their dance to such a degree she'd introduced her palm to his face.

Was it any wonder his first attempts to convince her marriage to him was a good idea had failed? No. And how hard had he really tried? Not as hard as he should have, that much was obvious. Instead, he'd let her have her opinions and offered little in the way of refutation. It had been easier than allowing himself to relive the heartbreak of being overlooked. Passed over. Easier than falling into despair at not having his feelings returned. He'd done that once and the fear of suffering through such a loss a second time was enough to make him step back, to let Temperance draw a line and he not cross it.

He'd thought it would be easier that way. That the hurt would brush past him like a shadow without burrowing deep and taking root.

He'd been wrong.

So horribly, horribly wrong.

And now she was leaving London forever. Leaving him.

It was no less than he deserved.

Chapter Nineteen

"Are you nervous about this evening?" Constance whispered, slipping her arm through Temperance's as the carriage conveyed them from Mayfair to Grosvenor Square.

"No, of course not." Which was a lie, of course. How could she not be? Temperance pressed the pale blue of her skirt down with her gloved hands. "I am simply not looking forward to this evening."

She did not bother to elaborate as to the why, especially with Mother and Father sitting across from them. Temperance dreaded the idea of saying good-bye to James. But to admit such to Constance would be folly. Knowing her sister, she would counsel Temperance to throw caution to the wind. To embrace love and tell James how she truly felt.

But that was only because her sister believed in the fairy tale. She believed true love would always win out in the end. And perhaps it did, if both parties shared said love. Unfortunately, such was not the case, as evidenced by James's newly blossoming courtship of Lady Charlotte. It hardly seemed sporting of Temperance to insert herself into the middle of that now, after having made it clear to James, she would not marry him enough times he had given up all hope of a future together.

If that had ever been a hope he'd harbored. She no longer believed it to be so. She wasn't sure if she ever did. Sentiments expressed did not always equal sentiments felt. After all, had Beauregard not claimed love and undying affection? He'd lavished her with sugarcoated words, poesies, and ribbons. None of which meant a single thing in the end, save to pull the wool over her eyes so she would not see whom he truly was.

"Temperance?"

She gave herself a mental shake. "I am fine, Constance. Truly."

They both knew it to be a lie, but thankfully, her sister let the answer stand. Perhaps she understood how desperately Temperance needed to believe in it, just for this moment. Just long enough to get her through this evening. To say good-bye to James and return his father's watch to him.

The ride to Sheridan House seemed interminable, each turn of the wheels and bump of the cobblestones counting down to the inevitability of this good-bye. Temperance had always despised good-byes. Endings of any sort, really. It was as if a possibility once hoped for had been irretrievably lost.

"Quit looking so downcast, Temperance. You must smile prettily and for heaven sakes, please keep your foolish opinions to yourself," Father said, glaring at her from the other side of the plush seats. "Plimpton is a viscount and this is the first titled gentleman that has shown any interest in either of you."

But her father's harsh words had little impact on Temperance. Her heart had gone numb to his cruel criticisms. If only she could make it do the same to the thought of losing James forever.

Her heart let out a painful throb reminding her such would never be the case.

That did not bode well for the rest of the evening.

Once they arrived at Lord and Lady Blackbourne's party, Father quickly begged off, likely to hunt down Lord Willanthorpe to complete whatever foolish deal they had conjured up with respect to her and Lord Plimpton.

Temperance sighed as she looked out from the edge of the ballroom at the throng of lords and ladies milling about her. Most of them held tepid relationships with each other, but the tightly knit group of friends that made up Lord and Lady Blackbourne's inner circle were different. They were like family, tightly entwined in each other's lives. The stories of what they had shared, the ties that bound them, were all but legend now, bandied about whenever large groups congregated to the point it was difficult to tell what was truth and what was fiction.

What it must be like to be a member of that particular circle. Temperance missed having such close friendships. Then again, her previous friendships had been nothing more than a mirage, hadn't they? Because the moment Beauregard's family made it clear she and her family were no longer desirable company, such relationships had quickly disappeared into the ether as if they had never existed.

Temperance did not look forward to returning to New York, no matter how briefly. The place held nothing but the residue of heartbreak and disappointment. Hopefully Daniel would not tarry long and they would soon be off to Nova Scotia. To her new life.

She just had to get through this final event before leaving London the day after next. Temperance had already packed her trunk, though no one had noticed save for Constance, who chose not to speak of it, almost as if her silence might prevent the day from coming.

She had taken only what was necessary. Such frills and fripperies that she trounced about in the ballrooms of London would be of no use to her in Nova Scotia. She'd packed only what would be serviceable, the dress she'd taken from the cottage she and James had shared, tucked away safely inside.

Would she ever be able to wear it without thinking of him? Unlikely. Then again, she thought of him regardless, so it hardly seemed to matter what she wore.

"You must stop sighing, Temperance," Mother scolded. "At least attempt to look like you are enjoying yourself. No one likes a sourpuss. Such behavior will not endear you to Lord Plimpton."

Temperance gritted her back teeth to prevent the sharp retort that sat like a barb on the end of her tongue. It mattered not what Lord Plimpton thought. Whatever plans her father and Lord Willanthorpe were conjuring would never come to fruition. She would be long gone by then. Far away from London.

And from James.

Her heart gave an agonizing beat. Would that ever go away?

No, the recalcitrant organ whispered back at her.

"Mother, I think I might like to take a turn about the room. Do you mind?"

"I do not think you should go traipsing about alone, my dear. I shall accompany you."

"Don't be silly," Temperance said, placing a restraining hand on her mother's arm. "Thanks to you and Father, everyone assumes my engagement to Lord Plimpton is all but complete. Constance, however, is a different story. You should stay with her. She is far more likely to garner a gentleman's attention than me."

Torn between her two daughters, her mother looked from one to the other until Constance spoke up. "Temperance is right, Mother. And I think I witnessed Lord Thatchbrook giving me a most agreeable look."

Temperance offered her sister a grateful smile then slipped away into the crowd before her mother could object. She needed room to breathe, to think, to say good-bye to the few friends she'd made in the time she had been in London.

To say good-bye to James.

Perhaps it made no sense to rub salt into that particular wound, but she could not make herself go without a final good-bye. Without letting him know she was leaving for good. But she had something to give him and tonight would be her last chance.

What an odd idea that they would never again lay eyes upon each other. Or lips. Or hands.

She shook her head. Heavens, this ballroom was warm. She needed an escape, a place she could sit quietly with her thoughts. A chance to shore up her courage so that she would not falter. Temperance made her way to the doors that led out toward the garden and slipped through the opening onto the terrace and down the stone steps.

She did not breathe until she found the shadows next to the grand townhouse. Ah, freedom. And yet, even that did not hold the fulfilling promise she had expected it once would. Instead, it felt...lonely. Is this what life in Nova Scotia would be like? Doubt crept into her veins and bled through her system. Was she making a most horrible mistake?

"Good evening, Miss Lindwell."

Temperance turned around, startled, her breath catching in her throat.

James stood on the edge of the shadows, resplendent in his evening finery, the white of his cravat stark against the black of his jacket and breeches. The midnight cast of his hair was silvered by the moonlight above. His eyes, bright despite the dark, twinkled as they often did with a hint of mischief. What a rascal he must have been as a young boy. The thought made her smile.

"James. What are you doing out here?"

He raised one eyebrow. "I might ask you the same thing. I hope it is not on my account."

She did not answer. She wasn't quite sure how to. It wasn't so much him she avoided, but her feelings for him. The tangled, twisted mess that they—*she*—had made of things. And the niggling sense that the choice she had made, the action she stood poised to take, would haunt her for the rest of her life.

"Hm," he said with a nod. "I shall take that as a yes."

"Do not take it personally."

He laughed. "It is hard not to. Shall I leave you alone then?"

Likely it would be less painful if he did. A clean break, as it were. The longer she spent in his company, the worse the pain of leaving became. But she could not make herself send him away. With her impending departure, each moment with him became precious, because it would be the last few she had. She wanted to say a proper good-bye. She needed to.

"No. Please, stay. Shall we sit?" She waved toward a low bench that lined the north edge of the garden. It was out of sight of the terrace, giving them an opportunity to visit without fear of fanning the flames of gossip.

"I would like that." He escorted her to the bench and waited until she was seated before flipping out the tails of his jacket and sitting next to her, not close enough to touch, yet not so far away that she couldn't feel the heat of his body reach out to touch hers. What an odd intimacy that was, to feel one another without touching.

"Are you enjoying yourself this evening, my lord?"

"No, not particularly. You?" He did not look at her when he spoke, but rather stared at the far wall of Sheridan House.

She did the same, mentally tracing the intricate stone and growing ivy that wound through the crevices to crawl upward to the balcony above. It was easier that way. The more she looked at James, the less sure she was about her decision to go, and she could not afford to falter now. She'd had her chance and refused it. A shadow passed across the window above, catching her attention before disappearing. A maid preparing the room for the night? The children's nanny perhaps?

Children. Another avenue her choices closed her off from. Sadness and regret pressed against her.

She swallowed and answered James's question. "You found me hiding in the shadows, my lord. I believe that should answer your question."

He laughed quietly and his gaze dropped to the ground in front of him. Oh, how she wished he would look at her. That she could feel the warmth of his gaze upon her. See the possibility of a different kind of future in his eyes. A future she had once feared, but that now no longer caused her such hesitation. Perhaps if it had been anyone else but James, that fear would rear its ugly head. A future with Lord Plimpton made her want to board the ship to the new world without a look back. But the idea of leaving James had her dragging her feet. Second guessing. Wishing she had enough courage to tell him how she truly felt. That she had changed her mind.

But it was too late for such things, wasn't it?

Since her arrival this evening, she had heard constant whispers and supposition that an impending announcement that he and Lady Charlotte would be affianced before the end of the Season was imminent. It had been enough to smother the rumors of what might have happened between them during their captivity. The ton, it was clear, had made their choice of whom they thought James should marry.

And it was not she.

Temperance had lost her chance. She had allowed her own reticence—her fear—to shut the door on the possibility that life with James would be different. Because James was a different man than the ones she had known. He was nothing like Beauregard. Nothing like her father.

James had treated her with respect. Protected her. Listened to her views, countered with his own, and engaged her in lively discussions of both. He did not belittle her strength or consider her inconsequential. Nor had he given her any indication these things would change should they marry. Because that was who James was. Open and honest, good to his very core.

He had been hurt before. She could see it in his eyes. He understood heartbreak and loss and yet he did not shy away from facing such again if the chance for something greater came his way.

Oh, if only she hadn't been so blind to this at the time. If only it hadn't taken time away from him to realize what a true gem of a man he was. Endless days and agonizing nights of wishing she could feel his arms around her. His body molded against hers. The heat of his passion. The sweetness of his smile. His wit. His charm.

God help her, she was such a fool! Was she too late? Did the slim possibility exist that maybe, just maybe, he might still harbor some feelings for her? He was here, after all? Didn't that speak well for them?

Temperance balled up her courage. "James—"

"Sometimes I miss being in captivity," he said suddenly, speaking over the whisper of his name. "Is that a strange thing to admit?"

She swallowed the rest of what she had been about to say, his claim taking her by surprise. "Yes, I believe it is. We could have died, after all."

James turned to look at her, a wry smile playing about his lips. Lips she wished to kiss, lips she wished to feel upon her skin, tracing a lazy trail of kisses that drove her near mad with wanting. "That part I do not miss. But I miss the simplicity of it. We had but two objectives—to escape and to make our way home."

"And you liked that sort of life, did you? Simple and straightforward?"

"I did with you," he whispered.

The words sank into her, deep and without restraint, finding her weakness for this man, for the things he made her want. For the decimation of past beliefs that no longer held true. Was it possible? Could he be suggesting—

A branch cracked behind her, interrupting the thought. But before she could turn around, everything went black as something was thrown over her head. A hand clamped over her mouth, smothering her scream of protest. Another arm wrapped around her waist and hauled her backward over the low wall. Beside her, she heard James grunt. His struggle, knowing he had suffered the same fate. The rush of fear, the familiarity of it, tore through her without mercy, though less for her own safety and more for James. It was happening again. Their captors had returned!

Would they kill James this time if he fought too hard? She wanted to call out to him, but the hand over her mouth prevented her from doing so.

A silky material bound her hands and feet and from the now subdued struggle from James, she guessed he had met the same fate. Relief washed over her that they had not hurt him. She was tossed over someone's shoulder and within minutes dropped onto the soft squabs of a carriage that took off at a fast gait.

One of the men sat next to her and lightly pressed something cold and hard against her temple. "Not a bloody word from either of you, or I'll pop a bloody cork in your doxy 'ere and that'll be the end of it. Understood?"

Silence from James. Yet even bound and a hood pulled over her head, Temperance could feel the coiled strength within him waiting for the right moment. He would not act rashly. He would never put her at such risk. But he would act. He would do whatever he must to protect her. Even at his own peril.

She must keep him from doing so. She would not have his life, the loss of something she held most dear, on her conscience. This time, she would save his life.

Even if that meant forfeiting her own.

Chapter Twenty

How could this possibly be happening again? From the second the sack had been thrown over James's head and a firm hand clamped over his mouth, while two others yanked him backward off the low wall, it was that statement that kept running through his mind. He'd taken every precaution. Hired a man to watch over Temperance any time she left her house to ensure her safety. Looked over his own shoulder. Searched through the crowded London streets for the never-to-be-forgotten faces of their two abductors.

In his heart, he did not think they would be stupid enough to return to London and try again. They were not all that adept at their job and with their identities known, even those two bumbling idiots must know a second attempt was an asinine idea.

Besides, this felt different. Though James could not see anything, he clearly heard more than two voices, though each one had an odd twist to it, as if they were putting on accents not natural to their mother tongue. They sounded staged. And he was certain it took three men to subdue him, and at least one other to grab Temperance. And the carriage had pulled up as they were being dragged away, which added another.

None of this made sense. Had another group of idiots deemed kidnapping them a solid enterprise, tagging off the idea of the first two? Not a very intelligent group, if that was the case, given how the first abduction had fared.

If so, they had clearly upgraded. This carriage was no hackney. The seats were plush and comfortable. Or they would be if he wasn't trussed up like a pig about to be put on the spit.

"Might I ask just what the meaning of this is?"

"Did I not clearly indicate that you were not to speak a word or I'd—"

"Pop a cork in my doxy," James said, interrupting. "Yes. You did. But that would be rather counter-productive, wouldn't it?"

Silence.

"He does make a point," Temperance said, her voice even, though James recognized a hint of fear lacing through its firmness. "It would be rather difficult to claim a ransom on a corpse."

"I have no intention of—" Their abductor stopped then started again. "I ain't gonna kill ya unless I have to. So...don't make me have to."

"And how do you plan to do that?" Temperance asked. "Shoot us? In the middle of Grosvenor Square? Toss our bodies out onto the cobblestone and make your getaway? Honestly, you did not think this through very well, did you?"

"Bloody hell," their captor muttered, and to James it almost sounded as if the man was as much impressed as annoyed. This was a far different type of criminal than the first batch they'd encountered. But something was off, he just couldn't put his finger on it yet.

After a brief silence, ten minutes, perhaps a bit more, the

carriage slowed then came to a stop. Outside a brief discussion occurred, though it was held too far from the conveyance for James to make it out. Had they reached their destination? Had this batch of criminals learned from the mistakes of their predecessors that going too far from the source of the money had not ended well and was likely not the way to go?

"Where are we?"

"Shut yer yap."

"I shall not. We have a right to know what you are about and where we are being taken."

"Says who?" The accent briefly disappeared. It was obvious these captors had hoped to keep their prisoners from providing any identifying details.

The door to the carriage opened and the man inside with them kicked James's boot. "Git out."

"And where might *out* be exactly? In case you haven't noticed, I've a sack over my head."

A muttered curse and their captor raised his voice, presumably to garner the attention of one of his cohorts. "Might one of you help his lordship from the carriage?"

A hand grabbed his arm but James braced himself against seat as best he could and refused to be pulled away. "I have no intention of leaving you alone in this carriage with Miss Lindwell."

"Oh bloodiest of hells! I told you this was a dumb idea." James wasn't sure whom the man inside with them directed that remark to, but he wholeheartedly agreed. "Take her first then. I'll deal with him."

"What do you mean *deal with him*? You shall not harm him. I forbid it."

Outside the carriage, someone barked out a laugh. Inside, their traveling companion sucked in a deep breath as if to hold back his temper. "I cannot very well shove you both out the door at the same time, so unless one of you is willing to leave first, we shall be spending a very long time in here together. Given that, I heartily suggest you decide which of you it will be."

"Not I," Temperance said.

"Nor I," James seconded.

"What the deuce! Bloody...bloody...Argh!" Their captor shoved past them and the carriage rocked as he jumped down to join his cohorts outside. A muffled, somewhat heated conversation took place outside for several long moments.

"Do you not find this situation a bit odd?" Temperance whispered.

"Indeed. Although what I find most odd, is that we cannot seem to be abducted by a group of individuals who possess any proficiency in their chosen field. How difficult can it possibly be to abscond with two unsuspecting individuals?"

Good criminals were apparently very hard to find.

Unless—

The carriage rocked once more as one of their captors rejoined them. This one, if James was not mistaken, was heavier than the previous based on the way the carriage swayed.

"We have made a decision."

Definitely someone new. The voice was deeper. Familiar somehow, despite their attempt to disguise it. In both instances, their abductors went out of their way to speak in a more common tongue, but each time they slipped and revealed themselves.

"A decision?" Temperance asked. "Does this mean you have come to your senses and plan to release us?"

"No."

"No you have not come to your senses?"

"No! I mean—that is to say—Devil take it! What I mean is that we have no plan to release you. Either of you. And as you have decided neither of you will be the first to depart this godforsaken conveyance, we shall leave you both in here for the entirety of your stay with us. So you might as well get comfortable until you come to your senses!"

The carriage jostled again as their captor stormed out, the door slamming against its frame with a loud rattle. The sound of a chain being pulled through the outer handle echoed within.

"It appears they mean what they say," Temperance said.

"Indeed." James bent over as far as he could, stretching his fingers until he was able to grab the sack over his head and pull it off. Cool air rushed in to touch his exposed skin. "Ah, that's better. If you bend down you should be able to remove your hood."

Temperance followed his suggestion, the result mussing up her lovely coif and giving her a tumbled appearance. It reminded him of how she had looked back at the cottage the night they had made love. Though she looked far less satisfied now than she had then, if he did say so himself.

"Much better," she said.

The carriage jolted and rocked again. They were on the move.

"Bullocks," James muttered. He shimmied over toward the door and lifted his hands to open the window, but it was sealed shut and a black covering had been thrown over it from the outside, preventing him from seeing where they were or what their intended destination was.

When he turned back to Temperance, she was looking about the interior of the carriage. A small lantern hung in the far corner, casting a wavering light over the interior. Despite her disheveled appearance, James had never thought her more beautiful.

"Temperance—"

She cut him off before he could tell her.

"Does this not seem strange to you?"

"Being kidnapped? Twice? Yes, I would say it quite strange."

"Exactly. Except this time is much different and—" She waved her bound hands at the interior. "Our accommodations are much improved, in case you hadn't noticed. What kidnappers have such an expensive conveyance at their disposal?"

Before he could agree, she continued on.

"Also, it is clear that during the first instance, I was the intended target. You were merely a casualty of being in the wrong place at the wrong time."

"I happen to think I was in the right place," James countered. "If I hadn't been, you may have met a different fate."

Temperance sat back in her seat and for a fleeting second, it looked as if she might argue his account, but she surprised him instead with a smile. "Indeed, you are correct."

"I am?"

"Of course, and I thank you for that, truly."

"You do?"

"Have I not said that before?"

James shook his head.

"An oversight on my part," Temperance said. "You were very brave. It was a comfort having you with me. I felt safe and protected. I knew you would never allow harm to come to me."

Something in James's heart eased and he smiled. "I sincerely doubt you would have allowed any harm to come to yourself regardless. It was you, after all, that kept me alive until I was well enough to return the favor."

"It was my pleasure." The smile she gifted him with warmed him from the toes up and for a brief moment, he forgot that they sat inside yet another carriage, against their will, facing yet another abduction.

"But my point is," Temperance continued, drawing James back to their current reality. "I do not think the two instances are related. It is clear their intention this time was to take both of us. This group is larger than the first and they are comprised of gentlemen, in case you hadn't noticed. They've tried to disguise themselves with their foolish attempts at accents, but it is clear such is rubbish. I do not believe we are being kidnapped, my lord. Do you?"

James shook his head, marveling at how swiftly her mind worked. Most people would have panicked, been frozen with fear. But not his Temperance. Not this intelligent, beautiful, quick-witted woman he had quickly grown to love. And need.

"No, I do not."

"And I believe the first man who accompanied us in the carriage may have been Lord Hawksmoor. He has a certain way about him that is difficult to conceal."

"I believe you are correct in that assumption."

Temperance leaned forward. "You do not have any gambling debts owed the man, do you?"

"I assure you, I am not a gambler, Miss Lindwell."

"Then whatever is this about? Why would his lordship abduct us in such a fashion? What does he stand to gain? I had thought he'd reformed himself?" She sat back and shook her head. "Oh dear, Lady Hawksmoor will be heartbroken to know of this. Especially now that she is with child."

"Is she? I had not heard."

"It is most recent." Temperance shook her head in dismay. "This is most distressing."

As much as James did not care to let her in on what he believed Hawksmoor and his brethren, the *Lords of Love* were up to, he saw no way around it. Not now that they had taken such drastic measures. For all that was holy, what were they thinking? With both he and Temperance missing from the party for an extended duration at the same time, tongues would wag. There would be no preventing it. He must correct the situation and get her back to the ballroom with all due haste. Regardless of how hard it was to let her go, he would not have her forced into something she did not wish for.

"Well, you may rest assured, The Hawk has no nefarious intentions toward us." James wiggled his fingers to motion her to move closer. "Here, untie me and I shall explain."

Confusion and suspicion colored her expression, but she complied, adjusting her skirts as best she could and kneeling in front of him. "I cannot wait to hear this explanation."

"Yes, well, you see," James began as Temperance struggled with the slippery knot. "It appears the *Lords of Love*—"

She stopped and looked up. "The what?"

Bloody hell. This admission was going to make him look every bit the fool. Another reason to find himself a new group of friends. James cleared his throat. "I am afraid that Lords Blackbourne, Huntsleigh, Hawksmoor, Walkerton, Glenmor, and Mr. Bowen have gotten it into their heads to play matchmaker."

"Matchmaker? For us, you mean?" She stopped and looked up.

She sounded truly surprised by the idea. Did the two of them together strike her as so unusual; even after all they had shared? "Uh, yes. For us."

"I see." She held out her hands toward him. "Here, pull my gloves off. It shall make this easier."

He would much prefer to pull everything off of her, to feel her skin against his once more, the enticing warmth of their heat mingling together with promise and intent. Ah, such a wonder that was. James let out a slow breath. Perhaps one day.

Perhaps not.

She'd made no mention to him of her intended departure from London. Or any change of heart that might cause her to stay.

He pinched the gloves at the tip of her fingers and she pulled away, letting them slip down her arms and off her hands, tugging to get them to slip beneath the silk ties at her wrist.

James continued. "Unfortunately, it appears they have taken the matter a bit far in their hopes of success by concocting this mock kidnapping."

Temperance smiled as she untied his bindings. "I am surprised they would go through the trouble. I had not thought anyone wanted my family to attach themselves to any member of the aristocracy."

"Initially, I believe that was true. But it appears you have worn us down, my dear."

A brief laugh. "I see. Well, do not tell Mother and Father or you shall never rid yourselves of them."

She held up her own bindings for him to undo. James did not rush as she had. Instead, he lingered. Reveled in the sensation of being able to touch her once more. Such lovely, capable hands she possessed. Slim and dainty, deceiving in their strength, much like Temperance herself.

"If their finding out means we get to keep you, I am willing to take the risk." Her silk ties fell away and James lifted one hand and brought it to his lips placing a warm kiss upon her knuckles.

"James..."

But she said no more and when he lifted his gaze to hers, her smile remained but her eyes had turned sad. Wistful.

"Apologies." But he did not mean it. He was not sorry. Not at all.

She said nothing in response but pulled her hand away and reached into her pocket. "I have something for you."

His chuckled. "Indeed?"

She glanced up quickly from where she still sat on the floor of the carriage, catching the lewd tone that had danced around his response.

She laughed. "You, my lord, have an indecent mind. Is it

any wonder you keep such friends as the Lords of Love, as you call them?"

The sound of her laugh, deep and throaty, slid over him like liquid heat. He bent down, bringing his face closer to hers, breathing in her scent, a heady mix of wildflowers. "My dear, clearly you read too much into my inquiry, a clear indication it is you who entertains such indecent thoughts, not I."

She lifted one eyebrow but did not pull away, allowing the closeness. "I think that may be the brandy talking. I can smell it on your breath."

James could not look away. She mesmerized him, causing him to fall into the dark pools of her brown eyes. "Would you care for a taste, Miss Lindwell?"

Her eyes widened, as did the smile he had missed so dearly over the past weeks. "I think we both know it would never end with just a kiss. We seem quite incapable of being able to control our baser urges with each other."

"I find I quite love your baser urges, my dear. As much as I love you."

The admission slipped out before he could stop it, pulled from him into the safe cocoon that surrounded them. His heart leaped to his throat and his brain worked furiously to find a way to call the words back, but found none.

Temperance, for her part, had ceased all movements, like a deer frozen in place, waiting to see if it was friend or foe that had caught them unaware.

"You love me?" The words whispered out of her, quiet and unsure.

"I...that is to say..." Nonsensical words tumbled out of him. He wished to say the right thing, to allow a graceful way out of the situation he had suddenly pulled them into. But there was no way out. He had said it. He had admitted it aloud and there was no taking it back because it was what it was. He loved her. He did. "Yes. With all my heart."

Chapter Twenty-One

⁓

"Forgive me."

Temperance shook her head as James offered the apology. She did not want to hear it. Did not want him to take those precious words back. Because she understood the truth of them. Understood that James was not a man who offered such sentiment easily or without meaning. He was a man of honor and principle. He stood true to his word and his words spoken were truth.

He loved her.

Such a wonder. But the impact of such left her tongue-tied, unable to respond. There was so much to say. So many things to tell him. To admit to. Where did one start? Her hand, still in her pocket, squeezed the object she had held onto since their return to London. A keepsake she had told herself to return a hundred times over, but never found the right moment to do so. She pulled it from her pocket now and opened her hand, presenting it to him.

"My watch." The words slipped out of him in amazement. "How—? I don't understand. I had left it behind."

"I know, but I couldn't let you. Not on my account. It was

too precious to you. I could see that in the way you spoke of it. The way you would reach into your pocket and hold onto it when you were stressed or worried." So many little things about this man she had learned in such a short time. But so many others she had yet to discover.

"Temp..."

She rushed on. "I left my jewels instead. I didn't want you to be left with any regrets." Tears pricked at the corner of her eyes, emotions she had tried to keep at bay rushing forward. Because, she did not want him to regret. As horrible as being abducted was, something wonderful had blossomed from it, something beautiful and unbreakable that she could no longer run from.

Somewhere along the way, James had unknowingly taught her that life held many avenues, and each one changed and altered depending on what you were willing to put into it. After Beauregard, she had viewed marriage as a gilded cage she could never escape. But James had taught her a life built on mutual love and respect held more freedom than she could ever imagine. That instead of being held down, one was lifted up. Instead of standing headfirst into the battering wind, one was given a shield. That one could be the shield for another.

Not once, in any of their interactions, had James tried to silence her. Never had he told her that her ideas and dreams were foolish and would come to naught. They may not always agree, but he had always listened. Debated. Allowed her to keep her own opinions even when they differed from his. He had never made her feel less. He had always made her feel like more.

And now he sat before her, offering her his love and all she had to do was find the courage to reach out and grab a hold of it. To embrace the idea that love and marriage and freedom could stand within the same circle and build each other up instead of tear one of them down. Yet, despite all ability to debate upon any number of subjects, she now found herself at a loss for words.

"I believe you offered me a taste of brandy, my lord," she whispered.

The hint of a smile tugged at the corners of his mouth. "Indeed, I did."

He lifted his free hand and titled her chin up, bringing their lips to touch, gently at first, almost tentative. Temperance's hands gripped his thighs, something hard and solid to keep her anchored, but it did little good as his kiss deepened and soon she was lost in the promise of his lips, the tantalizing wonder of his tongue, the heat of his breath mingled with her own.

She accepted the unspoken invitation, without hesitation. Without worry or fear. Those things no longer existed where James was concerned. This was it. *He* was it. James Harrow, Seventh Marquess of Ridgemont was everything she never knew she truly needed. He offered her a future where she could grow and explore and find happiness with a man who challenged her and loved her and would never leave or betray her.

But as this realization filled her, lifted her, the door to the carriage burst open and harsh lamplight shoved inside to interrupt the wonderful moment, stealing it away as James straightened quickly and Temperance turned, still on her knees in front of him.

Only to come face to face with Mr. Marcus Bowen and his inscrutable expression, unless one counted the dark eyebrow that slowly rose upward to disappear beneath an equally dark lock of hair.

For a brief moment, no one spoke.

It was Mr. Bowen who broke the silence, clearing his throat before he spoke. "Well, I can see I arrived at a most inopportune moment. My apologies Miss Lindwell, Lord

Ridgemont. It appears my companions got a little carried away in their exuberance to play matchmakers."

From behind him, someone spoke up in defense of their actions. "You're the one who said he loved her, Bowen, and that something should be done about that. Technically, this is your fault."

Mr. Bowen turned around and glared at whoever had spoken up. Lord Huntsleigh, Temperance believed, given he appeared to be the one on the receiving end of Mr. Bowen's potent stare. "Yes, *Ridgemont* should do something. Not you dimwits! For the love of all that's holy, Spence, the lady has already been through one terrifying kidnapping. Did you not think of that?"

"Oh." Lord Huntsleigh's chagrined face appeared over Mr. Bowen's shoulder. "He may have a point. That was not well thought out. My sincerest apologies, Miss Lindwell. We just thought that if you had a little time alone, you might come to your senses and agree to marry Ridgemont. He's truly not a bad sort. And a far cry better than sailing across the Atlantic to parts unknown. I hear Nova Scotia gets a fair bit of rain."

"So does London, my lord," she said, unsure of what else to say. What was there to say after all? Thank you? Because she was thankful. Their actions were ridiculous and possibly ruinous, but at the same time...lifesaving.

"Good point."

"But," Lord Blackbourne's head popped up behind Lord Huntsleigh and Mr. Bowen, aided by his superior height. "Nova Scotia does not have gentlemen willing to admit they were very wrong about you, Miss Lindwell. I'm afraid we have judged you harshly, simply because you have come from somewhere we are not familiar with. My wife has informed me that such thinking is...what is the word she used?"

"Idiotic," Lord Hawksmoor called from behind.

Lord Blackbourne cleared his throat. "Yes. I believe that was it. Please, accept our humblest of apologies. We can only hope to—"

"Oh, bloody hell, let me in there, would you."

Lords Blackbourne and Huntsleigh were pushed aside as Mr. Bowen slipped back into the shadows, offering a brief and uncommon smile as he went. In their place, Lord Rothbury appeared.

"Did you tell her, James?"

Temperance turned to look at James who had been as mute as she after being burst in upon, their magical kiss interrupted by their band of merry captors.

"Tell her?"

"That you love her?"

Temperance could not hold back the smile that came at Lord Rothbury's question. Had James told him? Or had it been apparent to the man he considered a brother in the same way it had been to Constance? How transparent they were.

And how foolish to think they could overcome something that had overtaken them in such an all-encompassing manner.

"He did," she answered.

Lord Rothbury smirked, his pale eyes flashing in the lamplight he had taken from Mr. Bowen. "And did you tell him that you loved him in return?"

"I did not."

"What the deuce?"

"Alex—"

"No," Lord Rothbury waved James's warning tone away. "Miss Lindwell, I understand you Americans have different ways of doing things that I will likely never understand, but when a man bares his heart, it is incumbent upon the person it was bared to, to respond."

"Well, my lord," Temperance said, finding the strength in

her voice that had deserted her earlier upon James's admission. "The truth of the matter is—"

"Temperance, you don't need to—"

"Yes, I do," she said, turning and pushing herself into a kneeling position once more. "I do need to because you deserve to know, James. You deserve to hear the words and know that they come from my heart. I do love you. And it is all your fault."

He smiled, that smile that melted her heart and sent heat spiraling to other parts she hoped they might get a chance to explore sooner rather than later.

"My fault?"

"Clearly. I had no intention of having anything to do with you or your ilk—"

"Our *ilk*?" Lord Rothbury interrupted.

She ignored him and forged on. "You changed my mind. You showed me how wrong I was, not something I admit to easily, I'm afraid. You proved to me that love was not a cage. That marriage was not a death sentence of the soul. That, with the right person, it could be a wondrous and magical thing. You are a good man, James. The best man. And I love you more than words can say. More than I ever thought possible. I am sorry it took me so long to get up the courage to say so. Can you ever forgive me?"

James took hold of her hand and pulled it to his mouth, imprinting the warmth of his kiss upon her skin. "Perhaps."

"Oh." Only perhaps? Her heart sank. Had she waited too long? Had he spoken his feelings in haste and now had second thoughts?

But his smile grew and reached out to touch every inch of her inside and out and the doubts flew away like a leaf on the wind. "If I am given a lifetime to do so."

"Then, Lord Ridgemont, might you consider marrying me?"

Lord Rothbury made a gargled sound. "*You're* proposing to *him*?"

"It seems only fair," Temperance answered without looking at the future duke. Her gaze instead remained steady on her love. On the man who had so captured her heart. "Given he had asked three times over and I foolishly turned him down each time."

"That's rather unconventional, Miss Lindwell."

"Well, Lord Rothbury, you should know by now, convention is not something I hold to with any strict adherence."

"Get away from the door, man and leave the two alone." Lord Hawksmoor grabbed Lord Rothbury by the shoulder shoved him away. "Apologies, Miss Lindwell. Please continue with your conversation. We shall await your departure at a safe, yet somewhat proper, distance."

And with a quick wink from the man known as The Hawk, the door shut quietly and the sound of several men being ushered away grew faint, leaving them in silence.

"Well," Temperance said, unable to meet James's gaze.

"Yes. This has been a rather strange and eventful evening, has it not?"

"It has at that."

Neither said anything. Temperance searched for words, for the courage that had allowed her to propose to him in front of everyone. Where had it gone?

"You do not need to marry me if you do not wish," James whispered. "I will not hold you to it."

His words cut into her and forced her gaze to meet his. "Have you changed your mind then? Have I waited too long?"

James shook his head. "I would wait for you forever, my dear."

"What of Lady Charlotte? There are expectations—?"

"Lady Charlotte will understand. I doubt she wishes to marry a man whose affection lies with another."

"No, not a fate I recommend to anyone," Temperance said, having narrowly escaped a similar one. "But she is a kind and lovely woman. Everything everyone expects you to marry."

"But she is not you."

"James—"

He didn't give her a chance to continue. He gathered her in his arms, pulled her into his lap, and pressed his mouth to hers in a kiss laden with all the hope and promise of a future of their own making. Her body crushed against his, molded into every curve and crevice, sweep and hollow. She cared little that the *Lords of Love* stood vigilantly only a short distance away. Every ounce of her demanded they be allowed this moment. This promise. This life.

Oh, the glory of being held by him once again. To feel his mouth move with hers, just as hungry, just as desperate. His hands buried in her hair, sending pins scurrying across the plush seats and the hard floor at their feet. Her hands searched for exposed skin, needing, wanting—

"Wait. No, we cannot," James said between breaths. "Not here. Not like this. This is..."

Temperance held her breath, waiting for the hideous claim she feared might come. *This is wrong.*

But no. His kiss had told the truth. His response, his words, his promise. He loved her. He had said so and he was a man of his word. She could trust him with her heart. She *did* trust him with her heart.

"I shall procure a special license, if you're amenable, my dear. We can be married in a matter of weeks."

"Days would be better." She loathed the wait. Every moment that passed between now and then would feel like a year.

James laughed and dropped a quick, searing kiss upon her lips. "I am a marquess, my love. Not a magician."

"I beg to differ, my lord. You have worked magic upon me."

"And I plan to do so again," he said, pulling her close and nuzzling her neck. "And again, and again and ag—"

She cut him off with a kiss. Letting him know that she believed. That she trusted. That she loved. And with her kiss, she made her own promise to him and to herself, that theirs would be a lifetime filled with magic and wonder and discovery.

When their lips parted, Temperance smiled and for the first time in so long she could not remember the last, her heart swelled with joy.

"I must confess, my lord, that I was grievously wrong about you."

James raised one eyebrow but amusement danced in his blue eyes. "Is that so?"

"It is. I fully admit that you are not nearly as pompous as I originally estimated."

"High praise indeed."

"And that I have fallen completely and irreversibly in love with you."

He smiled—and oh, that smile—she would never tire of it. And the kiss that followed, filled with promise and delights, she would never tire of that either.

Because as it turned out, sometimes the thing you feared the most, turned out to be just the thing you needed above all else.

And James Harrow, Seventh Marquess of Ridgemont, was exactly what she needed. Wanted. And loved.

Also By Kelly Boyce

THE SINS & SCANDALS SERIES

THE BRIDES OF FATAL BLUFF

SALVATION FALLS

Dear Reader

Thank you so much for reading **A HINT OF SCANDAL**, Book 9 in the *Sins & Scandals Series*. I had a great time writing James and Temperance's story. I think they were evenly matched in opposite ways that made for a ton of fun. I hope you enjoy their story!

This is the last book in the series, however, I feel there are a few more storylines left to be explored. After all, we still have one Lindwell twin left, don't we? And what about the Lindwell brothers, Colin and Daniel? And, of course, there is Lady Charlotte Overton. And let's not forget the Caldwell sisters!

If this is your first introduction to the series, **Book 1: AN INVITATION TO SCANDAL** is currently **FREE** on all digital retailers. I hope you'll check it out and discover where it all began!

To keep informed on new releases, check out my **website book page** or sign up for my **Newsletter** at **www.kelly boyce.com** to keep abreast of breaking news and new releases!

I love to connect with my readers through social media and email and you can find all of my relevant links (Facebook

Page, Twitter, Goodreads, Pinterest and Instagram) on my **website**!

Again, thank you for reading **A HINT OF SCANDAL** and I hope you will consider leaving a review at your favorite online retailer to help others discover **The Sins & Scandals Series!**

Wishing you all the best,

--Kelly